THE LE

Dedication

Meien artei eatil Vitaren aena paen en

My work is dedicated always to the Maker

Special Thanks To:

My editors: Rachel, for being the first; Mrs. Paris, for mentoring me in high school; Mr. Insley, for putting in many hours; and last but not least to Aria, for giving me great critiques. I would also like to thank my parents, for guiding me and shaping me into the man I am today. Finally, thank you Bill for providing me with the cover of the book. It's spectacular!

TABLE OF CONTENTS

The Legend of Braim
Prologue
The Sacking of Torrer

High on the battlements of Castle Torrer, Novadar patrolled, his boots thumping a steady rhythm on the granite stones. He peered into the night, glad that his watch was almost over so he could return to the warmth of the barracks. Keeping watch over the city's walls in the middle of the night was surprisingly hard work. It did not help that he was in full battle gear; his thick scale-mail shirt alone probably weighed fifty pounds; add the helmet, the gauntlets, the splinted boots, and without intense physical training the weight would be more than humanly possible to bear.

Novadar glanced up at the full moon and stars, then back down at the thick canopy of pine trees below, pausing for a moment to adjust his sword belt to a more comfortable position. He continued his rounds, and passed by one of the young trainees in his unit.

"All is well, Captain," said the young man, snapping to attention.

"Oh is it?" asked Novadar with a hint of a smile, "Straighten up, Patrick! Chin in, chest out, shield at your sternum, spear straight." The young man straightened as quickly as possible, and Novadar continued along the battlement.

All of a sudden meaty *smack*, accompanied by a soft gurgle and the clatter of a spear on stone, shattered the silence of the night. Novadar turned just in time to see the young soldier collapse with a crash, a black arrow sticking out of his neck. Arrows whizzed out of the shadows of the pines, barely missing Novadar as he ducked behind the battlements.

"The city is under attack," he roared, his clear, strong voice echoing between the towers nearest him. Novadar crawled to Patrick and rolled him over. The once vibrant young man lay quiet, still, lifeless. Novadar examined the arrow quickly, and his eyes went wide, "Goblins!"

Bells began to ring from every tower in the city; awakening her people, warning them to flee with their families and possessions to the keep. Pandemonium reigned inside the city. Novadar ran from man to man, and noticed that some of the new trainees from the outer villages were standing up.

"Get down you fools!" shouted Novadar. More arrows flew from the forest, the soldiers tried to dodge, but it seemed as if they were moving through honey. They fell in pools of their own blood.

Grappling hooks whizzed up and latched onto the ramparts of the city's outer walls.

"Quickly," yelled Novadar to his remaining soldiers, "cut the ropes or the city will be overrun!" Novadar grabbed a young soldier and said, "Take my position! I must go to warn Lord Braeln!"

The young soldier nodded, then drew his sword quickly, raised it above the wall, and severed a rope. The goblins who had been climbing screamed in terror as the ground flew up to meet them.

Novadar ran down the stairs of the wide battlement, barking orders as he went. He sprinted through the city's complex maze of streets and gates. Families and soldiers alike cleared the way for the hurrying captain. Finally, he reached the heart of the city: his Lord Braeln's tower. He labored up seven stories of staircases and burst through the door to his lord's receiving room. He knocked loudly on the door to the bedchamber, and Lord Braeln emerged, strapping on the last piece of his battle-armor.

"How goes the battle, Novadar?"

Novadar trailed after his lord toward the war room.

"We are holding off the enemy for now, my Lord," replied Novadar, "But I fear that our men are too few, and our foes seem great in number."

"Then we are now fighting a battle in the streets of our dear city, if not on the walls of the second level. I must go to turn the tide of the battle," said Lord Braeln. They entered the war room, which was ringed with Braeln's personal guard and many knights. Braeln turned to Novadar, "You must go down and help Risallia in the evacuation process. My wife is a strong, skilled leader, but sometimes too headstrong and free-willed. She has never been tested under the pressure of battle. Use your calm temperament to counteract any anxiety she may be feeling."

As Novadar turned to leave a soldier burst into the room. "Lord Braeln! The goblins have overrun the first level, and as we speak they are using a battering ram to destroy the gate at the second level!"

"Thank you soldier, you may return to your post," Braeln turned to Novadar as the soldier raced out of the room. "Novadar, I hope we meet again; may the Lord Vitaren go with you."

"And also with you, my lord," said Novadar.

*   *   *

Surprisingly, Novadar found an orderly line of people filing into the evacuation tunnel. Risallia, a beautiful woman even in her nightclothes, had a sword at her hip and a bow with a quiver full of arrows on her back. The baby, Braim, was slung across her belly.

"My lady, why are you wearing a soldier's armaments; it is not fitting for a woman of your station."

Risallia ignored him while she assisted an old woman down the steps and into the tunnel. "Careful now, mother Astrida. Find your husband and greet him for me. Ah, Novadar," said Risallia, as she turned to face the captain of the guard, "You are the very person I was looking for. Here, hold Braim for me."

Novadar took Braim carefully as Risallia took off the blanket and handed him the baby. The baby shifted and whimpered softly, but remained asleep.

"Novadar," she said, "I have another request to make of you."

"Yes, my lady?" said Novadar, uneasily.

"I want you to take Braim and lead the people to Rochaon in my place; I will not leave my husband to die alone."

"That is valiant of you, my lady," replied Novadar, "but I cannot grant this request. My duty is to my lord and-"

"His lady," said Risallia firmly, cutting him off. "Novadar, if you do not go, then I will find someone else who will."

"I am sorry, my lady, but I cannot do what you ask."

Risallia moved closer, as if she was going to take the baby back, but quickly drew her sword with her other hand and held it tight against Novadar's throat, "I am no longer asking," she motioned for a farmer who was holding the reins of a horse to come to her, and the man complied. "Get on the horse, Novadar," Novadar handed her Braim and climbed into the saddle. It was not until Novadar had Braim back in his arms that the farmer handed the reins to the tall man in the saddle. Novadar rode forward, following the last of the civilians leaving the fortress. He had planned to hand the baby off to someone else and gallop back out of the tunnel. Just as he cleared the entrance the doors slammed shut behind him, and his ears were greeted by the sound of cobblestones being hoisted into place. He was trapped.

*   *   *

From the shadow of the pine forest, a dark hooded figure watched with satisfaction as smoke began to rise from the central keep, accompanied by the screams of women, children, and men who had not escaped the city. The dark robe swirled around him as he leaped onto his horse and galloped northward, fast as the wind.

*   *   *

Far away, Novadar watched as the flag of Braeln, a silver star on a crimson field, floated down from the heights of the central keep tower. It was lost from view behind the walls of the city, but Novadar knew that it would hit the ground in the courtyard and be trampled, stomped, and spit upon by the goblin hordes.

As Novadar and the few people who had come with him turned to go, a lone arrow sailed from the fortress and struck Novadar in the middle of the back. Pain overwhelmed him, but he managed to throw his elbows forward and break his fall, saving the baby Braim from being crushed. As his vision faded, Novadar rolled over, and several of the men rushed to his aid.

"Leave me, I am finished. Take Braim to Teckor, as far from this place as possible." said Novadar. With that, Novadar died.

The city of Torrer had fallen.

The Legend of Braim
Chapter I
How It Started

The young man fired the arrow, and watched with satisfaction as it embedded itself in the neck of a goblin sentry. He quickly returned his longbow to its place on his quiver, then slid silently down the side of a dark ravine. The green-brown cloak of a Telnorian ranger allowed him to blend in to the ferns and dense floor of fallen pine needles. Pine limbs clawed at his unprotected hands, trying to pull the hood of his cloak back to expose his face, but Braim soon left the cover of the trees and emerged into the star-lit bottom of the ravine. He paused for a moment and scanned his surroundings for more sentries; they were all sleeping, or dead. The stench of the goblins filled his nose, bringing memories flooding back to him. His parents having been killed in a border village by a goblin raid, he was raised as a lonely child in a Teckor orphanage. Braim shook off the memories and returned to scanning the encampment.

Suddenly Braim's friend and partner, Aelundei, emerged from the forest next to him.

"This is merely a small encampment," said the elf quietly, "It will be easy to find the captains and commander. You get the captains. I will deal with the commander."

"I think not," whispered Braim, "you got the commander last time, remember?"

"Hey! That was a lucky hit, the guy was running away and you were just staring at him," said Aelundei jokingly.

"I believe you are mistaken," replied Braim mockingly, "however, I shall take out the captains, my Lord," Braim bowed to the elf and moved towards the nearest tent. He grabbed the tent flap and slid inside. Moving to the nearest goblin, he slit its throat. As the black blood spilled out, Braim could not help but think, *You've looted your last village, murderer.*

*   *   *

Moraina lay on her back and stared up at the ceiling above her bed, listening to the sound of her sisters breathing, reflecting back on the day. It had been a good day, up until the evening, and it was the events of the evening that troubled her.

Moraina had done her chores in record speed and was putting

8

away the last freshly washed dress when her older sister Lithia approached her.

"Moraina," she had said. "Saril, Brigim and I are going to a dance this evening. You need to do our chores for us."

Moraina had turned to face her and put her hands on her hips, "You went to a dance last night and the morning before; I always do your chores for you! If you really wish to go to this 'dance,' then you will need to find out how to do your own chores."

Lithia looked down her nose at her and sneered, "If you don't, then I will tell father where you go every afternoon!"

Moraina's heart raced. Had her sisters found out about her secret trip out to the forest every afternoon to practice archery? Or was Lithia merely bluffing?

Lithia saw Moraina's nervousness and pounced on her opportunity, "Yes, I will tell him you go to visit your boyfriend every afternoon, and that you and him go into his house alone."

"I do no such thing!" Moraina cried.

"Ah," said Lithia, "but he does not know that, and who do you think he would trust more; me, the adult; or you, a little child of sixteen?"

Moraina's father loved her dearly as the last daughter of his wife, yet he still trusted Moraina's older sisters more, and listened constantly to their lies. Her older sisters constantly played the Moraina's-just-a-small-child card. Moraina had winced at the emphasis on "little child," but had reluctantly agreed. She now had to wash the dishes, bring wood in for the oven, and wash her sisters' clothes. Moraina was almost used to doing her sisters' chores, but she still resented their having fun while she worked. When she finished, she decided that she would inform her father that her sisters had been leaving to attend dances, leaving her to do all their work. She slid down the banister to the ground floor of their house and marched to the closed door of her father's study. She halted in front of the magnificent oak doors and paused to run her fingers along the intricate carvings. Moraina's father spent many hours behind these locked doors, trying to discover a cure for Puerperal Fever, better known as Childbirth Fever among the unlearned. The disease had claimed Moraina's mother barely a week after delivering a stillborn son. Grief at the tragedy had driven her father to resign his prestigious position in the military and practically ignore his children for this futile quest. Gathering her courage, Moraina reached forward and knocked on the door.

"Who's there?" Her father's muffled reply emanated from deep within the study.

"It's your daughter, Moraina," she replied.

"What do you want?" the door to the room slid open and her father leaned halfway out.

"My sisters went to a dance, and threatened me that they would tell you I have been sneaking out to visit my boyfriend every day."

"You have a boyfriend?" asked her father, indignantly.

"No," insisted Moraina, "They saw me leaving to watch my cousins' brigade doing drill, and they accuse me of this."

Her father grew angry. He stepped out of the door way and loomed over her like he would have to his inferiors in the army. His dark eyebrows creased together, and his mouth grew tight and thin, "I have told you numerous times, Moraina, that you are not to visit your cousins Silas and Matthew. They are a bad influence!"

"They are not a bad influence, Father," replied Moraina, stubbornly.

Her father looked at her in angry shock, "Are you questioning my judgment?"

"Only your judgment of the character of my cousins," replied Moraina, flatly, "They have only taught me skills that I could use to defend myself."

"Skill with weapons is never decent for a woman," replied her father. She had her mother's stubbornness, and there was only one cure for that. He had to deal with her like he dealt with unruly men, through discipline. "I do not want to hear another rebellious word from you, young lady. You will do your sisters' chores, as well as your own, and you will not leave this house for a week." He closed the door to the study, and Moraina heard him walk away from the door. It would do no good to argue with him further.

Moraina had gone to the garden behind the house and retrieved her long bow, along with its quiver of arrows, from the back of the tool shed. This was the last straw, and tonight she was finally prepared to run away.

Moraina listened for her sisters' breathing to become deep and even; then she swung her legs out from under the sheets and stepped onto the wooden floor. She was already dressed in a pair of brown pants, a green shirt, and a black leather vest. Reaching under her bed, she also pulled out a pair of leather boots and a short sword. Every time she touched the hilt of the sword, she was reminded of her two favorite cousins, who had been like the kind, older brothers she had never had. Moraina had always been interested in activities that were traditionally unsuitable for a lady. Throughout her childhood she had tramped through the forests of Telnor province, following her cousins and learning from them everything about bows and woodcraft that they knew. As the pair had prepared to enter the army, they had also taught her everything they learned about swordsmanship, and last year on her sixteenth birthday, they had secretly given her the short-sword as a gift.

"So far, so good" thought Moraina as she slipped on the boots and buckled on the sword. Standing up slowly, she walked silently to the bedroom door, being careful to step over several dark objects that were strewn about the floor. *Were those bottles?* She shrugged off the thought and opened the door, making her way to the bottom of the last stair. Moraina stepped outside and breathed in the cool air of midnight as she scanned the courtyard behind her house. Crossing through the moonlit garden, she reached the shed in the back corner and retrieved her bow and quiver from their hiding place. She slipped the weapons onto her back, then scaled the courtyard wall, dropping into a neighboring alleyway.

"All is clear, and my sisters didn't even roll over," Moraina thought to herself, *"next stop, the ranger headquarters!"* She paused for a moment, *"On second thought, I should probably get my horse from father's stable first."*

Moraina walked toward the center of the city and her father's stables, marveling at how the mountain on which the city was built reached up to touch the sky, threatening to impale the moon with its snow-capped peak. She turned left into a narrow alleyway, unconsciously resting her left hand on the hilt of her sword at the thought of someone waiting in the shadows. She opened the door to the stable as silently as possible, but the horses still heard her and quietly offered her a greeting. She smiled as she opened the gate to her horse Prince's stall; his soft nose nudged her gently as she stepped inside. Moraina offered him a carrot, and he munched it gratefully as she groomed him. After Moraina cinched up his saddle, she grabbed Prince's bridle from its nail on the wall, but as she turned to put the bit in the horse's mouth she accidently got it tangled in her waist-length hair.

That's not good, thought Moraina as she wrestled her hair from

11

the clutch of the bridle, *No man's hair would be long enough to cause this issue.*

The young woman stepped out of the stall and drew her sword. She grabbed a handful of her nut brown hair and drew the razor edge of her sword across it. The brunet locks parted easily, and soon there was a small pile of hair on the floor. Moraina looked down at all that was left of her identity, and wept for its insignificance. Dashing the tears from her eyes, she threw the small pile of hair into one of the other horse's stalls, tied several cloths around Prince's hooves to muffle the sound on the cobblestones, then grabbed the reins to lead him out of the stable to the heart of the city. She closed the door to the stables behind her and walked away with the last memory of her old life, her trusty horse.

Moraina soon found herself standing before a large building attached to a walled courtyard. On the door there was a sign, written in a bold, hasty manner, which read: *Now Accepting Novices.*

"Well," she said, "It looks like I'm in luck," she tied Prince to the rail at the front of the building, grabbed the door handle, and stepped inside. The sudden light struck her eyes, and she stood blinking for a moment while they adjusted. She found herself standing in a large, square room, with a fireplace in one corner and an ascending staircase in the other. Between the fireplace and the stairs there was a massive door, with another sign by the same hand that read *Armory, Authorized Rangers Only, Keep Out.* On the wall opposite the front door there was a four foot high counter with yet another sign hanging next to it saying: *You Must Be Able to Look Over This Counter to Join the Rangers.* Moraina laughed inwardly, *Someone has a sense of humor.* Moraina walked up to the counter, navigating around several round tables and their chairs, but there was no one there. Then she noticed a fourth sign, this one saying: *If I'm not here, yell, and if I'm still not with you in a few seconds, yell louder!*

Moraina leaned over the counter looking left, then right, "Excuse me," she yelled. She waited patiently for a few seconds, but did not hear anything, so she did as the sign said and yelled louder, "Is anyone here?"

Then, a door behind the counter burst open, and an old man walked out. He was dressed in a nightgown, and his hair and beard looked uneven and messy. He studied Moraina through tired, bleary eyes and then asked gruffly, "What do you want, boy?"

"I have come to join the rangers," she replied happily, "I am skilled with the bow, sword and knife." *Hopefully, it is not just the fact that he is tired that hid my gender,* thought Moraina.

"Another foolish lad here to seek a dreadful death," said the man, "We will see if you live up to your tall and mighty words. We will test you tomorrow! Now go back home and sleep; you can come back tomorrow afternoon."

I cannot go back. She thought to herself, but out loud she said, "I need a room to sleep, may I stay here tonight?"

The man shifted his weight and replied huskily, "There are rooms upstairs to sleep in. Now let me return to mine!" With that he limped back through the door he had come from, slamming it shut behind him.

Moraina was troubled as she moved Prince to one of the ranger base's stalls, and as she walked up the stairs she wondered what kind of "testing" the man meant.

She entered a room and flopped down on the bed, but jumped up quickly, struggling to muffle a scream, as several dark shapes scurried out of the straw mattress. Rats. Moraina shivered as she drew her sword and started poking the bed in several different spots. It would be a long night.

*   *   *

The black of night was giving way to the gray of dawn as Aelundei and Braim finished their work and left the goblin camp.

"Our work is finally done," sighed Braim.

"That is the best news I have heard all night," chuckled Aelundei.

The two friends walked back to the horses that they had left tied to a tree and mounted to ride back to camp. When they arrived, they found a bear had gotten into the food supplies, which were scattered all over the forest floor. All the food was gone or ripped to shreds, except the flour.

"I can't believe I forgot to tie the food up in a tree before we left," said Braim, with a look of disgust on his face.

"Actually," said Aelundei, "I think you were busy repairing arrows from the last raid and asked me to do it."

Braim looked over at Aelundei, who looked back at Braim, and in unison they dropped their head into their right hand.

"Well, I'm not going to be the one who explains it to Gall this time," said Braim, "so, we better pack up and get back to Teckor before we're forced to hunt every day."

"You go get the horses ready while I pack the tents and salvage any remaining food."

They packed the tents and what remained of the food, then set off on the eight-day ride to the ranger's home base in the capitol city of Teckor.

The Legend of Braim
Chapter II
The Enemy Plans to Strike!

Castle Torrer was now overrun with goblins. In the lower levels of the fortress, goblins fought for food, armor, gold, and just for the fun of it. Goblins lay beaten in alleys, in the middle of rough and destroyed streets, inside houses with no roofs, and on the roofs of those that did. However, none of the goblins were dead, for the goblin king Grashnir had made murder illegal in the city of Torrer; punishable by slow, torturous death.

The middle levels of the fortress were slightly more organized, but only slightly. Instead of unconscious goblins lying around, there were mostly slaves who were done working their first shift and had a quick rest before their second shift.

The king's guard and their slaves dwelt in the top level of the fortress. In the highest tower of the top level of the castle, in the second highest room, was the goblin king himself: Grashnir. Grashnir was missing his right eye and one of his legs was lame. On the other leg and both arms were massive scars, but to say that he was no longer capable of ruling would be very, very far from the truth. If the dead could tell tales, one could just ask any of the hundreds of former officers who had been killed for the slightest mistake. He was the biggest, closest threat to the Telnorian kingdom. His desire was not to remain a mere threat, but to become their ruler. Yes, if Grashnir, king of the goblins, could have his way, he would destroy the Telnorians and rule over them with an iron fist. However, he did not have the power for such a taxing campaign. Grashnir looked up at the half circle of scribes seated around him. They were diligently writing, putting the finishing touches on the letter he had just dictated to them. Grashnir noticed that the oldest scribe, Ar-Kadeer, was writing slowly, and looking as if he were deep in thought. Grashnir walked over and leaned against the table directly in front of Ar-Kadeer.

"Scribe, read back to me what you have written," stated Grashnir flatly.

A look of terror came over the face of Ar-Kadeer. He looked down at the unfinished letter and then back at his king before picking up the letter and beginning to read. "To: Gartsamn, ruler of Braaztuhl; from: Grashnir, king of Torrer. Greetings, my fellow king; as you well know, the land of Telnor is a rich land, full of wine, ale, gold, and prosperous people to use as slaves. I propose an alliance to invade this land, and in return for your assistance I will give you a large share of the spoils of war."

"Go on," said Grashnir, though he knew the scribe had forgotten the rest.

"Oh, great ruler, have mercy on me!" said the ancient scribe, "For I cannot remember how you wished to end the letter."

Grashnir grinned disarmingly at the elderly goblin in front of him, "Very well, here is how I wish the letter to be ended. 'I have sent letters to several of the other goblin kings, and in one month they will meet with me at my fortress to discuss plans for the invasion, as well as shares of the spoils. Servants, food, beverages, rooms, and soldiers for protection will be graciously provided while you remain in my castle, but you are more than welcome to bring your own, if you wish. With all due respect, Grashnir.' And now that you have finished this letter, you are of no more use to me." With that Grashnir kicked Ar-Kadeer in the face, and the old goblin's chair fell backwards. Before the scribe could react, Grashnir rounded the table, seized him by the throat, and threw him out the window. Ar-Kadeer wailed pitifully as he fell five floors and collided with the cobblestones of the courtyard. Grashnir turned to see the shocked and horrified reactions of the remaining scribes. He laughed inwardly as they each began searching for errors, double checking with one another to ensure they had missed nothing.

"That," said Grashnir, with a grin, "is what happens to anyone who fails me one too many times." Turning to the window, Grashnir looked down at the still form of the goblin scribe far below. "Say hello to the reaper for me, Ar-Kadeer, I hope he's happy that I keep him in business."

Grashnir turned to the couriers that had entered the room during his conversation with Ar-Kadeer. "You know your assignments, get moving!"

The couriers scrambled forward, received the letters that the scribes had completed, and rushed out of the room, heading in pairs to the different goblin kingdoms scattered above Telnor.

Grashnir grinned; soon he could advance his plans. He marched out of the room and walked up to his personal chamber at the top of the tower.

"Servant!" yelled Grashnir in a harsh, gravely tone as he closed the door to his chamber behind himself.

The door opened again and a small goblin peeked in, hoping he was not going to bear the brunt of another of his master's destructively violent mood swings. "Yes, oh great and terrifying ruler?" the goblin said in a high pitched, timid voice.

"Bring food and wine," growled Grashnir. "And be sure it is the good stuff, from Telnor!"

"Yes sir!" said the servant as he turned to go.

"And you had better run all the way there or you will be joining the last 236 lazy servants in the bone yard," yelled Grashnir after the now sprinting servant. *"Cruelty,"* he thought, *"is the best part of being a ruler."*

Suddenly, Grashnir's thoughts were interrupted by the door opening. A tall figure entered the room, his large dark robe adding to the imposing aura that emanated from the man. His black gloved hands held the wine that Grashnir wanted.

"Excellent wine," said the voice of a man from deep within the hood. He poured one of the glasses and held it out for Grashnir to take. Grashnir looked darkly from the man to the glass then back to the man again.

"Who are you and what are you doing in my chamber without my consent?" asked Grashnir as he took a step backwards towards the cabinet that held his sword.

"I am known by many names. Some call me the Ambassador, others call me the Plotter, and those with a weak imagination call me A Man in an Imposing Dark Robe. But you will call me by my title: Lord." said the man after taking a sip of the wine, "I have an order for you from my master, one that you cannot ignore. You may do as I say, or, I could kill you and perform this task myself." The man handed Grashnir a glass of wine, "I truly hate goblins, they are so incompetent, so I would prefer you accept this enterprise peacefully."

"I am Grashnir, king of the goblins in Torrer! I bow to no creature, be he man, elf, troll, or goblin. You may leave peacefully, or I will throw you out!" Grashnir opened the cabinet and drew his sword, but as he turned to kill the man he was lifted into the air by some invisible force and slammed against the wall.

The man took a sip of wine and replied in a calm voice, "Take that as your final warning. Try it anything again and I will kill you. My master is more powerful than I, yet he wants you to be part of his plans, I cannot see why." He set the wine down on a table and took a few steps toward the now timid king. The man seemed to grow in stature, and the room grew darker to accompany the tone of his voice.

"Now, listen, filthy goblin. Here is what you must do. You already have sent letters to the kings of the many goblin kingdoms, summoning them here, except now, you work for me, and you do everything I tell you from here on out. Understood?"

Grashnir nodded, his pride finally conquered, and his Lord continued.

"Following your successful conquest of Telnor, you will bring all the goblin kingdoms together under your sole rule as you have already devised. Afterwards, you will join my personal legions and march north to destroy the elves. Once that is accomplished, we will turn to the east and destroy the Dwarves and the desert people. I will give you half of all the territory conquered, and you will reign as an emperor. Under my guidance, of course."

The Legend of Braim
Chapter III
Of Teckor and a New Friend

Orandaur's eyes opened. It was dark in the strange room, and it took his mind a while to catch up with the events of the past week. The memories of flight rushed back to him, and he was suddenly aware of the muffled sound of voices from the first floor. Rising, he buttoned on his new ranger cloak, strapped on his sword and knife, and crept stealthily down the stairs.

Gall, the old man he had met on the first night, was talking to two young rangers. Orandaur caught snatches of the conversation, something about bears and food, before slinking back up the stairs to grab his bow and quiver of arrows. The young man breathed a sigh of relief as he grabbed his bow. His family had been very close to finding him several times while he was in hiding, it would only be a matter of time before they checked here.

Orandaur descended the back stairs, not wanting to disturb the men's conversation, and stepped out into the dimly lit courtyard. He had just fired the last arrow from his quiver, when the door to the ranger base opened.

"Orandaur," cried Gaul, "These two rangers are considering taking you in as an apprentice. Come, let me introduce you to them."

Orandaur left the arrows in the target and walked a few yards to where the three men were standing. He bowed, and the two rangers bowed in return.

"The short one," said Gall sarcastically, "Is Braim, son of Braeln."

Braim grinned lopsidedly and nodded his head slowly. He was handsome, despite the raggedly cut hair and two scars on his face from a fight long ago.

"The tall one," said Gall, grinning, "Is Aelundei, the Elf."

Aelundei bowed again, "Monta tervedis, Orandaur," he said with a twinkle in his deep blue eyes.

"They wish to watch your skills with weapons before they take you into their party," stated Gall, "First, archery; then one of them will duel you to test swordsmanship; and then you will cook us a meal."

"But cooking isn't a weapons skill," replied Orandaur, incredulously.

"If you don't cook well, then everyone goes hungry, and the enemy wins," stated Gall in a matter-of-fact tone.

*   *   *

Braim watched as Orandaur turned and retrieved his arrows. The young lad moved a little slow, so Braim took the chance to question Gall about their potential apprentice.

"How long has he been at the ranger base?"

"He showed up in the middle of the night about seven days ago," replied Gall, "Every morning he comes out into the courtyard and practices archery for hours. Then he usually sits in the main hall and asks for news about the surrounding areas. He does seem a bit nervous though, whenever someone comes to the door."

"Hmm," said Braim thoughtfully, "I wonder what dark secret is hidden behind that young face."

Orandaur walked to the shooting line, and looked over to the three men on the sidelines. Gall nodded, and Orandaur reached a hand up to the quiver slung low on his back.

The boy's first arrow slammed into the bull's eye, and Braim whispered to Aelundei, "Beginner's luck."

When the fifth arrow hit just outside of the bull's eye a few seconds later Aelundei replied, "It looks like he knows what he's doing."

After the eighth arrow, Braim was amazed. "You know, he's pretty good." Then the twentieth arrow hit the target, and Braim said, "Only five left, look for the accuracy to fade now that he's tired."

But the accuracy did not degrade, and when the twenty-fifth arrow hit the bull's eye, even Aelundei could think of nothing to say.

Gall turned to the two rangers and grinned, "What did I tell you? He's good. Let's go have a look at the target now."

Orandaur walked to the target with them and stood next to it with a solemn face, one end of his long recurve bow resting on the ground, the other propping him up as he leaned casually on the weapon.

"That's the best shooting I've seen from a rookie yet," said Aelundei. "How long have you been practicing archery?"

"I have been practicing archery for five years now," said Orandaur with a shrug.

"Well, let us see how well you can wield the sword," said Braim. "Would you like to duel against me, or my elf friend, Aelundei?"

"If half the myths I've heard about the skill and speed of the elves are true, I would only succeed in humiliating myself if I sparred Aelundei. Therefore I choose you, master ranger." Orandaur drew his short sword, putting his hand on the broad side of the fullered blade.

"I will go easy on you," said Braim, self-assuredly.

"That may be harder than you think," said Orandaur with a wolfish grin.

"High and mighty words for a novice," said Braim, as he too pulled out his sword, "but pride comes before the fall."

"Hold!" interjected Gall. "You will not be using your real swords." He ran into the armory and brought out two wooden training swords, "These are wood, with metal weights inside. You might bruise each other a bit, but it is better than cutting each other into fish-bait."

They dropped into fighting stances and circled, each looking for a weakness in the other's defense.

Braim struck first, bringing his sword up into the air and sending it whizzing down at Orandaur's unprotected head. But Orandaur was agile. He sidestepped and swung his sword up toward Braim's neck.

Braim brought his sword up just in time to block Orandaur's counter attack.

"Is that the best you can do?" asked Braim sarcastically.

"I'm just warming up," said Orandaur darkly.

They backed off and circled again, looking for gaps in each other's defenses. Braim charged, swinging his broad sword at Orandaur's feet, trying to sweep the boy's legs out from under him. But Orandaur jumped over the sword as he brought his sword down toward Braim's head. Braim dodged to the side and then jumped into the air, as Orandaur also tried his hand at cutting Braim's legs. Braim kicked Orandaur in the chest, knocking the would-be ranger onto his back. As Orandaur struggled to his feet, Braim brought his sword down toward Orandaur's stomach. Orandaur, seeing that he could not get up fast enough, rolled out of the way just in time to avoid the sword. Moving quickly, Orandaur spun around and kicked Braim's feet out from under him as the ranger touched the ground. Orandaur's mind flashed quickly back to the lessons his cousins had taught him, and one line in particular screamed at him, *If you want to beat a guy who is stronger than you, you have to fight dirty.* Orandaur punched Braim between the legs and brought his sword down one-handed at the ranger's chest.

21

Despite the intense pain, Braim managed to bring his sword up in time to parry Orandaur's blow and reply with a cut at Orandaur's neck. Orandaur leaned back and let the sword hiss by, using his backwards momentum to roll over his shoulder and onto his feet. Braim staggered upright and charged Orandaur. Orandaur could barely move his sword fast enough to parry the blows that seemed to rain down from all sides. He could not even think of getting a return blow in. Finally, Braim knocked the sword out of Orandaur's hands, swept his legs out from under him, and placed his sword on Orandaur's neck.

"Dead," said Braim grimly, then a smile broke onto his face, and he extended his hand to pull Orandaur off his feet. "You fight dirty. You'll do well in the forests hunting goblins, with more practice," Braim added.

Aelundei and Gall walked over and clapped Orandaur on his back.

"Very good, Orandaur," said Aelundei, smiling, "that is the longest any novice has lasted in a duel with my accomplice here, you put up a great fight."

"Truly said, my friend," said Gall. "Once this young man has toweled off his sweat, he shall light a fire and cook us the finest meal you two have ever tasted!"

Braim threw a towel at Orandaur, laughing as it wrapped around the young man's face. "I hope you cook better than Aelundei," he said with a smile.

Orandaur toweled off and grabbed his weapons, but Braim and Aelundei hung back.

"We could use another sword to do the dirty work," said Aelundei, "Since you are obviously getting fat and slow."

"I am not fat and slow!" protested Braim mocking a look of pain, "Let's see how the city boy handles a cold night in the woods. Perhaps a fat and slow companion will be better suited to you than a terrified city boy."

They caught up with Orandaur and Gall just as they were turning to go into the ranger base. Gall spoke on and on in his gruff bass voice about the armory and how obsolete the equipment contained within its walls was. They followed him through the armory to the kitchen, where he sat down at a large table. Braim and Aelundei followed his lead.

Gall said, "Orandaur, prepare soup, for that is one of the best

22

meals for a trio of hollow-legged rangers in the woods."

"Yes, Gall," said Orandaur, as he began to prepare the food.

When the soup was prepared, Orandaur sat in the shadows while the men talked and ate.

The conversation flowed through many different topics, from war to politics, and eventually to the predicament of the ever-dropping number of rangers.

"Our numbers are at an all-time low," said Gall. "For every lad that joins, we lose at least five of our best. We cannot continue if this will be the path. More men would rather join the regular army, wear the armor, and stay at home with their loved ones."

"The army allows a man to stay in his home, only going on duty one week out of three. You rangers have a full time job on the distant borders of our land. Also, soldiers can win glory on a battlefield because they do not wear green cloaks and sneak around slitting throats in the night. We rangers never get credit for turning whole armies because no one hears about it, only the large battles where two armies face off and try to crush each other," Gall shook his head sadly as he finished his tirade.

"Well," said Braim. "I guess I never thought of it that way. I have no loved ones and nothing to lose, so it does not bother me as much as the average man."

Gall looked around, and spotted Orandaur sitting in the dark corner. "No sulking in corners is allowed here, Orandaur. Among us rangers, everyone is equal. Come! Take a seat with the men."

Orandaur grabbed a chair and sat down with the other rangers.

"So, Orandaur," said Gall, "We've talked a lot about ourselves and our worries. Tell us a bit about yourself!"

"There is not much to tell," said Orandaur, flatly.

Braim looked at him questioningly, but shook it off and changed the subject. "How many rangers have been by the ranger station this month, Gall?"

Gall leaned back in his chair and crossed his arms, "I'm afraid you have been the first group this month. Returning groups have been fewer and farther between, either patrolling rangers are fewer in numbers or they have been resorting to purchasing their own food and gear in areas closer to the borders."

"If that is the case," interjected Aelundei thoughtfully, "then perhaps the king will reopen the bases near the border that he closed over a decade ago."

"If only that were the case," said Gall sadly.

The four companions talked for a little while longer, and after everyone was stuffed to their fullest, Braim stretched back in his chair, "This meal convinced me that we could use a better cook than Aelundei. Orandaur, we'll be taking you under our wing until you have finished your training. Be ready to travel to the borders of Telnor at the crack of dawn."

The Legend of Braim
Chapter IV
Negotiations of the Goblins

Grashnir stood and looked out over the diverse group of goblin kings that were seated in his banquet hall. They ranged in height from just under four feet to almost five feet tall; some were dressed in rags and crude armor, others in fine and elaborate silks; all had green skin, flat noses, and rough black hair, characteristic of their race. At Grashnir's right hand sat Gartsamn, the repulsive king of the crude goblins from Braaztulh; he had outrageously demanded one half of all the Telnorian women and children as slaves. Directly across the room from Grashnir sat Torag-Jun from the far eastern kingdom of Varenvar, who had demanded one third of the land, on the basis that his country was half desert, which inhibited growth. Most of the other rulers had been happy to join in the plans for invasion just so they wouldn't be left out of the killing, but there had been some, like Gartsamn and Torag-Jun, who had caused the negotiations to be a long and difficult process. Each goblin ruler had wanted more land, or more gold, or more slaves than the last. Finally, they had reached an agreement. Since there were 12 of them, they had settled on one twelfth of the spoils each. And once they were all settled in after they had conquered Telnor, then it would not be very hard for Grashnir to have the other kings assassinated, and set himself up as supreme emperor. After the Telnorians were destroyed, Grashnir could have the man in the dark robe assassinated, and forget all about his "master's orders."

"I raise a toast," said Grashnir as he lifted his wine, "to our new alliance, and to the death of Telnor!"

"To the death of Telnor!" cried many of the kings, but the goblin rulers from the north lifted their voices in unison in the Dark Tongue; Grashnir mentally translated their words in his head as he heard them, "to the overthrow of Grashnir."

Grashnir also noticed that many of the goblin rulers, especially the rulers from the north, had their servants taste their wine or ale before drinking. Then, seeing that they had not been affected, they kicked their servants out of the way and began drinking and tearing at the food with ferocity that matched starving wolves. Grashnir saw that his guests had begun to eat, so he joined in and began to devour the food in front of him.

Idiots, thought Grashnir, *if I had wanted to poison them I would have used poison that would take days to kill them.*

After a few hours and numerous requests for more drinks, the rulers were escorted to their rooms by some of Grashnir's goblin servants. Most were so drunk they forgot to have their servants inspect the rooms for traps. Some, however, had controlled their liquor and were still wary of Grashnir's hospitality. They instructed their servants to go in and inspect the rooms carefully for nasty surprises and stomp on the floor to check for hidden trap doors.

Grashnir watched them all with interest. *Just you wait until the victory celebration when I have you back. It will be an event worth dying for!*

The kings slept well that night. Grashnir had given them rooms with good views and goose-feather beds looted from the Telnorians. When they awoke in the morning, they were all invited to Grashnir's planning room, which had a large table with a map of Telnor and all the outlying goblin kingdoms. The goblin leaders all gathered around the large map. Then Grashnir said, "Good morning, fellow kings and rulers. I trust you all had a good night's sleep?" All the rulers nodded and growled in answer, smiling as they thought of the soft feather beds.

"Now, great rulers," said Grashnir, "we must develop our strategy for the mighty invasion of Telnor."

The Legend of Braim
Chapter V
Back to the Bush

The sun was just beginning to rise as Braim and Orandaur led the three horses from the stables to the front of the ranger station. Gall had loaded enough food to last the trio over a month. Braim and Orandaur sat on their horses waiting for Aelundei to finish saying his goodbyes to some of the rangers who had arrived during the night.

"Is he always this way when you're trying to leave?" asked Orandaur.

"No," answered Braim, "sometimes none of his friends are here, except for Gall, who can never leave."

"What confines Gall to the city?" asked Orandaur.

"Long ago," said Braim, "Gall and one of his friends went out on a border patrol in the northern province of Bordras. While they were sneaking into the enemy camp they were ambushed, led into a trap. Gall and his friend were fighting well until the captain came out of his tent. Gall's friend shot the captain in the right eye, but the captain just kept coming at them until they had to fight him with their swords. They fought for a long time and were almost overwhelmed by the goblin captain and his troops, but in the end they managed to cut him down, and they fled, barely escaping with their lives. They were able to make it to Teckor, where they were treated for their injuries. Gall's wounds prevent him from riding on horseback and he also developed breathing problems, so he can never go out and fight again."

"What happened to the goblin they shot?" asked Orandaur.

"Most military officials in Telnor believe the goblin died," said Braim, "but Gall and his friend don't think so. Three months after the battle, Gall's friend went back to the site of the ambush. All he found was his arrow, broken in half."

Once he had finished his story, Aelundei walked out of the inn and mounted his horse. They rode out of the city at a slow trot, trying not to awaken anyone. Passing through the main gate, they rode under the canopy of the silent forest.

"Well," said Aelundei, "we're finally back to our 'home away from home'."

"When do we fight the goblins?" asked Orandaur.

"We'll find them as soon as we get out to the border provinces between Telnor and the goblin lands," said Aelundei, "You were pretty anxious about getting out of the city, Orandaur."

"I never really cared for big cities," said Orandaur, "Being around that many people makes me feel cramped and nervous."

"Ah," said Aelundei, "you make me think you are trying to hide from something. Have you ever had an extended visit to a dungeon?"

"No," said Orandaur, "never have, and hopefully never will." As he said this there was a sinking feeling in his stomach at how close Aelundei's guess had been.

$$*\qquad\qquad*\qquad\qquad*$$

Orandaur's mind was in a whirlwind. Aelundei and Braim were teaching him so many things about the ranger corps and its job of protecting Telnor's borders that he could hardly keep track of it all. As the trio made camp on the fifth day into their ride, he decided that a nice bath would help to straighten everything out.

Braim and Aelundei rarely bathe, Orandaur reminded himself as he slipped quietly out of the camp, *However, they have to ensure the camp is in good order, scout for nearby threats, and plan their next lessons for my training. I can afford to take a quick dip.* The camp was near a small river that wasn't on the map, and Orandaur followed it downstream from the site so he wouldn't foul the party's drinking water. Aside from the one instance during the first day on the trail, Braim and Aelundei had not mentioned any strange activity on Orandaur's part. He assumed this meant he was doing a good job of concealing his true identity of Moraina. He quickly banished the thought. Even remembering a thought of his former life could distract him from his mission, to stay as far away from his family as possible.

I've stopped walking, he suddenly realized. With a shake of his head he started resolutely forward once more, *I cannot think of these things, I need to keep my head in what is happening around me.*

Arriving at a spot where the creek was shielded on both sides by thick clusters of filbert trees, Orandaur decided this was as good a spot as any to disrobe and quickly rinse off his grimy body. Removing his weapons and outer garments, Orandaur laid them among a thick cluster of saplings. He untied the cloth that Moraina had tied around herself to flatten her chest, and rinsed it off in the

28

creek before dunking his whole body beneath the cool water. As he emerged from the water, he suddenly felt exposed. Realizing this had been a poorly-conceived plan, Orandaur quickly retied the cloth around his chest, and was hurriedly donning his homespun tunic when a branch snapped behind him. Orandaur whirled around and drew his sword in the same motion, adrenaline coursing through his veins. On the opposite bank of the creek, five roughly dressed men with wild beards stood, grinning malevolently. Orandaur's eyes went wide and his blood turned to ice as he realized they were all armed.

A man wearing rancid furs, possibly their leader, stepped forward and began to wade into the creek, "I figured you were a runaway woman the instant I saw you," his hand rested on the head of an iron mace that was shoved through his worn leather belt, "Me and my men would love the company of a young lass like you. Come with us to our camp, nice and quietly, maybe we can teach you a few things."

"Back away from me, you scum," said Orandaur coldly, struggling to keep his voice, and hands, steady.

"You're a feisty one, I see," said the leader, "Well, you won't be so temperamental when we've finished with you." The other men guffawed, fanning out and moving into the creek to support their leader.

Orandaur slashed out with his sword as the ugly man reached forward to grab him. The leader dodged, but the razor-edged weapon still opened a large cut along his forearm. "Grab 'er," yelled the leader as he covered the wound with his other hand, trying to staunch the flow of blood.

The young ranger struck as fast as he could at the first man to follow his leader's orders, but the ruffian was a good fighter. He took the blow on his battered shield, then stepped in close before Orandaur could follow up and grabbed his sword-arm. More rough hands grabbed Orandaur from behind, and his blade was pulled from his hands. Despite struggling valiantly, he realized that he could not break free.

The leader approached Orandaur and leaned in, his breath reeking of undercooked flesh and cheap chewing tobacco. "I will enjoy personally beating you to near-death, then selling you to the desert slave traders, where they will whip that temper out of you. Men," began the bandit, "let's get this creature back to camp, and grab-" an arrow cut off his sentence as it slammed into the ugly man's throat, staining his black beard with bright red blood.

29

More arrows flew from the forest, and the other ruffians quickly forgot about what their leader had started to command them in their haste to cross the creek and reach the safety of the trees on the other side.

Orandaur rushed over to his clothing and pulled his pants on, tucked in his shirt, and strapped on his belt. Just as he finished, Aelundei emerged from the foliage next to him. "Braim is continuing to pursue those highwaymen; they must be dispatched for the protection of other wayfarers in Telnor. I will escort you back to the camp."

Orandaur could not talk, he only nodded as he retrieved his quiver and bow.

"What were you thinking, sneaking off on your own in dangerous territory?" questioned Aelundei, exasperated, "Braim and I warned you that this area is well known for harboring outlaws."

Orandaur looked down and shuffled his feet, "I'm sorry, master Aelundei, but I was in great need of a bath, and I am rather fond of my privacy."

Aelundei spread his arms wide and looked at the surrounding forest, "Welcome to the great outdoors, Orandaur. Nobody out here cares how you smell, as long as your stench is not worse than that of the goblins we are hunting." He softened his tone and lowered his voice, "When we reach our main campsite, then feel free to go swimming near the camp in the Mulleno River, but until then, no more dangerous escapades. Privacy is not to be valued over safety."

With that they returned to the camp, Orandaur was silent all evening, slowly mulling over how his actions could have revealed his secret, and how they almost cost him his life.

* * *

It was late morning on the eighth day after leaving Teckor when the trio rode into the campsite that Aelundei had mentioned. It was a pleasant place to camp, guarded in the front by the great river Mulleno, and one of its tributaries known as Beaver Creek. The site was guarded from the rear by a thick grove of pine trees that were tangled with blackberries and had only one entrance, just big enough for the horses.

As they set up camp, Braim took the first watch while Aelundei and Orandaur set up the single person tents. About an hour later, when the tents were ready, and the meal had been cooked and eaten, Braim signaled for the conversation about politics to stop.

"Orandaur," asked Braim, "what is the basic strategy for finding and attacking a goblin raiding party from a home camp?"

Braim watched the young ranger's face. Orandaur was intelligent, and Braim knew he would produce the correct answer in short order. Suddenly his apprentice's countenance lit up, the young lad had remembered.

"Our camp is used as the focal point. Rangers sally forth from the central location. If a goblin camp is discovered, they call the nearest ranger to their area, and back at camp they prepare a raid on the enemy."

"What if the enemy is still moving?" plied Braim, urging his pupil to continue the scenario.

Orandaur thought for a moment, then responded confidently, "One ranger follows the party until they make camp, alerting as many other rangers as possible, and then returns to his camp to coordinate the raid."

"Excellent," Braim grinned, satisfied with his student's understanding. "Aelundei, I'm afraid you're riding alone today, I'll take the novice for his first patrol."

"Very well," said Aelundei, resignedly.

The three friends saddled their horses, strung and tested their bows, then set off in different directions.

As they rode, Braim quizzed Orandaur about the basic procedures for approaching a band of goblins.

"What shall we do if we come across a goblin camp while on horseback?" asked Braim.

"If you come across a goblin camp while mounted," said Orandaur pausing to think, "ride back along the same track and tie up your horse to a tree. That way if your horse whinnies, the goblins won't hear it and be alerted to your presence."

"Good," nodded Braim. "What happens next?"

"After dismounting," asserted Orandaur, "One returns to the camp on foot, moving very slowly to watch for sentries, then find a good location to sit and observe the enemy group."

"Excellent."

An hour passed without seeing any goblins, so the two rangers turned back toward camp, Braim questioning and teaching Orandaur the entire way. They found a bear sitting in the middle of their camp site sniffing for food and digging up the fire pit. Braim slowly dismounted and led his horse away. Orandaur did the same. They both nocked arrows to their strings and drew back, aiming at the bear. The ranger and his pupil fired at almost the same instant, Braim's arrow striking the large bear in the throat, Orandaur's arrow hitting just behind the shoulder. The bear roared in agony, turned towards the rangers, and charged.

"Run!" yelled Braim to Orandaur.

Orandaur turned, ran a short distance, and jumped up into a pine tree. Braim, however, stood his ground, and fired another arrow into the chest of the charging bear. He dropped his bow and drew his large sword.

The bear stopped as it heard the sound of the sword and saw the sharp object in the young man's hands. Its tiny brain sensed that there was no fear in the human that stood defiantly before him, but the small two-legged creature was between him and his escape. The bear lowered its head and resumed its charge, closing the gap between man and beast like a brown bolt of lightning.

Just as the bear was about to slam into him Braim leaped to the side, swinging upwards with his sword at the same instant. The sharp blade cut the bear's main arteries in the throat, and blood spilled swiftly out of the cut.

The bear, confused and enraged by his pain, spun swiftly and batted at Braim with his front paw.

Braim backpedaled at the unexpected reaction, but tripped over a large rock. The young man fell backwards and hit his head violently against a tree. He slumped to the ground, unconscious.

Orandaur cried out. He tried to nock an arrow to his bowstring, but his hands were shaking. The bear ignored him and lumbered towards the still form of Braim, growling ominously as it snapped its jaws, yet obviously weaker from the cut in his neck. Deciding that arrows were useless at this point, Orandaur leaped from the pine, drawing his sword and charging the bear. The brute turned to him with a weak groan. He began stumbling towards the young ranger in training. Orandaur neared the bear, yelling at the top of his lungs. Suddenly the bear stood up on its haunches, swinging one of its front legs wildly and batting the sword out of Orandaur's hands, knocking the boy to the ground. Orandaur rolled to his feet and drew his knife as the bear ambled towards him.

This is it, thought Orandaur grimly, *This is where I die, but I will not let that bear get Braim or me without a fight.* Suddenly, an arrow flew through the air and struck the bear in the throat. Three more arrows followed, and the bear fell and breathed its last.

Aelundei galloped into the entrance of the clearing and leaped off his horse. He took the knife out of Orandaur's hands and threw it to the ground.

"Til fîmu!" said Aelundei, angrily, "Stupid people. I leave you for one hour and you try to get yourselves killed fighting bears!" Then Aelundei noticed Orandaur's hands shaking violently. He dropped the boy's hands and turned to the still form of Braim.

"Get up, Braim," said the elf, "death by bear is not the way I want to see a friend go."

Braim slowly returned to consciousness, and blinked lethargically. He looked back and forth between Aelundei and Orandaur, "What took you so long?" he said to Aelundei.

"What were you doing trying to fight a bear with a hand and a half sword?" asked Aelundei in return, "You would have died if it weren't for Orandaur."

"And that would have been one less orphan in this world; no one would care."

"I would care, Braim. I would miss you terribly."

Braim looked at Orandaur and grinned, "Why didn't you watch my back?"

Orandaur laughed, "You were the one who told me to run."

"Oh yeah, that's right."

*   *   *

Two hours later the three friends were sitting around a pleasant campfire, eating the delicious bear soup, Braim and Aelundei bantering back and forth about Braim getting knocked over by a half-dead bear.

As Orandaur listened to the conversation he wondered how they could be joking about a near death experience already, and also what type of people he had gotten mixed up with. After the meal was done, Braim dunked the cooking pot into the river to rinse it out, while Orandaur and Aelundei cut some of the remaining bear meat into strips and made jerky.

"Well, the day is almost done," said Aelundei, looking up to the setting sun.

"It really turned out to be a nice evening," said Orandaur.

"Yes, it did," said Aelundei, "Before we retire to our tents, I must tell you something."

"Yes?" asked Orandaur, suddenly nervous.

"Remember what we taught you about camping in enemy territory. During the night, we keep a watch over the camp. Whoever is on watch stays awake during his portion of the night listening and watching for anything out of the ordinary, hence the name." said Aelundei. "Tonight, I will take the first watch and Braim will take the second."

"Which means I get the last watch," said Orandaur.

"Correct," said Aelundei, "but you must not forget this: when you keep watch, only put small amounts of wood on the fire at a time. It is extremely dangerous to run out of wood during the night."

"I will remember," said Orandaur.

*   *   *

One month later Orandaur fired the last arrow from his quiver and grinned with pleasure as it slammed into the space near the bull's-eye. He was getting more and more of his arrows into the center of the target, the difference between now and when he had first met Braim and Aelundei was dramatic.

Before he could get the smile off his face, Braim walked up and put a hand on his shoulder, "Orandaur, you are doing much better at archery than you were last month, but there is still much to be learned.

"You have reasonably good accuracy and release speed, but you must work on your form. You need to get your left arm a little more bent. The bowstring is snapping hard against your left fore-arm, but that is preventing you from feeling it," he reached down and tapped Orandaur's left vambrace, "Don't let it slap that, the leather and steel are there to protect your arm from other things.

"Also, you must let the string roll off of your fingers instead of jerking them open all of a sudden. Smooth release will help your accuracy that much more. Work on that when you shoot again, but that is enough for today. Head over to Aelundei for swordsmanship, I am going to get dinner."

Braim strapped on his bow and quiver, then began saddling his horse.

"Wait! Can't I come with you and work on stalking again?" called Orandaur after him.

Braim turned from his work and snapped, "I need some time to myself right now. Work on swordsmanship."

Aelundei walked over to Orandaur and put a hand on his shoulder as Braim mounted his horse and rode into the forest, "This is the eighteenth anniversary of the night that Braim's parents were killed. Afraid of weakness, he tries to hide it by running away from others. It is his custom to withdraw into the woods for solitude, where none can see his feelings exposed. Do not worry, he will be back in a few hours; come, let us spar."

Perhaps Braim just needs a woman to comfort him, thought the part of Orandaur that was still Moraina. He shook his head as he stepped into the center of the clearing, *Knock it off, girl, you'll never maintain your disguise with those thoughts in your head.*

Aelundei drew his sword and stepped over to the camp's clearing.

"Braim has always taught the sword training, so you have learned the style of a swordsman from Telnor Province. You have only been under our tutelage for a month, yet you have done extremely well for only this small amount of training. What I am about to show you is the style of the elven warriors of Elleavemar. As a human, you will never be able to reach true mastery of my style, but I feel that you will do well enough.

"In the elven style, we hardly ever parry, and when we do parry, we use our opponent's strength against them; swing downwards at my head and I will show you."

Orandaur timidly brought his sword down at Aelundei's head, but the elf batted it to the side with a mere flick of the wrist. Orandaur's eyes went wide as he realized how easily his mediocre attack had been deflected. In battle, every ounce of strength that could be conserved drastically increased the odds of survival.

"See? I used just enough strength to deflect your sword down towards the ground. It works best when your opponent actually wants to see you six feet under, and he's putting all his strength behind the swing in hopes of bashing through your guard and helmet, or if he is at least trying to cause you as much of a headache as possible. That way, the sword might actually get slammed into the ground and add a few precious moments onto your enemy's reaction time. In a real fight, this could be the difference between life and death, or victory and defeat."

"Aelundei," said Orandaur, "why can a human never master the elven fighting forms?"

Aelundei chuckled and replied, "There are two reasons. First, humans live a far shorter life than the elves; in fact, elves are immortal. We never die unless killed by the sword or lose the will to live and just perish. Secondly, all elves have an organ between the two halves of our brain called Sílenil. When an elf is in a life or death situation, the organ triggers a state of mind called by my people Illnorean, or The Speed. When an elf reaches the age of one hundred, his brain is fully developed, and he is taught how to use Illnorean at will. It takes a lot of strength, and if you are not careful, you can kill yourself from using it too long or from pushing yourself too hard while in it. But it speeds the reflexes so that everything seems to the elf as if it is moving through honey, slowly. I have actually been able to grab an arrow out of the air before it hit me, but I can only hold Illnorean for about twenty minutes of light fighting or a little more than ten minutes of heavy combat. I don't use it often, so I have gotten weak; the more an elf uses it, the longer he can hold it in battle and the harder he can fight in it."

Orandaur looked at Aelundei and then down at his sword. "Can't you just practice more often?"

This time Aelundei laughed at the absurd statement, "It's not that simple. An elf must go through intense daily reflex exercises before he begins to see an increase in his abilities. You humans do not have the proper equipment, and none of your warriors could provide the speed necessary to make up for this fact. We are wasting time bantering with useless words. Come, let me show you the basic drills for learning my people's fighting style."

Though I cannot master the elven fighting style, thought Orandaur resolutely, *I must at least attempt to.*

Aelundei drilled him for the better part of an hour on basic footwork and stances. Finally, he stepped toward Orandaur and drew his sword. "You have heard of the elven fighting style and tried to learn the basic techniques, but since you are obviously curious, I will demonstrate it to you in full speed. Attack me, try breaking through my defenses, I will not counter attack."

"Are you serious?" asked Orandaur incredulously.

Aelundei nodded with a grin and then settled into his battle stance as his eyes began to glow gold.

Orandaur readied himself, then stepped forward with a vicious downward chop. Aelundei's feet didn't budge, but his blade moved in a blur as it flicked up and redirected Orandaur's attack. Recovering, the novice ranger cut sideways at the elf's midriff. Aelundei again parried the blow without moving his feet, batting the short sword up and over his head. Orandaur rained blows down on Aelundei's defense from every angle as rapidly as he could. Finally after a minute of this drill Orandaur held up his hand.

"Enough," he said between pants, "If all elves fight this hard, do you ever lose battles?"

Aelundei exited Illnorean, the golden glow in his eyes slowly fading, "Yes," he nodded, "my people do lose battles. Like I said, if one holds Illnorean too long, it may result in death. Often times elven warriors actually have to sleep after battles, and then we are more vulnerable."

Orandaur, his curiosity piqued, began to ask a question, but Aelundei raised a hand to stop him. With a nod of his head toward the creek he stated, "Time to work on sword sharpening. Grab your whet stones and come join me."

Aelundei walked over to the creek and sat down on a mossy log near the bank. Soon Orandaur joined him, placing his whetstones next to the log before himself sitting down.

"Aelundei," asked Orandaur thoughtfully as he started drawing his stone across the edge of the blade, "You mentioned earlier that after hard battles elven warriors 'actually sleep.' Are you saying elves don't sleep, either?"

"Well, yes and no," said Aelundei as he moved from his position to sit on the ground with his back against the log. "Normally when elves are tired, they lay down and go into a state of rest, in which they still see and hear everything around them, but they cannot respond unless they leave the resting state. In the state of rest their body recharges, but if an elf has been fighting really hard for a long time, or if they've used Illnorean for too long, or if they've run from one side of the elven kingdom to the other non-stop, then they fall asleep. When an elf sleeps, he sleeps very hard, and don't get between him and food when he wakes."

Orandaur inadvertently shifted away from Aelundei slightly, "Are you all possessed?"

Aelundei rocked his head back and laughed. His eyes were back to their usual blue color again, "No, elves cannot be possessed by demons. We were once messengers of Vitaren, called spirits by some, or angels by others. We were sent down to earth in lesser form, to protect the works of Vitaren from the Dark One. Perhaps different would be a better word."

"Well, I guess that would work, too."

Aelundei dropped his head back against the log and sighed, "You should concentrate on sharpening. Keep working and you may even get your sword sharp enough to shave with it." Orandaur began sliding the stone down the length of the blade. All was quiet.

*   *   *

Braim released the arrow and watched with satisfaction as it sank up to its fletching slightly behind the deer's front left shoulder. The wounded creature leapt away into the brush and disappeared. Braim sat down and waited. It would not be long before the deer collapsed; he had pierced the heart, and probably the lungs, any ranger worth his salt knew where his arrows struck.

As he sat and waited he thought back on his life. He had accomplished nothing with his life, he was worthless. For every village that he saved, another one was lost. And of all the villages he wished he could have saved, there was one in particular that haunted his every dream. More than anything in the world, he wished he could somehow travel back in time to save his parents. He could coordinate defenses, lead the villagers, and eliminate most of the enemy forces with his archery skills.

His thoughts drifted from his parents, to his friends, and finally to his newest companion.

There is something different about that lad Orandaur, thought Braim, *Something very special, but what?*

He debated several different explanations in his mind, from Orandaur being demon possessed to him being the son of a god.

There is no such thing as demons or gods, or Vitaren, no matter what Aelundei says.

He got up quickly, trying to shake the strange thoughts out of his mind, and followed the blood trail of the deer. The trios' supplies were running low, but with the addition of this deer meat they would be able to stay out for at least another week or two before riding back to Teckor. He shouldered his bow and began walking swiftly and silently, making hardly a noise.

The Legend of Braim
Chapter VI
Planning

Grashnir laughed to himself. It would be almost too easy to kill the other kings after they were all settled in Telnor. But for now, he would wait and vent any anger on his servants and slaves. He stood watching the last of the other rulers walking away or being carried on a litter as they set off for the various city states and mountains that they ruled. They had decided to step up their raids and put more capable generals in charge of the raiding parties. Then, about a month before the invasion, they would slow the raids down to a trickle before falling on the unprepared Telnorians, mowing them down like a farmer harvesting his crops. He laughed to himself again at the thought of possibly being able to kill the rangers who had blinded his eye and maimed his leg, leaving him with the multitude of scars that he now bore. He cursed the rangers and headed back to his quarters. He stomped up the stairs and stormed into his room.

"Servant!" Grashnir bellowed, "Get in here."

"Yes, master?" squeaked the servant. He looked at his ruler and realized he was in a bad mood. He cowered.

"Congratulations," said Grashnir, "you've just been promoted to chief of the servants. Go and get acquainted with your new position."

"Yes, oh master." Maybe his master was in a good mood. Then his heart fell as he remembered how long the last chief of servants had lasted, three hours.

Back in the large, warm room, Grashnir's mood improved as he thought of how he could torture the whole ranger corps. He laughed inwardly; *all the apprentices will be flogged and then sentenced to a life of hard labor. The masters will be slowly roasted alive on a spit and then those two who thwarted my plans last time will be forced to walk back and forth on a bed of nails while carrying bags of rocks on their backs.*

"Servant!" yelled Grashnir.

"Yes, master," said a new voice. A tall, proud, goblin walked in the door and bowed.

"Hmm," said Grashnir, "I see that chief servant thought further ahead than the last one by assigning me a new slave. Good for him, he might live a few hours more. What is your name?"

"My name is Jorguel, master," said the servant.

"For your first task as my new servant, I need you to run and summon all my generals; and about twenty smart, cunning, evil-minded goblins who are willing to learn how to become assassins, to my war room."

"Yes, master. I know just the ones," said the goblin as he bowed and left the room at a run.

When Grashnir reached the war room he saw that some of his generals were already there. They came to attention and saluted as soon as he walked into the room.

"At ease and take your seats," said Grashnir as he walked to his seat and sat down. "Servants, bring us drink and bread."

He watched with some amusement as the servants scampered to fulfill his bidding, almost falling over each other in their mad rush to not be the last one out the door. The last of the generals, his twenty assassin candidates, and Jorguel walked in.

"Greetings, my future assassins," said Grashnir. "Stand at attention in the back of the room until I have finished with my generals." Turning to his generals he said. "Generals of my mighty and glorious army, I have summoned you here to brief you on the next few months of planning. You will step up your efforts of raiding a little, and train your troops with wiser tactics. Instead of just handing them a sword and telling them `here's a sword, go kill Telnorians,' expecting them to learn or die. We must do everything in our power to make the Telnorians spread themselves thin. We must learn to work together and to be more brutal, more cut-throat.

"If we organize better and learn how to position body guards so the accursed Telnorian Rangers think they are killing the captain or general of the raid, then we may be able to slowly squeeze the life out of the Ranger corps.

"The smartest and most cunning of my generals, who survive to see another day, could perhaps earn promotion to, say, "Second in Command of the Invading Forces." Grashnir noted that several of the generals' heads perked up at the sound of those words.

After an hour of instructing his generals about their roles, he ordered them to their regiments to commence training.

"Now, my assassins," said Grashnir with a scowl to the twenty goblins who had waited, unblinking, for the past hour, "I have some special tasks for you, but only after you have proven yourselves as assassins to me. At tonight's meal you are to each knock out with poison a high ranking goblin officer. You must not kill any of them.

However, I would like you to put twenty of my generals to sleep for a few hours. After that, seek out Vronalf, the assassin at the castle here. He knows you are coming, and he will train you in the art of assassination."

The Legend of Braim
Chapter VII
Orandaur's First Goblins

Early in the morning, Braim woke Orandaur from his sleep. After eating a cold breakfast while preparing the horses, the trio mounted their horses. Braim waved goodbye and rode east, while Orandaur and Aelundei rode west, they were to meet with him back at camp for lunch. Trainer and trainee had ridden for about an hour when they heard the trill of a Jerrar-bird, the warning call Braim had agreed upon.

"Sounds like Braim found a goblin camp!" said Aelundei, "We better tie the horses here."

Once they had tied up the horses, Orandaur followed Aelundei to the tip of a narrow ravine, and peeked over the edge. After only a month of training Orandaur's mind was already subconsciously noticing the details that a skilled ranger was supposed to look for in a camp. The camp was a large one, with about a hundred goblins cooking, eating, and fighting over plunder and slaves from a village they had just raided. Orandaur had never seen a goblin before, and he studied them closely. They were short people, with pale green skin and no nose, slits on the front of their faces serving the purpose. Their clothes were simple, and their armor simpler. All of a sudden, Orandaur was startled by something slipping out of the forest and lying down next to him. Then he realized it was Braim.

"It's a good-sized camp," whispered Braim. "They have prisoners, and there are more goblins than meets the eye. They used to have sentries in the woods, but I took care of them and made it appear like wild animal attacks."

"How did you do that?" asked Orandaur.

"I'll explain it back at camp," said Braim. Then he turned to Aelundei, "Are you ready to draw sticks, my friend?"

"Ready as I'll ever be," Aelundei replied. "However, they have prisoners we will have to rescue, and that makes things slightly more difficult."

"Glad to see someone is optimistic!" Braim chuckled.

"There's never been an obstacle that we haven't tackled," reminded Aelundei with one eyebrow cocked, "Besides, it will be a great opportunity for Orandaur to learn about sneaking prisoners from right underneath a goblin's warts."

Braim picked up two sticks from the ground, one shorter than the other.

"Orandaur, we need you to switch these two sticks around," explained Braim, "And then we will draw them out of your hand. Whoever gets the short stick watches the enemy camp until you and the person with the long stick return from our camp to participate in raiding the raiders."

"Why are we leaving the camp we just found?" asked Orandaur incredulously. "Why do we not engage them in battle now?"

"Have you been with us over a month and not learned anything?" asked Braim, raising his hands and looking at the sky.

"Calm yourself," said Aelundei to Braim. Then he turned to the blushing Orandaur, "Look at the odds: over one hundred goblins, even though they are just over three feet tall, against three rangers. Even Braim wouldn't attempt that."

Braim shot him a dark look, but remained silent.

"I see," said Orandaur, nodding.

"I knew you would," replied Aelundei, smiling.

Orandaur held out the two sticks, and the two rangers drew them from his hand. Aelundei drew the long one, and Braim drew the short one.

"Well then," sighed Braim, "I get the watch, you two go get your rest and bring some food for me."

"See you later," said Aelundei, then added with a mischievous grin, "we'll try to remember the part about food."

*   *   *

Back at camp, Aelundei briefed Orandaur about the fast-approaching raid.

"What did you observe about the camp?" asked Aelundei.

Orandaur recounted everything he had seen to the elf about the number of sentries, the approximate number of troops, as well as the location of the raid leader and also where his captains would be.

The elf smiled and nodded, "Excellent, Orandaur. Tonight when we return, we first need to take out the sentries; this is accomplished by shooting them. Then we sneak into camp, and slit the throats of the leaders along with their body-guards; first the bodyguards, and then the leaders that they are trying to protect. Why do we not immediately target the leader?"

Orandaur thought for a moment, rubbing his chin with his fingers. His head suddenly jerked upright as he answered jubilantly, "If one targets the leader first, he may awaken the bodyguards!"

Aelundei pointed his finger and grinned, "Precisely. Braim will take out the commander, you will take out the captains, and I will rescue the prisoners, understood?"

"I think I got that all," said Orandaur.

"Good, now go and get your rest, Orandaur," said Aelundei, "it's going to be a long night, and when I wake you up, you will need to throw together a cold dinner for three while I get the horses."

As Orandaur went to sleep, he could not help but hope that all went well.

*   *   *

Orandaur was roused several hours later by Aelundei, who was shaking him and saying, "Orandaur, it's time to go." It was extremely humid despite fall having sank its claws into Telnor, and crickets chirped in the background as the young ranger packed the saddle bags. First he grabbed the beef jerky, then threw in a couple of water skins and the whey bread. Orandaur much preferred bread cooked with yeast to the whey bread, but there was not enough room in the saddlebags. Then they put everything into the bags, and started out on the ride to the site of the goblin camp.

"Aelundei," queried Orandaur, "I brought all of the jerky and whey bread to give to the captives, do you want to take that with you into the camp to give to them or leave it with the horses?"

"Smart idea," said Aelundei, both eyebrows raised. "You are already beginning to think like a ranger. Did you bring any water skins?"

"Yes," replied Orandaur, "I filled five of the big ones in Beaver Creek."

"You can leave the food in the saddle bags," said Aelundei, "but I will take the water with me."

When they arrived at the goblin camp, Aelundei filled Braim in on the plan, and then the three rangers went to work. Orandaur went to the opposite side of the ravine from Braim's viewpoint, accompanied by Aelundei, who had concluded that was the best avenue of approach to the chained-up slaves in the center of the goblin camp. He then nocked an arrow to the string of his bow and

44

drew back, sighting on one of the few sentries who were awake. Orandaur took a deep breath and released the arrow, which flew so fast across the ravine it seemed to grow out of the throat of the guard. The goblin fell to the ground with a silent gurgle. Aelundei and Braim did the same from their positions. He pulled out another arrow and did the same to the only other guard left after his friend's deadly salvo. Then he drew his knife and slid silently down to the bottom of the ravine. The first thing he did when he reached the bottom was retrieve his arrows, then he went to the nearest tent and entered.

Orandaur stood over the first bodyguard in the tent. Moraina could have never taken a life, yet Orandaur had already killed several. His hands shook as the knife neared the throat. This goblin was only doing his job. Did he have a family that he was trying to support? Was he forced to fight and guard his superiors? Then Orandaur remembered the villagers chained together in the center of camp, and his hardened to match the resolve on his face. Quickly he stabbed the knife into the throat of the goblin, and the black blood spilled out. The small creature gurgled silently and was dead. Trembling, the young ranger withdrew his knife. That creature had injured and killed innocents, even burned their village to the ground. He deserved to die. With tears coursing down his cheeks, Orandaur moved to the next goblin and stabbed it in the throat.

Meanwhile, Aelundei was seeing his own action. As soon as his arrow left the string he began to move down the slope, confident that after one hundred years of practice he was able to hit a stationary target at twenty yards. He crawled down the slope, retrieved his arrows, and slew the guards of the slaves silently with his knife. Startled by the sudden fighting, a few of the captives started to cry out, but their quick-thinking companions stopped them.

"It's ok," said Aelundei softly as he made soothing gestures with his hands, "I am a member of the ranger corps, and I've come to get you out of here." Reaching to the water skins at his side, he untied their leather straps to hand them to the captives, "Here, take these."

The slaves drank the water he gave them most gratefully, and he used the distraction of them passing around the skins to wrap their chains in cloth to muffle the noise. Yet even with this precaution there were over thirty men, women and children. He paused, should he dare attempt to saw the chains off here? Or would it be safer to lead them away now? Sawing them off here would take too long, yet leading them away could awake the entire camp. Throwing caution to the wind, he decided to move them now. Gesturing them forward up a less steep portion of the ravine, the elf drew his bow and an arrow, and then watched the camp intently. Orandaur moved from one tent to the next, Braim left the commander's tent to begin killing the captains, yet none of the foot soldiers stirred. As the last of the freed slaves cleared the edge of the ravine, Aelundei silently thanked Vitaren before following them. Moving to the head of the procession, he motioned with one hand, "follow me."

Braim also had some action. When he had finished off the guards on his side, he had moved silently to the tent of the goblin chieftain. When he made it to the tent he found two guards, one on each side of the tent flaps, asleep at their posts. He drew his hunting knife and eased them silently into a sleep from which they would never awake. Then he slid silently into the tent, moved like a shadow around the two body guards inside, and prepared to kill them as well. Then, on a sudden impulse, he moved to the bedside of the chieftain, and slit his throat. Then he moved back to the two bodyguards, and slammed their heads together. Next he bent over each of them one at a time and slammed the pommel of his knife into the back of their skull. Smiling, he grabbed a bottle of ale that was in the tent and poured it on them. *That ought to leave them a headache, but I'm sure their sergeant will allow them a long time to sleep after discovering them with a very severe hangover tomorrow morning.*

It was some time later when the three of them came together at the pre-arranged meeting place. Aelundei had successfully removed the slave's chains. Braim had eliminated the chieftain and several captains, and Orandaur had killed all the other captains.

"Well, another job well done," said Aelundei, "we have all the captives, we have eliminated the chieftain and all his captains, and it looks like we still have about an hour of semi-darkness. Braim, I want you to take Orandaur and show him how to cover our tracks. I shall take all three of the horses and put those of the captives who are unfit to walk in the saddles. We'll meet again at the camp. Orandaur, I want you to make breakfast when you get there."

Orandaur was staring blankly at his hands, stained black by goblin blood.

"Orandaur, did you hear me?"

Orandaur looked up, startled, "I killed living creatures." The reminder of the evening's combat was too much. Turning away from the group of former captives, he vomited into the forest.

Aelundei walked over to him and poured water over Orandaur's hands, cleaning the blood away, "Killing is wrong, and it is not the will of Vitaren, but you must snap out of it. Goblins were originally elves, but they were bribed by the enemy and tricked into serving him, and Vitaren cursed them. They are evil, Orandaur, and can only work evil. You did right in ending their lives and bringing less punishment on their souls." Aelundei looked into Orandaur's eyes. "Right now I need you to concentrate. These people need our help, and I don't need another person to take care of."

Orandaur nodded sheepishly, his cheeks burning, "I understand."

With that Aelundei set out with the freed captives, Orandaur and Braim beginning to cover the tracks of the party.

Braim carefully taught the fine points of the art of hiding tracks while they worked, and all was going well until the two rangers heard the sound of a goblin pursuit party.

"Sounds like they're after us!" said Braim, "Quick! Get into the trees."

No sooner were they hidden among the shadows of the pines than about twenty goblins entered the clearing that they had just been in. They found the tracks of the slaves and were about to take off after them when Braim had an idea. "Orandaur, shoot the leader. I'll go around to the other side of the clearing and shoot a couple arrows from there. Shoot twice and then keep moving." Braim disappeared into the woods. Orandaur selected some arrows from his quiver and aimed at the leader of the hunting party. He shot the leader, another goblin, and then started to move to another spot. Just as the goblins were about to make it to the spot that Orandaur had been a few moments ago, two more goblins were felled by Braim's arrows.

"I bet all of you idiots together can't find me," yelled Braim from the forest.

This seemed to confuse the goblins. They had just been shot from the opposite side of the clearing than where the arrows had come from first.

They turned around, and then half of them went toward the spot where Orandaur had been and the others went toward Braim. When they had almost reached the spot Orandaur shot four more arrows from his new hiding spot, each one hitting its mark.

"Not over there, you idiots, over here!" yelled Orandaur, emboldened by Braim's words.

This sent the goblins into a panic. They suddenly thought that

47

they were facing a force much larger than they really were facing, but just as they were about to run Braim let loose the whole force of years at honing his archery skills, Orandaur trying to copy. They fired as fast as they could and stepped out of the cover of the trees so that the goblins could see them. When the ten or so remaining goblins realized that it was only two rangers shooting them, they charged, yelling curses in the harsh language of the goblin-people. The two rangers kept firing arrows and insults until the creatures were almost on top of them, then drew their swords and cut down the remaining few.

"Well, that's all of them," said Braim, "You did a great job, Orandaur. Do you understand why we stepped out into the clearing?"

"Yes, I do," said Orandaur, "We did it so that the goblins would realize there were only two of us. They then got confident and charged us. It is done so that all the goblins are exterminated and none go back to sound the alarm and possibly betray our position."

"Good, very good," said Braim as Orandaur blushed, "now, we need to pitch the goblins into the woods and continue covering our tracks."

They did as he suggested then continued on their way, but deep in the bottom of the pile something moved. As soon as the rangers were gone, a goblin crawled out of the pile of its dead comrades and started to limp back to the goblin camp.

*   *   *

Braim and Orandaur made it back to camp quickly and told Aelundei of their encounter with the enemy. Aelundei was uneasy about the goblins being smart enough to come after them.

"It's not like goblins to come after us once their leaders have been killed," he said, "They normally race back to their territory, the overrun ex-province of Torrer. Orandaur, are you sure that you got all the goblins that were in tents?"

"Yes," said Orandaur, "I am sure. Perhaps one of the leaders was smart enough to put one of his troops into the tent where he was instead of himself."

"Excellent deduction," said Aelundei, "that would explain why the goblins came after you. If that is true, we need to get these farmers out of here immediately, before the enemy can try a counter attack."

"I do not think a counter attack is imminent," said Braim, "besides, we covered our tracks as well as we could and I was instructing Orandaur on every fine point in the technique. No, I do not think a counter attack will happen any time soon. We need to give the villagers a few days to recover from their ordeal before we move out."

"Braim, just because you've had years of practice, doesn't mean you are not subject to mistakes or failure," said Aelundei, "The best of us, even I, have had a time where we have made mistakes or failed in a certain task. I say we leave this place immediately and head in the most direct line to the nearest castle in Telnorian territory, which would be Castle Rochaon, a three-day's ride as the eagle flies."

"I second that," said Orandaur, "Braim, I'm not trying to sound better than you, and may the gods above help us if I were in charge of this operation, but I agree with Aelundei, we need to get out of here in a hurry."

"I guess I have no choice but to come with you two then," said Braim. "Let's get away from here."

Grashnir was highly pleased with the way things were going. So far, eleven of his generals had tipped over. From a distance, they appeared to be dead, but upon close examination they were proven to be asleep; they were still breathing and their hearts were still beating. He had been surprised when the first general had fallen asleep after the first few bites. He had laughed inwardly when all the others had also fallen asleep. Just then, another of the generals' heads started to nod and then his head fell forward onto his food. *There's number twelve*, thought Grashnir, *my future assassins are doing extremely well*. Grashnir also noticed that with every general that had fallen over, one of the potential assassins would smile. *That's something that will need to be fixed*, thought Grashnir. Then all at once, as if it had been carefully rehearsed, eight more of his generals toppled over backwards, their chairs hitting the floor almost in unison. As soon as the generals were confirmed to be alive, Grashnir stood and started to clap. "Congratulations, my new assassins, well done." At that all the assassins stood and bowed together.

"However," growled the goblin king, "You made one fatal mistake. As each one of the generals that you poisoned hit the floor, or fell into their food, you smiled. In enemy territory you could be killed for smiling at the fall of your target. You must learn to control your expressions. Now then, run and report to your new teacher, Vronalf."

He made a mental note that none of the assassins ran to fulfill his bidding. Instead, they started to slink out of the room and then jog silently down the hall. *Just like my new servant*, he thought.

With that, Grashnir sat back down and recommenced his dining. Then he had his slaves carry the snoring generals up to their rooms.

As soon as he finished eating, he went up to his quarters and pulled out his old sword from its shelf on the wall. He drew the sword and examined it. It was a cruel-looking, single-edged scimitar. The hand guards were the shape of scorpion claws, and the pommel was elongated, curving back around to form the stinger of the huge insectoid. The grip was wrapped in black leather that resembled the body, and two almond-shaped rubies were set between the hand guards as eyes.

We'll be invading Telnor in a few months, thought Grashnir, *Better get my weapons sharpened.* He then reached back into the shelf and pulled out four knives that were almost identical to the sword. He spun a knife experimentally to test its balance. *As perfect as it was a decade or two ago*, he thought. Turning swiftly he threw the knife. It hit the door just as his servant was opening it. The goblin didn't flinch at all as the knife struck, still quivering, an inch from his hand. "Master, the king of Braaztulh requests an audience."

"Why does he request another audience?" asked Grashnir with a frown.

"He claims that you set up robbers along the trail," said the servant, "I tried to tell him that if you had wanted to rob him of the possessions that he had brought with him, you would have just taken them at the castle. But he wouldn't listen to me, your highness."

"Very well," said Grashnir, "show him up to the big room." As the servant jogged off to fulfill his master's bidding, Grashnir was silently cursing his luck. Of all the times for robbers to attack the other rulers, this was the worst. As he strapped his sword and knives onto his belt, he reminded himself that Gartsamn had one of the largest armies of all the goblin kings, rivaled only by his own. He must not lose this ally. Then he walked out the door and went up the stairs to the highest room in the tower at the center. The room was called the big room because it was extremely large for a room that high up in a tower. When he reached the door of the room he was completely sure of what he would have to say to Gartsamn to convince him that the robbery was purely coincidence. He would even offer an armed escort to take him back to his castle. He opened the door and entered the room. He noticed that the tiger, named Graklen, was pacing in its cage faster than usual. He also noticed that king Gartsamn was sitting in the seat closest to the tiger, poking it with a spear.

"I would be greatly pleased," said Grashnir, "if you would stop stabbing my dear Graklen and sit away from him." He noticed that Gartsamn jumped at the sound of his voice and almost dropped his spear.

"Ah, Grashnir," he said, "I have come to tell you that I was assaulted by robbers on the way back to my kingdom. They bore your insignia, and robbed me of my possessions on your behalf."

"What proof do you have," asked Grashnir, "other than my

insignia, which could easily be stolen or replicated, that points toward me arranging your robbery?"

"It was confirmed when they ordered me to halt on behalf of king Grashnir, ruler of Torrer," replied Gartsamn. "What further evidence do I need?"

"I have met with other robbers," said Grashnir, "that have ordered me to stop on behalf of some king or another, and they have all been fakes, save two."

"That still does not prove your innocence," said Gartsamn.

"Listen to me, Gartsamn," said Grashnir, "If I had wanted to rob you of your possessions, then I would have done it in the middle of the night, in the middle of my castle surrounded by thousands of my men. Then I would have thrown you in prison to rot, just like I did to the former king of my kingdom."

"You are giving me the same speech as your servant," said Gartsamn, "I will not listen to you and your lies, Grashnir."

"How much did you lose when they robbed you?" asked Grashnir, growing angry, "I will repay it and send a royal guard with you that is twice as strong as the one you lost."

"Here is what I lost," said Gartsamn "I lost three Telnorian servants, fifty of my best goblin warriors, and the copy of the map to Telnor that you gave me."

"Here's what I plan to do," said Grashnir "I will give you three good servants, 100 of my elite soldiers to see you back to your castle, and a new copy of the map to Telnor as well. And I will offer you a position of high authority when we invade Telnor, say, second in command of the invading forces. Will that make you happy?"

"Pocket change," said Gartsamn folding his arms with a sneer.

Grashnir knew he would have to offer more. Reluctantly, he expanded on his previous deal, "Very well," Grashnir said with a sigh, "I will give you nine servants, 150 of my soldiers, and a new copy of the map." He paused and then added, "I shall also throw in three barrels of ale to lighten your mood."

"Deal?" asked Grashnir as he spat on his hand.

"Deal," replied Gartsamn as he also spat on his hand and shook Grashnir's.

The Legend of Braim
Chapter IX
Separate Ways

After the rangers had gotten the refugees awake and fed, they saddled the horses and set those who couldn't move quickly on the saddles. The trio and their new companions headed out to the nearest province, Rochaon. Rochaon Castle, near the center of the territory, could usually be reached on foot in four days from their location on the border. Due to the poor condition of the former captives, Aelundei had figured it would take closer to five days to cover the distance to the castle. They were now on day five and they were still around twenty five miles from the castle. Braim had lagged behind to make sure they weren't being followed; so far, nothing had made him worried. As they walked, rode and shuffled along, the captives were starting to get tired again; Aelundei knew that it would soon be time to stop and rest. He walked over to Orandaur and voiced his thoughts, "I think you should run back and check on Braim again."

"I was just thinking the same exact thing." said Orandaur, "Would you like me to take him some food, as well?"

"That is a good idea." said Aelundei, "He could use some company, too."

With that, Orandaur moved to get some food from the saddle bags, but before he could leave with it a child on the horse asked "Are the goblins coming?"

"Of course not," said Orandaur, "Ranger Braim has the situation taken care of, my dear."

"Thank him for saving me" said the little girl.

"I'll make sure I do that," said Orandaur. Then Orandaur sank into the forest and disappeared.

Meanwhile, Braim was thoroughly bored. He was all alone in a forest, and even if there had been someone there, they wouldn't have been able to see him. There wasn't even a sound except for the sound of birds in the distance. Braim would walk for a while then stop and listen for the slightest sound of pursuit, but there never was a sound of anything at all. He was walking along, when suddenly, Orandaur seemed to materialize out of a tree a few feet in front of him. Braim jumped and said, "Orandaur, let me know next time you sneak around in the woods! You are lucky I did not mistake you for a goblin!"

"I must be getting good at this stealth stuff if I can scare you," replied Orandaur with a smug grin, "Anyway, I brought you some lunch and company!"

"I always love both of those." said Braim as he took the food and ate, "How are the refugees doing?"

"They are doing fine," said Orandaur, "but they keep throwing their heads back over their shoulders and looking for a sign of pursuit."

"So far I haven't seen or heard anything." said Braim "And it sure gets quiet and lonely back here. Not even the birds are singing anymore, it gives a certain thought of evil when all I hear is silence."

"Wait a minute," said Orandaur, strangely uneasy, "did you say that the birds weren't singing?"

"Yes," said Braim, "it struck me as odd when the birds fell silent about an hour ago, but I think it's merely our presence." He stood up when he finished his food, then stiffened as he heard a noise.

"What do you," began Orandaur, but stopped in mid question as he saw Braim put a finger to his lips. He lowered his voice to a whisper and started again, "what do you hear?"

"Goblins," said Braim, "and lots of them. Hurry, run to warn Aelundei, I'll hold them off for a while."

The last thing Orandaur saw as he bolted off into the darkening woods was Braim nocking an arrow to the string of his bow and melting into the forest.

*   *   *

Braim drew back on the string of his long bow as the first goblin in the party of trackers was about to turn the corner of the clearing. He was fifty feet up near the peak of a pine tree. If he had not been waiting for the immanent attack he would have enjoyed the climb. But this was a matter of life or death and he was not in the mood for enjoying anything, especially not while his friends were in danger. As the first goblin rounded the corner, Braim loosed five arrows in rapid succession. The party of goblins was around twenty, he would only have five arrows left after this group was finished. He hope the goblins were far enough away that he could retrieve his arrows.

As the first five goblins to round the corner fell, the rest dropped to the ground in an effort to dodge any further missiles. *Like shooting chickens,* thought Braim grimly as he began to fire arrows as fast as he could. When seven more of their companions fell, the remaining eight goblins jumped up and ran for the trees. Two more fell, pierced by the ranger's arrows, before they made it to safety. Braim slid down from his pine as quickly as he could. The goblins, hearing the noise of Braim's descent, charged him at the bottom of the tree. Braim was able to loose two more arrows into the charging goblins, but was forced to drop his bow and draw his sword, taking on the remaining six in a melee attack. He downed two of them with a single swing of his sword, stabbed one through the heart, and was able to bring his sword up just in time to block a blow from another goblin's sword. He kicked that goblin below the belt then beheaded it as it was falling. The remaining two turned to flee, and Braim was barely able to scoop up his bow to finish them off before they could escape. As the last goblin fell, he grabbed his sword and cleaned the black blood off it with a goblin shirt, before sliding it back into its sheath. He then retrieved all of the unbroken arrows and prepared for the next wave.

*   *   *

Aelundei was walking along, listening to the refugees conversing in hushed tones, when all of a sudden Orandaur appeared next to him. He jumped in surprise, "Orandaur, let me know next time you sneak around in the woods! You are lucky I did not mistake you for a goblin!"

"I think you have been listening to Braim talk too much," said Orandaur, out of breath, "Aelundei, we have to run fast and hard. The goblins are after us!" The villagers' conversations all stopped, and they looked at the two rangers, fear plainly visible on every face.

"What?" asked Aelundei, in disbelief.

"I took Braim his lunch," said Orandaur, whispering, "and when he finished, we heard the sound of goblins in pursuit. He told me to run ahead and warn you. Even as we speak he is buying us time."

"Then we must hurry," replied Aelundei in a similar tone, "tell the villagers to run or ride at a steady jog."

"Aelundei," said Orandaur, squaring his shoulders, "I do not know the way to this castle you call Rochaon. One elf alone could take care of the villagers. I want to go back and help Braim."

"You are not going back," said Aelundei, firmly, "I will not allow it."

"Aelundei," said Orandaur, clenching his jaw, "I promise not to actually engage the enemy; all I have to do is follow their trail and leave markers for you to follow in the event of Braim's capture."

"I do not care if you engage the enemy or not," said Aelundei, "how do you know that they are not still following us?"

"I am not that stupid," said Orandaur, "I would never be unaware enough as to run straight into the enemy. I am going, and nothing you do or say is going to be able to stop me!"

Aelundei was prepared to argue back, but when he saw the look in Orandaur's eyes, he realized that he was telling the truth. *Humans*, he thought, *are worse than mules in the morning!* "Orandaur, get the villagers running and come back to me when you are done."

"Yes, Aelundei," replied Orandaur, running to do as Aelundei had said.

*   *   *

Braim charged the goblins with a mighty battle cry. He had killed about fifty of them by now, twenty-three with the bow, and the rest with his sword. But the goblins had finally grown wise on him. As their companions fell, those behind leapt over their fallen comrades and dog-piled Braim, pulling him down with sheer weight of numbers. As he went down, he drew his knife and roared his defiance, determined to take out as many as possible. He would fight to the very end.

*   *   *

Orandaur rode Prince faster than he had ever ridden before. It had taken him a long time to convince Aelundei to let him go, but in the end he had prevailed! Now he was riding like the Devil himself was after him. He hoped he was not too late to rescue Braim. As he rode, his mind absently returned to his life before running away, this time he forgot to suppress it. He remembered how it felt to wear a dress instead of wearing men's clothes and having to disguise his voice. He remembered going to the few parties that his sisters had allowed him to go to, he remembered wondering about which boy would dance with him. He remembered being Moraina. Her mind returned to the present and she realized that a tear was running down her cheek. She dashed it away angrily and kept riding, it would do no good to meet Braim crying.

*   *   *

Braim slashed at the goblins until his knife was taken away from him. Then he started hitting goblins with his bare hands. He finally managed to escape the dog-pile that he was buried in, for he fought valiantly. But every goblin he killed, two more took their place. He reached down now and picked up a goblin sword. It was not well balanced and very rusty, but it would have to do. He slew about ten more goblins, and then they dog-piled him again. He roared as loud as he could, then he was punched in the side of the face. The world went black.

*   *   *

Drallgn, now commander of the raiding party, surveyed the wreckage that was before him. *It looks like a battalion of trolls ran through here*, he thought, *more like two battalions*. Two goblin soldiers walked up to him, carrying an unconscious human in ripped-up clothes between them. They dropped the human and saluted. He returned the salute.

"Commander," one of the goblins said, "here is the man who destroyed half our battalion."

"Where are the others?" he asked. Seeing no understanding, he explained. "There has to be more than just this one human, fool."

"No commander, there were no others" said the goblin.

Shaking his head in disbelief, Drallgn looked over the battle field again. "How many dead and wounded are there, soldier?" he asked.

"There are nine-and-seventy dead, six-and-twenty wounded and two-and-ten dying, Commander."

"That is over half of what is left of this raiding party!" said Drallgn, "If they all fight like that then we had better turn and run for the border. Put the dead into a pile and burn them. Dismissed!" As the soldiers ran off to do his bidding, he turned and walked away, shouting orders to lieutenants as he went. Then, what was left of the raiding party turned and marched off; leaving a column of smoke behind them. This had been the worst raid that Drallgn had ever been in.

57

When Moraina made it to the scene of the battle the fire was burning down to red hot coals. She started walking toward the fire, but her toe hit something in the long grass. She bent down to investigate, and came up with Braim's bow. A memory flashed into her head, *Braim clapped her on the shoulder after she fired the last arrow downrange. "Good job, Orandaur," he said with his typical wide grin, "your speed is really improving." He raised his own bow as he explained a better technique, his muscles rippling as he drew back the string. He was so attractive.*

Her heart began to sink as she started to walk into the middle of the battlefield. Then she saw a sword lying in the grass. It was Braim's sword, covered in black goblin blood.

Braim parried a series of blows, then lowered his sword as he stepped back, a cocky grin plastered on his face. "Much better, City Boy, keep improving, and you might eventually be able to beat somebody."

Moraina looked down and shuffled her feet.

"Hey, keep your chin up, Orandaur," said Braim as he tapped her chin with two fingers. Growing serious, he continued, "I'm proud of your progress, you are the best apprentice I've ever had."

"He's also the only apprentice you've ever had," interjected Aelundei from across the clearing, happily.

The trio laughed heartily, the cares of their dangerous lifestyle melting away.

Moraina knelt down, clutching the sword and bow to her chest, weeping uncontrollably. The full weight of Braim's imprisonment or death descended onto her shoulders, and she was left to bear it all alone.

The Legend of Braim
Chapter X
Grashnir's Army

All throughout Castle Torrer, the sounds of preparation could be heard. The clang of the blacksmith's hammer forging swords, spears, axes and armor; the steady ringing of a sharpening wheel; and if you had good enough ears, you would have been able to hear the new assassins working on stealth. Grashnir heard it all. He heard the blacksmith, the grinding of the sharpening wheel and the new assassins. He also heard the surprised yelps of the unwary goblins that were caught off guard and surprised. He smiled every time he heard a yell. He smiled even further when one of the assassins tried his luck on him, and yelled as Grashnir suddenly spun around and put a knife to his throat. "Never try to sneak up on your king, the master of backstabbing, idiot," said Grashnir, and then he left the goblin standing in the hallway, dazed. As Grashnir walked around surveying the preparations, he eagerly looked forward to the battle and being able to personally kill his enemies. He walked up next to a forge and watched the smith and his assistant working on a half-finished sword. Though goblins were not generally known as skilled craftsmen, the smiths of Torrer were able to turn out some very good weapons. He walked over and picked up an axe, which had just been equipped with a handle. He swung it a few times to test the weapon, then brought it down with force on a barrel, splitting it neatly in half.

"Good axe," commented Grashnir as he handed the weapon to the blacksmith and walked off.

He made his way down to the courtyard to watch the weapons drills. This was the first time that the goblins in Torrer had actually trained soldiers in combat, and it had taken some time for Grashnir to find a good instructor. But in the end, he had prevailed, and the results were very good. Welmn was a talented instructor, and the new weapons school had turned out a few battalions in the two months it had been in operation. He watched Welmn yelling commands "Up cut," he yelled, "head-slash, cleave-head!" Whenever a goblin was too slow or didn't execute the movement the way Welmn wanted it, he hit them across the back with a bull whip. Learn to fight properly, or get whipped.

He turned and walked off to view the preparations of designing siege engines to destroy the Telnorian castles. They would not try to drag the siege engines with them, the goblins were just trying to get used to building them and making them fling rocks as far as they could with as much power as possible on impact. So far, the trebuchet had been the best catapult tried. They could not get them to work perfectly, but still, they worked better than any of the other catapults. Grashnir watched as a trebuchet crew got another rock into the giant sling and fired a shot at the small house that they had commandeered for a target. It missed, but it was about ten feet closer than the last twenty or thirty times that they had fired the device. Of course, a castle would be a lot easier to hit than a house, so therefore, this amount of inaccuracy was not of concern. He turned around and went to check on the class that was supposed to be happening with his assassins at that moment.

He opened the door and entered the small room. They were in the middle of a class on how to use a grappling hook. Vronalf was in the middle of explaining how to land hooks on rock walls as quietly as possible. When the king walked in, the class paused for a moment but quickly resumed. Vronalf gathered up his gear as he said:

"Let us now go out to the castle's ramparts to test what we have learned."

Grashnir followed the group out to the high wall, and listened as the master assassin explained the grappling hook throwing techniques to his class.

"Remember," said Vronalf, "for a wall of this height, you need to throw the hook overhand. For a wall about ten, maybe twenty feet shorter than this, then you can throw it underhand. Do not throw it too much higher than the wall; otherwise it will come back down on the rampart with too big of a noise. Make sure you bloody well throw it when there are no guards around or you'll get killed." With that, he proceeded to watch all the assassins-in-training throw their hooks, and start climbing up. The first goblin to throw his hook made it twenty feet up before he fell when the hook came loose; his legs broke when he hit the ground. The others learned from his mistake and tested their hooks for any sign of movement before climbing; they all made it up safely. At the top the assassins waited as Vronalf and Grashnir each threw a hook, and ascended. Once that was accomplished, Grashnir commanded them to continue training hard and then left, heading for his quarters.

When Grashnir made it to his room, he sat down in his chair and thought expectantly towards the day that he would crush the aggravating Telnorians and take control of the rest of the goblins' countries. That was why he needed the assassins; he would poison the leaders one at a time, with poison that would look like severe illness. Then, when they died, he would use his clever tongue to get himself in charge of the countries. It was all so simple. The only glitch with his plan was the small, stubborn goblin kingdom of Karadancth. The goblins of Karadancth were people who dwelt high in the mountains on the border of the elf lands. Their people would not easily be swayed. However, he could worry about that when the time came. Right now, the only thing that worried him was the issue of the rapidly disappearing stores of Telnorian wine.

"Servant!" He yelled.

"Yes, great ruler?" said the servant, as he bowed deeply.

"I want you," said Grashnir, "to bring me some of the Telnorian wine and a chalice for it. While you are at it, bring me bread too."

"Yes, Master," said the servant as he bowed again and jogged off to get what his master had requested.

Grashnir leaned back and thought of his plans for destroying the country of Telnor and waited for his wine.

The Legend of Braim
Chapter XI
The Chase

Moraina slowed her pace, not wanting to make Aelundei kill the horses while trying to catch up. She leaned out of Prince's saddle and cut another chunk of bark out of a tree next to her. She hoped Aelundei would notice the trail she was blazing. Turning in the saddle, the young woman checked the large bundle that was tied behind her, it was still snug and secure. She had wrapped Braim's bow and sword in his cloak, but every time she checked the package, it reminded her of him. No one had yet guessed that she was a woman in disguise; Aelundei had gotten pretty close a couple of times, but Braim was still clueless as to her identity. She was glad Braim was not a people person. Tears began to well up in her eyes as she thought of Braim. If she had not been worried about being turned in and sent back to her father, then she would have told Braim of her true identity long ago, for she had grown to love him. Knowing that he would disown her immediately, she could never tell him, so she had had tried to spend more time watching Aelundei and learning from him. Now all she wanted to do was confess it and weather what was due to her. In the culture of Telnor, if a boy ran away from his father, he was returned and the father was viewed as a bad father. If a daughter ran away, it was a completely different story. She would be returned, yes, but then she would be married to a man with children so she would be too busy to run away again. She hoped Aelundei wouldn't send her back, but she didn't doubt that Braim would insist on sending her away. Braim probably had some other love out there that he cared about; why leave her for a crazed runaway?

$$* \qquad * \qquad *$$

At that very moment, Braim was being dragged along by a green, wart-faced goblin about three-quarters his size. He didn't mind this silent captor, he was better than the one who had been handed his leash a few hours before. Every two or three hours the goblins would rotate, and Braim would have a new guard. The previous soldier had despised Braim, pulling and jerking him along, often times dragging him face first through mud puddles and thorn-bushes. To keep his mind off of trying to get loose and break the cruel goblin's neck, he had tried to imagine what his parents had been like. His father would have been slightly taller than he was, with red hair and bright green eyes. He was the village blacksmith, and a humble man, using his strength to help others, not himself. His mother would have been not quite as tall as Braim, she would have had blonde hair, and hazel eyes. She would have been quiet and soft spoken, except on issues that she felt strongly about. They would have been the perfect couple. Just then, there was a commotion at the head of the column of goblins. It had something to do with a human, and a lack of meat!

*   *   *

Aelundei dismounted from his horse. He had ridden him hard for over an hour, and it was time to give him a break. The elf loosened the girth of the saddle a little to let Valostala breathe easier. Then he tightened the cinch on Braim's horse, mounted the saddle, and set off at a steady canter. It was a good horse, but there was no comparison between it and his elven horse. His horse was long-legged, light and agile. It had a smooth, gentle gait, and yet if anyone other than the three people he trusted tried to ride her, she would sense the change and the thief would curse the day he was born. Braim's horse was not so long-legged, and it was also not so light and agile. Braim's horse could probably hold a canter all day and hardly break a sweat. Aelundei's horse was built to hold a gallop for several hours. Aelundei had almost done that, but he had to make sure that Braim had a mount after they rescued him. He wondered how Orandaur was doing in his quest. He had been a good student and had learned very quickly. Somehow, Aelundei knew he was doing fine. He then shifted back into full awareness of his surroundings as he noticed a cut in the side of a tree as he cantered by. He turned the horses around, the elven horse following without a lead-rope. He rode up to the gash and leaned out of the saddle to examine it. It was made by a mounted person, being too high to be made on foot and at that angle. He also observed that it had been made by a knife almost identical to his. Orandaur had been blazing a trail for him, and it was close to being a day old. He did not remember teaching Orandaur about trail-blazing. Orandaur was smart, surprisingly skilled, agile, and able to learn. He would become a ranger of the first degree when he completed his apprenticeship.

The sun was sinking low as Orandaur made camp and settled down with a cup of pine-needle tea. A small, sheltered fire crackled next to him, though no warmth was needed in the middle of a fair Telnorian summer. He had never recalled feeling so exhausted, or alone. He shuddered as he moved closer to the fire, knowing it was his only companion. He hoped Aelundei would arrive soon, so he could help come up with a better plan than just following the trail. Orandaur gazed up at the plethora of stars in the sky as he considered his course of action. The goblins were heading toward the former province of Torrer. That would present a major problem; since the castle had not been destroyed when the goblins overran it, and they now used it as a base. He and Aelundei would have to find a way inside. On most Telnorian castles the dungeons were located on the level below the ground. And there was usually a torture chamber in the central keep. So Braim could be in either of those two places. Orandaur was glad he had two great rangers as masters.

*   *   *

Braim was almost glad that the leader of this raid was a strong leader. There had been an argument about having a feast, and Braim would have been the main course! That argument had been settled, and now Braim was being locked to a tree stump by two chains. He found a nice patch of grass and tried to get as comfortable as possible; hoping the instigator of the argument wouldn't come back searching for free food. It was going to be a long night.

*   *   *

Aelundei didn't stop riding until the sun was completely set and even his eyes could barely make out the trees. He set up camp underneath a tree with a blaze on it. This blaze was only about four hours old. He settled down by the fire and began to plan for the next day. There was no doubt in his mind that these goblins were heading for the old province of Torrer, which was where the majority of the goblin raids came from these days. No doubt that was probably where some goblin ruler had set up his kingdom and was probably scheming something big for Telnor.

The Legend of Braim
Chapter XII
Alliance with the Trolls

Grashnir climbed up the side of the mountain in his bear skin cloak and a loin cloth, which cleverly concealed a dagger. The dagger would do absolutely nothing against the thick skin of the trolls, but it was there to reassure his generals and other high officials that they shouldn't settle in and prepare to take over if Grashnir didn't return quickly. Grashnir turned to look at his only companion, the servant Jorguel, who was now carrying a large spear and rucksack full of food, wine, and gold. All of which had been gathered from Telnor.

"Servant," said Grashnir, "you do not appear to act like my former servants, instead, you seem to have the bearing of an assassin or former ruler."

"Yes, master," said Jorguel, "I was trained as an assassin as a young goblin."

"Interesting," said Grashnir, as he trudged up the slope behind his servant. *He has the aura of something more than an assassin. There is more to this story.* "Then what brings an assassin into the lowly vocation of a king's servant?"

"The king would not be interested in the story of his lowly servant," stated Jorguel, raising one eyebrow.

"A lowly servant obeys orders," replied Grashnir with a snarl.

"Your wish is my command," replied Jorguel with a nod of his head, "I was once heir to the throne of Zelgranf, but I had a younger brother who was able to bribe and coerce most of the military into supporting him in a coup. After our father died of suspicious means, he usurped the throne and sold me to one of your soldiers."

"Very interesting," said Grashnir with a snarling grin, "You did not think to kill your brother when he was in Castle Torrer?"

Jorguel frowned and nodded, "I wanted more than anything to kill him. I could feel bloodlust and revenge rising within me. Yet if I had killed him, I would have risked insulting the most powerful king of the goblins, and that would not be a very wise political move."

He longed to kill his brother, yet he did not let revenge cloud his judgment. My servant could be a powerful ally, but let him prove his loyalty, first. "You were a fool to not watch your brother closely," spat Grashnir, "But prove your loyalty to me, and perhaps I could rectify your lowly estate."

The two goblins came to the top of a ridge on the mountain, and there they could see the cave in front of them, guarded by two trolls.

The trolls, with green-gray skin that was extremely thick, stood slightly hunched over with their small heads sticking forward. They had no nose; instead, they had two little holes above their mouth that seemed to tilt in towards each other, their beady little eyes resembling two black holes in their heads. Each carried a huge club studded with bits of iron and skulls, and wore a large loin-cloth that almost scraped the ground. Even at a slouch they still stood about nine feet tall, their short legs and long arms gave them the appearance of being shorter than they really were.

Suddenly, one of the trolls stiffened and raised his head up in the air, a sniffing noise accompanying his movement.

"Hal' pueney lifle wart fache scumb," said the troll in a booming, deep voice, "ta'e no' a step farther more!"

Then the other troll, squinting its eyes and leaning even more forward, made a totally contradictory statement, "Steph ou' off the fog and show yu'selfs"

The first troll turned to the other troll and hit him on the top of the head with a fist, "I done an' tol' dem to take no steffs mor forwar'. I mak der rulesh 'roun hur!"

The second troll reached out and shoved the first troll back against the side of the cave, while bellowing: "Yu maik no rule hur, Big Bosh Xim makes der rule hur!"

The first troll lunged with a speed that was surprising for one with such short legs and tackled the other troll, while roaring at the top of his lungs. Pretty soon both trolls were yelling about random things and trying to beat the life out of each other. Grashnir and Jorguel had to plug their ears and get out of the way as the trolls rolled around on the edge of the flat clearing that was in front of the cave. Then a third troll stormed out of the cave, kicking both trolls and bellowing so loud the boulders shook. The other two trolls stopped fighting, turning their heads to look at the third troll.

"Stoff yur brawl nowr!" he yelled, "yur just given me arn head hake. Big Bosh Xim wants yur two to go dowrn and eport to herm 'medjetlee!"

The third troll suddenly stood up straight, seeming to grow another foot as he sniffed the air, then leaned forward to squint in the direction of Grashnir and Jorguel.

"Steff forwar' out of thurt forg an' show yeselfses Gorbluns" bellowed the troll.

Grashnir turned his head to Jorguel as his servant hid his spear behind a tree.

"Stay behind me and keep your head down at the floor," whispered the king, "Do not speak unless a question is asked directly of you. If we have to run, run with the wind. The trolls cannot see further than fifteen feet, but they can smell better than tracking hounds." With that, the two stepped forward, and marched up to the troll who squinted down at them and then bellowed

"Whart buissnesh have yur gort in the realm of Big Bosh Xim the Great?" He asked, glaring down at them now and grabbing one of the discarded clubs of the two guards.

Grashnir motioned to Jorguel to copy him while he bowed low to the troll, as is the custom for "lower" beings when they meet a troll in its territory

"We have come on a mission to Big Bosh Xim," said Grashnir, "To deliver a plan that will make him greatly pleased."

"What this plan you speak arf?" asked the troll, uncertainty covering his ugly face.

Grashnir remained bowed to the troll and said in a slight trollish accent, "The goblin creatures will be invading the human creatures' country called Telnor, a country that is green and soft, much better than a cave on a snowy mountain. I would like yur Big Bosh Xim to help the invasion in exchange for part of the spoils of the takeover."

"Furry wal," said the troll, dropping the club and turning to enter the cave, "follow me."

With that, Grashnir and Jorguel stood and followed the troll down into the mountain, walking through an intricate series of tunnels that had once been a dwarven kingdom, but was now in the possession of the trolls. The conquerors had added a few tunnels, but the existing tunnels were large enough to fit the giant, clumsy creatures. Legends among the goblins said that the dwarves built the giant tunnels to allow the passage of their catapults and other war machines from one end of the underground kingdom to the other, but their own strategy had brought about their demise.

The small party walked past great caverns, full of trolls lying on the ground, eating, or fighting over some stupid issue or another. The halls were dimly lit by bonfires scattered randomly throughout the city. Finally, after about half an hour of walking, they came to two great doors, wrought of polished silver that gleamed even in the dim light.

Why are there no guards? thought Grashnir as he looked around nervously. Trolls were dull, yet even they understood the need for guards.

Their troll guide straightened to full height and knocked on the door three times before shouting, "Two lether creatures reques' ardinence with Big Bosh Xim the Great!"

From the other side of the doors came the sound of a wooden hammer striking a brass gong, and a giant voice saying, "Enter!"

The doors swung inward, and the troll urged them to enter the chamber on the other side.

Grashnir surveyed the hall with one quick glance; it was a large hall, with four sets of pillars running the length of the great throne room. In the middle of the room was a large fire that lit even the edges with its dancing red light. Across the fire, was a huge, granite throne. On the throne sat not a Mountain Troll, but a Great Troll.

That's impossible! thought Grashnir as he and Jorguel were led around the fire to stand before the Great Troll's throne, *Great Trolls only live in the Frozen Waste, far to the north of the Elven Lands!* Suddenly great hands descended on their backs, and the goblins were violently throne to the floor.

"What business do you have in my realm?" asked the Great Troll, glaring down at them, "Do you come to spy on us, and find out how large our army is? Or do you come to slay me? For if you have come to slay me, then it is a hopeless cause, stand and look at me!"

Grashnir and Jorguel stood, watching in awe as the Big Boss stood to showed them his size and strength. As he stood, they were surprised by how strong and tall he was. He was almost fifteen feet tall, with short legs and medium-sized arms, his great chest rippling with strength. His skin was black as a moonless, starless night, muscles bulging, stretching the thick membrane as he flexed his arms and legs. Suddenly the troll seized his war hammer from its place beside his throne, swung it up over his head, and brought it down upon the floor of the cavern so forcefully that it left a dent large enough for either goblin to lie down in.

Grashnir realized that the troll had not *forgotten* to place guards, he simply didn't need them.

"As you can see, puny, lesser goblins," he said as he set the hammer down and sat on his throne again, "I am far more terrifying

69

and clever than the average dull-witted mountain troll, and in my battle armor I appear even fiercer. Tell me, why did you come?"

Grashnir and Jorguel bowed low, then rose as Grashnir said.

"Oh, great and mighty ruler, we have come not in folly to attempt to slay you, but in an effort to obtain peace, and help," with this he turned and motioned to Jorguel, who walked forward and set the rucksack next to Grashnir.

"This," said Grashnir as Jorguel reached into the sack and pulled out a bottle full of dark red liquid, "this is Telnorian wine, made by the most skilled craftsmen in their land. Here, take the bottle and we can have a drink," Jorguel pulled a cup out of the sack, poured wine into it, and then handed the bottle to Xim, who waited until Grashnir had drank his glass before raising the bottle to his lips and downing its contents.

"Mmm," growled Xim, "that is indeed good wine, where did you say it came from?"

"It is from the kingdom of Telnor, which the goblins will soon invade," said Grashnir, "but wait, your highness, there's more. This," exclaimed Grashnir as Jorguel reached into the sack again, pulling out a loaf of bread and some meat, "Is Telnorian bread and some meat from the livestock of their country. Here, take some," he ripped the bread into two pieces, handing the largest piece to Xim.

Again, Xim waited until Grashnir had finished his bread before eating his. Upon completion of that task, Grashnir cut the meat up and gave most of it to Xim, who by this time didn't wait for Grashnir to eat but ripped into the beef with a vengeance.

"That was very good food," exclaimed Xim, "although I would prefer the meat raw. You said that these also came from this place called Telnor?"

"Aye, that I did," said Grashnir, a sly grin crossing his face, "but there is one last thing I wish to show you before we discuss the terms of the treaty." He nodded to Jorguel, who grabbed the sack by its bottom and dumped the remaining contents on the floor.

Xim gasped as he saw what came out. Before him was a small pile of gold, jewels and bright iron.

"How did you come across such merchandise?" he asked in disbelief.

"I have come across this pretty pile of shiny items by armed conquest, in the form of raids across the Telnorian border," grinned Grashnir, seeing that there would not need to be much negotiating to get what he wanted, "And," he added, "If you help me and twelve other goblin warlords take this country of Telnor from its present owners, you can have all the wine, bread, meat, slaves and shiny things that you will ever care to see. But before we do that, we must negotiate the terms of our agreement."

The Legend of Braim
Chapter XIII
Castle Torrer

S everal hours after dawn, Aelundei found the site where
Orandaur camped. The fire was crackling, and there was a
griddle over it, with six delicious-looking pancakes cooking.
Aelundei dismounted and tied Valostala and Rochle next to Prince,
who was tied to a tree, contentedly munching on an apple. Then,
Orandaur emerged from the tent with a plate and fork, and flipped
three of the brown cakes up onto his plate.

"Do you want any of these pancakes, Aelundei?" he asked as he
looked up from the griddle.

Aelundei was surprised that Orandaur had known it was him
approaching the tent without looking. He looked thoughtfully at
Orandaur for a moment before replying, "Yes." He turned to walk
over to his saddle bags and get his own utensils, "Orandaur," he
asked as he walked back to the fire and food, "how did you know it
was me riding up to the tent?"

"Oh, that," said Orandaur, looking relieved for a brief moment, as
if he had nearly been caught in a lie, "Simple deductive reasoning,
I've learned a lot from you, you know. Human bandits do not venture
this near to the border; the risk of meeting goblins is too great.
Goblins do not ride horses, and I heard two, therefore, it could only
have been you."

"Very good!" exclaimed Aelundei looking from Orandaur to the
horses and back again, "but how did you know it was me and not
someone else riding Valostala and Rochle?"

"That part is the easiest," said Orandaur, looking up from the
pancakes long enough to put four more on and then to look at
Aelundei, "One reason is the fact that no one whom you do not trust,
can ride Valostala, and ever hope to regain full use of his body." At
this Valostala snorted and pawed the ground with a hoof. "And two,"
said Orandaur with a smile on his face, "No one is as quiet as you,
even when you are not trying to be stealthy."

"Very interesting," said Aelundei, who had just finished his
pancakes and was reaching for two more, "You are a fast learner,
Orandaur."

"Thank you, Aelundei, some things just seem to come naturally,"
said Orandaur, "such as swordsmanship; I had hardly used a sword

before in my life, other than playing with my cousins, and then I nearly beat Braim in the testing duel, which came as a complete surprise to me."

"That certainly came as a surprise to me as well." said Aelundei, "Braim is an expert swordsman who has never been beaten in a duel with any other ranger who's challenged him, although he never bragged about it. Then again, he was never one to talk to people he didn't know, and he doesn't have a lot of friends. But those friends he does have are extremely loyal; you and I are living proof of that."

"Speaking of being extremely loyal," said Orandaur, dousing the fire with dirt and then pouring water over it, "What is our plan of attack? I have a somewhat vague idea that the goblins who have him in chains are heading for the ex-province of Torrer, but I've never seen it and I have only heard stories of its fall."

"I have been through that area and have seen the castle only once," said Aelundei with a faraway look in his eyes. "But that was before Braim's parents were killed and their, I mean, that province was wrested away."

"Wait a moment," said Orandaur, leaning towards Aelundei with a look of wonder on his face, "did you say Braim's parents were the Lord and Lady of that province?"

Aelundei put his head in one of his hands and then looked up, "Yes, but Braim must not know this until he is ready to take the province back and avenge his parents' deaths. I must be the one to tell him and help him to convince the king and other lords that he is the rightful heir to the position." He paused for a moment, contemplating some difficult thought before voicing it, "He must also find a wife to help govern and to assure that there is a descendant to take over when he dies. That may be the most difficult task in the list."

I, thought Moraina, *can take care of that.* But outwardly, Orandaur showed no sign of slipping back into the thought process that had taken him two days to finally get under control.

"Anyway," said Aelundei, "we can do no planning until we arrive on the scene and survey the castle. Let's break camp and chase that elusive friend of ours!"

*   *   *

That friend of theirs was just now arriving at the fortress that his parents had given their lives defending, though he did not know it. At the sight of the castle, Braim gave up all hope of rescue from his friends. Torrer was certainly a sight to inspire fear now, several levels of fortress climbed up to a tower in the middle, perched on the highest foothill of the mountain range that had once protected Telnor from the goblins, but was now partially overrun. Torrer's once clean granite walls were now covered in slime and poison ivy. A few goblins were practicing climbing up the walls with their hooks, and many yards away, several siege engines were being tested. A small house that was obviously the target was surrounded with small boulders that had all missed their mark by a few yards. Once the small contingent of goblins that was leading him entered into the city, Braim could see the full size of the inside of the fortress. It had a central street running through it with houses crowding against the walls on both sides. Just inside the gate was a large courtyard, where a battalion of goblins was training under a cruel-looking goblin holding a whip and yelling commands. The contingent turned left and started towards the gate to the second level, which appeared to be wrought from iron and wood, but was covered in the same green slime as the walls. The second level was also lined with houses, some of which were marked by their signs as taverns or shops. They turned right, went up a set of stairs to the top wall, which was about eight feet thick at the top with a thirty foot drop to the street below. They continued on the wall until they came to another set of stairs. These stairs turned left and went in a gate to the third level, which was lined on only one side with what had once been barracks, but were now just walls and doors. Again, they turned left, and went past another battalion of goblins; these were holding crossbows and firing at targets up on the roofs of houses. After walking quite a ways down the street, they came to a gate leading into the fourth level. The fourth level was at the top of the foothill and was just a wide open space with buildings that could have been stables and a giant tower in the middle. Braim was led across the courtyard and into a large gate at the base of the tower.

Upon entering the tower there were three choices; a person could turn right, left, or go straight through a door. The leader of the party of goblins went straight, opened the door, and entered the room. The room was an extremely large room; in fact, it appeared to be a banquet hall. There were many large tables in the room with chairs around them, except for one. The one table was the largest table there; it was also elevated so the people sitting at the table would be able to observe all that went on in the room. Braim also noticed that the table only had one row of chairs, and the chair in the middle of that row was the biggest, most cushioned, chair in the room. While Braim stood there observing the room, he had a strange feeling that this was where he belonged. Shaking off the feeling just as the guard behind shook him and told him to keep moving, Braim started forward and followed the party up a spiral stairway to the next level of the tower.

The prisoner and his escort finally reached a room that was in the third-to-highest level of the castle. Once there, they took his chains off, opened the door, and threw him in. Braim heard the slam of the door and the click of the key turning in the lock before his head hit the floor, and the room went black.

*   *   *

Aelundei and Orandaur slowed from a canter to a trot and then to a walk as they neared a great river that was known as Mulleno river, the very river that served as part of the southern border of Torrer.

"Well, I guess we'll have to ride up and down the river looking for a bridge." said Orandaur, peering across the river to the shore that made the giant pine trees on the other side look like pine needles. "That or we could turn and make for the mountain pass. I don't think the horses could swim that far."

Aelundei, with eyes as sharp as eagles, peered up and then down the river. Pointing to an object downriver that only he could see he said "No, there are two thick ropes over there, let's go see what it is."

The two rangers, master and apprentice, turned their horses and trotted into the forest in the direction Aelundei had indicated. After riding a few minutes with the river's flow, they dismounted, tied their horses to a tree, and walked stealthily over to the two thick rope cables. As they approached, they looked right and left to make sure there were no guards or other goblins in the area and then walked up to the huge wooden posts that held the ropes, which were both about the size of Aelundei's forearm.

Aelundei peered out into the river, and then a frown crossed his face.

"What do you see, Aelundei?" asked Orandaur with concern riding his voice.

"It looks like the goblins are building a huge bridge across the

Mulleno," replied Aelundei, who reached up and grabbed the rope, swinging up onto it, "I will be back."

"What?" asked Orandaur in disbelief at the elf's words, but Aelundei didn't seem to hear; he was already running across the rope like it was a wide street.

Orandaur turned and walked back under the edge of the forest, then leaned up against a pine tree, with his longbow strung and an arrow in his hand.

*   *   *

Aelundei had heard Orandaur's question, but it wasn't every day that he ran across long ropes, so he didn't want to take his concentration off of his present task to answer.

After running about a hundred feet on rope cable, Aelundei made it to his destination, a long wooden bridge that was halfway finished. The pine boards still smelled fresh and newly cut, so Aelundei guessed that the workers came at night. The bridge was about twelve feet wide, and it felt very sturdy, only the biggest of floods could take this bridge out of commission. As Aelundei looked around, he noticed a large bundle of wood, the planks about a foot wider than the gap between the two ropes; he also realized that the planks were bound together by leather straps. A plan began to form in his sharp elven mind.

*   *   *

When Braim came to, he found himself on a cold, rough, uneven stone floor. He got up and surveyed the situation. The room was very small, probably ten feet by seven feet; one of the walls was slightly curved and had a small, barred window. He turned and noticed that there was no bed, only a small pile of straw, which smelled very rank. Other than the window and the straw there was nothing to make the room anything other than what it was: a prisoner's cell. Braim walked to the window and looked out. It was a western facing window, because the sun was setting away from him; in all directions that he could see there were forests of pine trees, dotted by the occasional cluster of oak, maple, or birch. To the southwest, Braim could just barely see a mountain range that would be the border with Telnor. Due west, the pine forest slowly gave way to rolling grassy hills, occasionally dotted with short, dead trees, and when he turned his eyes to the north-west, he could see another mountain range. This one, though just as far away, if not further, than the Telnorian mountain range, seemed to loom towards him, wanting to crush him and the free land of Telnor. Braim shivered at the sight and hoped he would never have to go there.

With that, Braim turned and walked back to the spot where he had fallen to the floor. He lay down, curled up, and for the first time since his childhood, he wept.

*   *   *

Moraina awoke, looked around, and quickly confirmed that she had fallen asleep while waiting for Aelundei's return. She wondered what it was that had roused her and then grabbed her long-bow and the arrow lying on the ground next to it as she tried to find out. A steady noise of rattling wood hit her ears and she quickly nocked the arrow to the string of her long-bow, drawing back while moving out of the cover of the pines. She was grateful that the long-bow was not as strong as Aelundei's or Braim's. She had tried to draw back the string of Braim's once quickly discovered why it was such a feared and respected weapon. As she broke free of the forest, the pine-needles scraping her hands and face, she saw what was making the noise. Coming across the river from the bridge was Aelundei, pushing a bundle of planks that was slowly growing smaller as it unrolled. Moraina slowly let her bow go slack and returned the arrow to her quiver.

"What are you doing?" she asked when Aelundei got closer.

"It appears that the goblins have been staging raids from this bridge as well recently," replied Aelundei, rolling the last of the leather-bound planks out to form a temporary bridge to the stronger one. "If we dismount and lead the horses across, then we should be able to get to the other side of the river and be that much closer to Braim before that storm hits." He pointed to a large, dark mass of clouds that was slowly growing on the horizon.

"I will go and get the horses," said Moraina, "who will go first?"

"I was thinking that I should go first, leading Valostala," replied Aelundei, looking at Orandaur strangely, "because she is calmest and the other horses trust her to lead." He finished, and Moraina turned to go, but before she could take a step Aelundei stopped her.

"Orandaur," the elf said, now looking at the person he knew as Orandaur like he was a strange creature, "your voice sure has been sounding different these days, are you alright?"

"Yes," said Moraina, her heart rate accelerating as she cleared her throat to change her voice back to Orandaur's, "I have some allergies that affect my voice, but it will be perfectly fine." She knew her face was beet red; it took all her willpower to not pull the hood on the cloak to hide her blushing.

Aelundei looked at her suspiciously, but nevertheless accepted her story and continued checking the temporary bridge to ensure that it was safe for them and the horses.

Moraina ran off, untied the horses, and led them over to where Aelundei had built a ramp up to the bridge. Aelundei took Valostala and looked Orandaur in the eyes.

"I will go ahead," he said quietly, "and if there is no trouble then you are to follow. And Orandaur" he said, his mouth turning up in a mischievous grin. "Einye alas chalo. Síela víarala verena en!"

"What?" asked Moraina, wondering what on earth it meant. But Aelundei had already turned to go up the ramp; he did not seem to hear her question.

After Aelundei had made it about fifty feet, he turned and motioned for Moraina to follow. She gently urged Prince to walk up the ramp, Rochle obediently following. Moraina looked down, and, seeing that the water was not moving very fast, decided that it would be a perfectly safe and easy trip. The horses, sensing her ease at crossing, took comfort in the fact that the human was calm and followed obediently.

Upon arriving at the bridge, Moraina mounted Prince and rode up to where Aelundei and Valostala were patiently waiting. Moraina looked at Aelundei and realized that he had a wide grin.

"I told you to not look down," he said, his grin growing wider, if that was at all possible.

"What?" asked Moraina, not recalling Aelundei saying anything that she had understood.

"What I told you as I walked away," he said, his grin not able to get any bigger, though his eyes told Moraina it wanted to, "what I said means: don't look down. There is a dangerous current!"

Moraina realized with a sickening feeling that the calm surface of the water was just a wolf in sheep's clothing.

Aelundei threw his head back and roared with laughter as

Moraina unleashed on him.

"You could have at least told me in the Common Tongue!" she yelled, slugging him in the arm with a fist.

Aelundei kept laughing until he was out of breath, and then laughed some more. He stopped suddenly a few seconds later when a drop of water landed on his face, that one drop soon followed by more. The storm that they had seen in the distance had closed in on them. Then the torrent of rain began. It was so heavy a down-pour that it was like someone was standing above them and emptying a huge, endless, pail of water.

"We had better hurry to make it under the safety of the pines!" Aelundei yelled, his cloak already soaked through.

Moraina nodded back, her teeth chattering as flashes of lightning and peals of thunder added to the storm's ferociousness. They turned and started to walk quickly for the shore opposite from where they had come. The river started to rise quickly, water started to flow across the bridge at the spot where they had been a few moments ago.

They were only a few yards from the end of the bridge when the wind struck. It was a wind so strong and hard that it made the rain run almost parallel to the ground. Moraina was swept off of her feet and thrown off the bridge. She dangled precariously over the side, holding on to a piece of rope, slowly sliding to the end. Her body was slowly running out of strength and quickly running out of hope. She wanted to give up, to just let go and let the river take her. Then, when she had finally given up hope and was about to let go, a warmth seeped into the back of her mind. Then she heard a voice, quiet and reassuring. It spoke in a language that she did not know, yet strangely comprehended, *Moraina, you must hold on, Braim must be rescued, and Aelundei cannot do it alone.*

But the wind is too strong, the rain too heavy, and the bridge so slippery, replied Moraina in her mind, *I just want to give up and surrender!*

I am Vitaren- the maker of all things, answered the voice quietly, *I have made the wind, though my enemy has perverted it, and there is nothing too great for me to do; see, watch!* There was a soft light, and the wind seemed to split around Moraina and Aelundei, resuming once it went past the horses. The rain fell all around them, but not on them.

Moraina's eyes grew wide at the sight, trying to wrap her mind around what type of being had the power to do such things.

There was a quiet laughing sound in Moraina's mind, and then the voice returned.

See, said Vitaren, the warmth in Moraina's head spreading to the rest of her body, *even the wind and rain must obey me!*

But, Vitaren, Moraina asked, *why can I not see you?*

Blessed are those who by faith can believe what they do not see, Vitaren's voice started to go softer, *and remember, my daughter, even in your darkest hour, there is always hope, even if it is a fool's hope.*

No! Moraina's mind screamed, *don't leave me! I have too many questions!*

Just believe, Moraina, believe and have hope; I will come again. With that the voice was completely gone, but the warmth was still there and the wind continued to go around them, though it howled and screamed.

"What happened?" shouted Aelundei, as he pulled her back up onto the bridge.

"I'll tell you when we get to a dry campsite!" Moraina shouted back, pointing to the pines still only a few yards away, "but I'm not sure if you'll understand; even I'm not certain."

*   *   *

In his tower cell, Braim was far less comfortable. The rain and wind were coming in and had turned the room into a smaller version of what was happening out side. It would be a long, cold night.

The Legend of Braim
Chapter XIV
Armor for the Trolls

Grashnir and Jorguel, followed by twelve mountain trolls, walked into the now sunny courtyard that was next to the main gate of the city. They passed a battalion of training goblins, and were surprised at how few of them were making mistakes now. They walked up to the second level, and then to the third, where they passed a second battalion of goblins; this time they were training with crossbows, and there were only a couple who missed the target. They continued up through the fourth level and started walking to the tower at the center. Before entering the tower, Grashnir turned towards the trolls, all of whom were carrying great bags of slag iron. After seeing that they all still had their bags, Grashnir turned to Jorguel.

"Take the trolls and show them to the various blacksmith shops. Explain to the blacksmiths what they are to do, and then explain to the trolls, as simply as you can, that the blacksmiths need to measure their size to make armor and weapons for them. Once you have completed this task, come and report to me in my room in the tower." he said, not once taking his eyes off of Jorguel, "do you understand?"

"Yes master," replied Jorguel with a bow. Turning to the trolls, he jogged off to do his master's bidding.

Grashnir turned, entered the tower, and marched up to his room. While walking to his room, Grashnir's mind reflected on his trip. It had not taken long at all to reach an agreement with Xim, the ruler of the trolls, so Grashnir and Jorguel had left late the same day they had arrived.

All is well, thought Grashnir, *we have nearly reached the tree-line, and the trolls still haven't started fighting. Then the snow started falling. Within minutes, the light sprinkle of snow became thick enough to quickly cover the tracks of the party behind them. The deluge was followed by a wind so hard it knocked even the trolls to the ground, spilling their burdens of unrefined slag iron everywhere. Despite the blizzard rapidly growing worse, the puny brains of the trolls rationalized that someone must have pushed them down, and instantly began to blame one another. The loud kerfuffle escalated into an all-out brawl; the noise of the troll's bellowing* vibrating the mountain itself. Suddenly the fist-fight stopped as the trolls heard a low rumble from far up the mountain.

"'Ey," said one of the trolls thickly, "Oo's gutt's rumlin?"

All the trolls vehemently denied this horrible accusation, and soon began to argue over which one of them the source of this was rumbling.

"Quick," exclaimed Grashnir, alarmed, "Get into a tree!"

The two goblins rushed for the nearby tree line, leaving the trolls still arguing as a wall of snow and ice rushed around a ridge, leaping forward to wrap the party in its chilling embrace. Grashnir and his servant barely reached the trees when the snow impacted the trolls. The pair managed to scramble into the lower branches as the avalanche hit them. Jorguel was a faster climber; he was several limbs higher than his king when the massive white wall enveloped them. Somehow the tree survived the onrush of snow, and the movement of the white current ceased. Jorguel tunneled his way out of the snow by climbing up the tree, then returned to free his master. As the two goblins stepped foot onto the hard-packed snow, there was no sign of the trolls.

"Do you think the trolls are dead, master?" inquired Jorguel.

"No," replied the king with a sigh, "Give them a few moments, and they will be on the top of the snow arguing again."

One by one the trolls managed to claw their way free of the snow. Despite Grashnir and Jorguel's best attempts to stop them, the trolls soon returned to fighting.

Suddenly Grashnir yelled at the top of his lungs, "Stop this nonsense at once!"

The trolls froze, and looked at the goblin king with surprise. Grashnir stalked over to the location that he thought the slag iron would be and pointed at the ground. "Dig around here until you find your bags. I do not want to hear another argument come out of your mouth for the rest of this trip!" The dull-witted creatures remained still for a few moments as they digested what he had said, then scurried to follow the angry king's order. Within moments they uncovered the bags near the spot Grashnir had chosen, then followed his lead into the forest.

Grashnir's mind returned to the present as he reached the door to his rooms. He walked in and sat down.

No sooner had he sat down when a knock sounded heavily on the door.

"Who is brave enough to knock on my door?" demanded Grashnir, a foul mood growing rapidly in the bottom of his black heart.

The door opened slowly and a shaking goblin warrior entered timidly. "K-king-g G-g-Grashnir, s-sir."

"Yes, what is it?" shouted Grashnir at the stammering warrior. "Speak clearly or I will give you a lesson in flying from the top window of the tower!"

The goblin straightened and saluted. "My king, I am captain Drallgn. I was third in command of a raiding party last week, and I came to report our spoils."

Grashnir rolled his eyes and sat down in a chair, rubbing his temples with his left hand, "Continue."

"We c-captured no slaves, took th-three barrels of wine and ale, s-s-six loaves of bread, four cows, and some small gold trinkets and jewelry."

"Hmmm, very unimpressive for a raid," said Grashnir, "Where are your superiors?"

"They were killed," replied Drallgn, "Along with over 130 other goblins, sir."

"What?" said Grashnir, enraged, "What did you do? March them into the middle of a Telnorian Army?"

"No sir," replied the captain, "We were attacked by rangers."

"How many?"

"One, sir."

"One ranger snuck into the camp and killed that many goblins in the middle of the night without being stopped?"

"That is how he killed the leaders and two-and-ten others, sir. He came in and snuck our prisoners out in the middle of the night, and then he killed the leaders. The next morning twenty more goblins fell in pursuit of him and the escaped prisoners, then the rest of the party arrived to engage him in open battle."

Grashnir sat, stunned at the incompetence of his leaders and troops. "What happened to the ranger? Did you take him alive?"

"Yes, sir."

Grashnir's strange mood system went from murderous rage to almost happy at the sound of those words. "Excellent! For that, you are promoted to a general! Now, come over here and have a drink of wine with me."

The relieved goblin approached, glad to be out of danger, but

Grashnir grabbed him and threw him out the open window. "That is for your incompetence!"

Another for the Reaper.

Jorguel entered, "I shall get a crew to wash off the stones in the courtyard, do you need anything else, master?"

"Yes," said Grashnir, "I want you to find out where the ranger is being kept, and then send me four soldiers to accompany me there."

"It shall be done as you say, master."

Now, all Grashnir had to do was wait for the soldiers to come, and then the torturous moments of fun would begin.

The Legend of Braim
Chapter XV
Of Torture

Braim was awakened by the sound of footsteps outside his door, many footsteps. He then heard goblin voices, they were talking about him. The footsteps stopped, after Braim heard two sets of goblin sandals going to one side of the door, and two more going to the other side of the door, that meant that there were at least four goblins. Braim wished he had Nelya, his hunting knife, to hold onto as he waited for fifteen minutes until he heard two more sets of sandals approaching. Braim pressed his ear against the door and listened silently.

"I want you four soldiers to go in there and tie the human up!" demanded a harsh, gravelly voice that sent tingles up and down Braim's spine.

"It shall be done as you command us, great King Grashnir," said a timid goblin voice.

"But, Lord Grashnir, that human took out whole battalions on his own, what can four of us-" This voice was silenced by a fist hitting flesh and a groan. Then four sets of feet approached the door.

Braim backed as far away from the door as he could, and then laid down, pretending to be asleep, but with his eyes slightly opened. The door slowly started to open inward and then four goblins entered, shutting the door behind them. They advanced slowly, and he saw that their confidence grew when they thought he was sleeping. Then, as soon as they were all within range, Braim kicked his legs out and roared the Telnorian battle cry.

"For Telnor!"

All four of the goblins let out cries of dismay as they fell in heaps on the ground. Braim leapt up, yelling the battle cry again even louder than before, grabbed a goblin and hurled him into the wall. The goblin screamed as he flew towards the wall and then went silent when he discovered that granite *is* harder than skull bone. The remaining goblins ran up to the door, tried to open it, and found it was locked. They cried out, and turned around just as Braim slammed into them, knocking two out with one blow to their jaws. The remaining goblin tried to punch Braim in the sternum, but Braim caught the punch, broke the wrist of the goblin, then swung it over his head. The goblin flew through the air with a wail, smashed into the barred window, and sunk to the floor. Braim started to take a few steps toward the goblin he had thrown, the only goblin with a weapon that entered the cell, but stopped and whipped around when he heard the door slam open.

There, standing in the cell as if nothing was going wrong, was the cruelest-looking goblin Braim had ever seen.

A quick glance revealed everything that Braim needed to know about the creature. He had a sword in his hand, which appeared to be a curved, single-edged scimitar. Around the goblin's belt were four knives almost identical to the sword. He also noticed that the goblin was of slight build, walked with a limp, and had an iron patch over his right eye. Gall's story was confirmed.

"Listen, human dog," said the goblin, his harsh, gravely tone identifying him as Grashnir, "If you give up now, and yield all the information I ask for, life will be slightly less painful for you!" Grashnir started slowly walking towards him, Braim waited till the sword was almost touching his chest then moved like lightning. He knocked Grashnir's sword out of his hand by punching it on the flat part, raising his hand to smash the goblin's face into a green pancake. But his hand froze in mid-air as he realized that there was a knife pressed against his neck.

"Make one more move, ranger," said Grashnir coldly, "and you will be as dead as the humans who tried to defend this fortress."

"I have nothing to live for," said Braim, a look of determination set in his face. His fist introduced itself to Grashnir's face.

*   *   *

Aelundei and Moraina were riding along, staying well to the side of the wide road that led to castle Torrer. As they rode along, they both cleaned and sharpened their swords. Moraina looked over and noticed that there was a thin line of flowing script etched into Aelundei's sword.

"Aelundei," said Moraina, "what is that writing that is etched into your sword?"

"That," replied Aelundei, looking down at the sword, "is called Nílva Rivilen, or insight-script. It is supposed to bring out the personality of the bearer and his sword. It is done by singing a special song over the sword as it is made. In Elleavemar, the elf lands, every elf must make his own weapon before he is deemed ready to fight."

"What does it say?" asked Moraina, leaning over to study the strange writing.

"It says some things that are embarrassing to me," said Aelundei, "but if you really want to know, I can read it for you." Moraina nodded at this suggestion and Aelundei continued. "It says, *Meien Raeva Reavel rí, tava Aelundei, ontaren Toivoa. Alera meien halos Rada!* It translates to the common tongue as 'I am Great Cut, sword of Aelundei, hope of nations. Flee from my bearer's wrath!'"

"That is written on the sword when you sing a song?" inquired Moraina, suspiciously.

"Tell me, Orandaur," replied Aelundei with a grin, "Do you believe in magic?"

"Magic only exists in children's tales," scoffed Moraina, "Stories meant to send shivers down your spine around the winter fire and prevent those who cannot fend for themselves from venturing into the woods at night."

"You could never be more wrong," responded Aelundei, chuckling. Suddenly he felt a shiver run down his spine, "Did you feel that as well, Orandaur?" He asked, still not quite certain what it was he had felt.

"Yes" replied Moraina, then she paled as she realized what the tingle meant. "Aelundei, I think someone just seriously hurt Braim!"

"We had better pick up the pace then," cried Aelundei, sheathing his sword and urging Valostala into a canter. Moraina followed suit, and they were soon speeding through the forest, hoping that they would not be too late.

*   *   *

The two remaining goblin soldiers tied Braim's hands behind his back as he lay on the ground, and then roughly forced him to his feet. Grashnir rubbed his face where Braim had punched him. He wanted desperately to kill the young man, but he needed information. Instead of slitting the ranger's throat, he had taken the punch, then driven his knee into the fork between Braim's legs and followed up with a punch to his stomach. The goblins were now marching Braim, who was still in pain, out of his cell and into a hallway in the mighty tower. They took a flight of steps down one level and then turned right, entering into an open door. A third goblin closed the door behind them, then helped to tie Braim's hands and feet to two leather thongs on either side of a long table.

"If you have not yet guessed," stated the goblin-king enthusiastically, "It is my pleasure to inform you that this is my torturing room. You will be slowly put through a series of painful experiences and will eventually tell me everything that I want to know. The table on which you now helplessly lie is what I call the stretcher. Soon, we will flip it up so you hang upside down, and then we will slowly, ever so slowly, tighten the leather straps you are tied to. When you are about to snap in half, we will loosen them and start over. It sounds like an enjoyable experience, does it not? It will be enjoyable for me at least. We will start the interrogation by asking you your name. Do you want to play stubborn, or do you want to give in and tell my friends and I this harmless piece of information?"

Braim did not answer with words, instead, he spat in Grashnir's face.

"Pull!" said Grashnir. Instantly, two goblins flipped the table up on its swivel so Braim was almost up-side down, the third pulled the lever that tightened the straps.

"I see you have chosen the hard way of things," said Grashnir, his harsh voice seeming to get harsher. "I was hoping you would choose the easier method; bleshtem voc," he yelled, switching into Dark Tongue for a second.

Again, he yelled in the Dark Tongue "Skramme!" The goblin at the tightening lever seemed to know the Dark Tongue, for he immediately pulled the lever.

*　　　　　*　　　　　*

 Moraina and Aelundei felt more tingles in rapid succession, each one urging them to ride faster.

"Aelundei," said Moraina "I think they're torturing Braim!"

Aelundei nodded; apparently he had already reached the same conclusion. "I hope we make it to him in time to save him!"

*　　　　　*　　　　　*

Indeed, Grashnir was torturing Braim, but to no avail. Every time he tried to ask him a question, Braim would say nothing. Instead, he would spit in Grashnir's direction. And every time Grashnir did not get an answer, he would tell the goblin at the lever to pull down and tighten the leather straps. Finally, Grashnir could take it no longer. He turned to a lighted furnace that was in one of the corners of the room to retrieve a red hot poker. He turned towards Braim with a wicked smile on his face.

"I told you that you should have chosen the easy way," said Grashnir, lowering the hot poker until it was almost touching his skin.

"I never was one for taking the easy way out of things," said Braim grimly, as he stared at the wall opposite where he lay. Then, Grashnir lowered the metal poker, the sound and smell of burning flesh filled the air. Braim clenched his teeth and restrained from crying out, but inwardly his body was screaming. Grashnir, seeing that even this had not produced a reaction from the young man, left the poker on Braim's skin a moment longer than he would have if he had been torturing any other human.

"Tighten!" He snapped as he turned and put the poker back in the fire, waiting for it to heat up again. Five more times, he tried to burn the information out of Braim, and five more times the leather stretching Braim was tightened. Braim was about to give in and tell Grashnir as much as he knew about the king's standing army, when a coolness seeped into his mind, spreading to the rest of his body. All of a sudden, the room was filled with a bright white light, Braim looked at Grashnir and then at the other goblins, but they did not seem to notice it.

A clear, soft voice started to speak from the light. "I am Eien Moran," said the voice, and, as if sensing the question forming in Braim's mind, it said, "which means 'Light Among Dark' in your tongue. I am the fastest messenger of Vitaren. I was sent to assure you that no matter what happens, our Father will be watching over you. I was also sent to give you this."

With that, a pair of hands reached out of the light and tied a necklace made of leather with a brilliant emerald on it around Braim's neck. Braim looked down at it; it seemed to shimmer and sparkle from some unknown source, and it had an inscription on it. The inscription read: "Eatil pelvaren toivoa Yava~Cling to the hope of salvation."

Braim looked up, but the light was gone, one word echoing around the room: toivoa, 'hope.' Then Braim had to grit his teeth as the red hot poker returned to his body again, along with the same question Grashnir had repeated five times before. "How large of a standing army does your country posses? How long does it take to mobilize the reserves?" but Braim answered the same as he always answered, he spat in Grashnir's face, which just happened to be in range this time.

*   *   *

Moraina and Aelundei finally decided to let themselves and the horses rest.

"How much farther is Castle Torrer?" asked Moraina, hoping they were getting close to rescuing Braim.

"Well," said Aelundei putting on his thinking face. "If I remember correctly, we should have about a day and a half ride from here. That will give us half a day to plan the escape and find out the length of sentries' shifts, before we go in, find Braim, and rescue him, before he gets killed."

"Two more days of torture?" asked Moraina, her eyes beginning to mist at the thought of Braim enduring that much pain. "Is there some way we could speed up our travel?

Aelundei was about to deny that thought, but then he turned and saw the tears beginning to spill over Orandaur's face before Orandaur could dash them away with his cloak. "Of course," he said, "We can travel at night as well, but we must give Prince and Rochle time to rest and regain their strength. We should wait half an hour and move on. You can switch back and forth between Rochle and Prince, and Valostala can carry me all night. All we have to do is take a few breaks, maintain a slow canter, and Valostala can last much longer.

"See, Orandaur, *Síela toivoa aena en, aels hír íralen toivoa so en* ~there is always hope, even if it is a fool's hope. Come now, let us eat!"

Moraina turned and followed Aelundei, the last of the tears drying up. She wondered how much longer she would be able to maintain her masquerade as Orandaur.

The Legend of Braim
Chapter XVI
Training of the Trolls

Grashnir slammed the door to his room behind him and stormed over to his favorite chair. He had spent the whole night trying to interrogate the stupid human, but the young man was the toughest nut Grashnir had ever tried to crack. Other than informing Grashnir that he wasn't one for easy things he had only said one thing.

"When my friends find me," the boy's words seemed to echo around Grashnir's head, he could almost see Braim's stern visage in front of his face, "We will hunt you down, and then you will be killed slowly."

Grashnir got up and paced angrily back and forth in his room, trying to think of some way to get into that boy's head. Then, he realized something. The boy had said his friends would find Grashnir and kill him, and that could only mean one thing. The boy knew rangers that would be stupid enough to come and try to rescue him. An evil thought started to form itself into an evil scheme. And then the evil scheme started to form itself into an evil plot.

"Jorguel," shouted Grashnir, his random mood swinging back to at least a semi-good one.

"Yes, oh king?" asked Jorguel as he entered and bowed, surprised that his master had actually used his name.

"I want you to go and get me the three trolls who have finished battle armor, and about thirty goblin warriors who have finished their training," said Grashnir, then carried on with another thought. "Make sure there are fifteen sword-goblins and fifteen crossbow wielders, tell all of them to assemble in the courtyard at the base of the tower."

"It shall be done, my king," said Jorguel, bowing again and jogging off to do his master's bidding.

Grashnir stood, grabbed his sword, four knives, and walked to the bottom of the tower; stopping only once to check on the ranger, whom he had left lying on the table in the torture room. He noticed that the human was not sleeping; instead, he appeared to be looking down at an object on his chest. Grashnir made a mental note to check what the fool was looking at when he came back to resume the interrogation in an hour or so. He walked away and was soon at the door to the bottom of the tower. He opened it and stepped out into the warmth of the early morning sun rise. The three trolls were already standing in the courtyard, conveniently positioned with large gaps of ground in between them. Grashnir made another mental note to promote Jorguel, or something like that.

He looked the trolls up and down, surveying his smith's handy work. Each troll had a simple metal breast plate with a thick, nail studded leather strap connecting it to a metal plate on their backs. Their helmets fit tightly to the head, the nose bar and a metal plate on each side of the head protected the troll's face while still allowing them to eat and drink. Grashnir also noticed that they each had thick shin and calf guards to protect their legs. Each troll had also been outfitted with new maces. The maces were about five feet long, as thick as a human thigh, studded with cruel metal spikes all the way around, covering the upper three feet of the mace. Grashnir guessed that they knew how to use the mace, but he wasn't sure. He walked over to one of the trolls.

"You," he said to the troll; the troll looked down at Grashnir stupidly with its beady eyes. Grashnir continued, "What is your name?"

"I's Trug-bar," said the troll, hitting his armored chest with his empty fist.

"I would like to see how well you fight," said Grashnir, "go and destroy that building over there." He pointed to one of the deserted stables.

The troll turned, barely able to see the building that Grashnir was pointing to. He bellowed as he ran towards it. Instead of doing as Grashnir had thought he would, which was using his mace to smash through the crumbling building, he continued to run and smashed his body through it. Stones flew everywhere as Grashnir dropped his head into his hands. This would take a little more explaining than he was used to.

"I flaten der buldign" said Trug-bar, walking back up to Grashnir.

"I wanted you to use your club," said Grashnir, annoyed.

Trug-bar turned, and saw that there were still a few pillars standing. He ran back to the building and smashed the remaining pillars with his mace. He turned around and walked up to Grashnir again.

"I hav dun as 'ou sai' likkle goblign," said Trug-bar, a stupid look of accomplishment on his flat face.

"Very good," said Grashnir, surveying the wreckage, "but next time, swing your club lower to the earth."

"Yeh, shir!" said Trug-bar, he took a practice swing and narrowly missed Grashnir, who had taken a couple steps backwards in anticipation of that act.

Grashnir then repeated the same process with the other two trolls; soon there were no more stables on the top level. The buildings were replaced by piles of rubble, making the courtyard a much larger place than before the demolitions had occurred. Grashnir then turned to the thirty goblins who had assembled while the trolls demonstrated to the king what they could do.

"I need the three with the highest ranks among you to step forward." said Grashnir, and watched as three captains timidly stepped forward. There were two goblins with swords and one with a crossbow. "You three will each be head of a patrol. Including yourselves there will be one troll, five archers, and five sword-goblins, on each patrol. Your mission is to find any rangers that may be out in the territory near the castle, kill them slowly, and bring their bodies back here. Do not come back until you have killed a ranger or are summoned to the castle. Do you understand the task?"

All three of the goblins nodded and said "yes, sir," though not in unison. They then turned, gathered the goblins they needed, and marched out of the castle.

"Let's see those rangers make it in now," mumbled Grashnir to himself, rubbing his hands together before turning and entering the tower, followed silently by Jorguel. He walked up to the interrogation room, and, seeing one of his generals walking by, he grabbed him.

"General," growled Grashnir, "I want you to see to it that the watch is doubled, and only trained goblins are up on the wall."

Grashnir continued on to the interrogation room. He opened the door and walked in, Jorguel shutting it after he too entered. Grashnir walked over to the furnace, stoked the flames, and proceeded to the table.

"Well, hello, my favorite guest," said Grashnir, smiling wickedly, "did you have a good night's sleep in your nice feather bed?"

Braim mumbled something, and Grashnir leaned in to hear what it was. Suddenly, Braim turned his head and spat in Grashnir's good eye, which was only a few inches away.

"Ah!" yelled Grashnir, losing his temper, "Tighten, tighten again."

Jorguel pulled the lever two clicks as Grashnir punched Braim in

93

the stomach and then hammer-fisted him in the fork of the legs. He stormed over to the furnace, grabbed the glowing poker, and then stomped back to Braim. Grashnir stabbed the hot iron poker against the human's skin, yelling for the millionth time. Braim screamed in pain, but Grashnir yelled louder than his prisoner. "What is the size of your king's armies? What is their form of warfare? How long will it take for the army to muster when attacked?" He had had enough of this stupid ranger's stubbornness. He then decided that there was a better plan for getting information from this boy, he could squeeze it out. Remembering the mental note he had made that morning, he drew his sword and walked around the table to Braim's head, careful to stay out of range of the human's spitting. With his sword, he opened the flap of his shirt to see what the young man had been looking at that morning. But all that was there was Braim's chest. He returned the sword to his sheath and walked over to the fire, moving the poker into the hottest part of the coals and thinking about his plans to get the ranger to talk.

The Legend of Braim
Chapter XVII
The Rescue

Aelundei and Moraina continued to canter along all day, meeting no enemy soldiers until Aelundei's sharp elven ears heard crashing trees in the distance. They reigned in their horses as the crashing got louder.

"We have to get further from the road now!" said Aelundei, a look of worry across his face.

"What is it?" asked Moraina as they turned and rode off the road.

"Get an arrow ready," whispered Aelundei, following his own instructions before he could finish talking.

Aelundei and Moraina watched the road, practically invisible and yet able to see everything that went by on the road. All of a sudden, a troll and ten goblins walked by on the road, totally oblivious to the fact that there were two rangers hidden in the nearby undergrowth with arrows trained at their heavy armor division.

"What is that huge creature?" whispered Moraina, hoping that the creature didn't have acute hearing.

"It's a troll," whispered Aelundei back, then indicated that Moraina should be quiet.

"Yeah, it's too bad stupi' ole Grashnir had to go and give us orders to not come back until we had killed ourselfs a ranger," said one of the five goblins with crossbows to one of the goblins carrying only a sword.

"Yeah," said the one with the sword, "I can't wait for the big invasion of Telnor that Grashnir's plannin' with the other goblin kings and these 'ere trolls!"

"Quiet!" barked a goblin that seemed to be the leader of the group, "We could be walking past that stubborn ranger's friends now, we don't want to miss them and get slowly killed by king Grashnir!"

"Shoot the troll in the neck, and then shoot the archers," whispered Aelundei, drawing his elven bow all the way back to the iron tip of the arrow.

Moraina aimed for the unguarded neck of the troll, drew back, and released. The arrow sailed through the air, narrowly missing some trees, and bounced off the thick hide of the troll, who turned to see what had hit him. That was exactly what Aelundei wanted. He released his arrow, which buried itself halfway into the troll's small right eye. The troll let out an airy bellow, wobbled around for a few moments, and fell on six of the goblins. The remaining four were cut down by Aelundei and Moraina's arrows as they took off running in the direction of Castle Torrer, which was conveniently in the same direction as Aelundei and Moraina's hiding spot.

"Well," said Aelundei, returning an arrow to his quiver, "That made short work of them! Now we need to dispose of the troll's body," he grimaced at the thought.

"Perhaps," said Moraina, "we could each get a section of tree and try to use them as levers to roll the troll's body off the road?"

"Excellent idea," replied Aelundei looking at Moraina, "you really are the one to come up with simple solutions, I was thinking we'd have to burn the brute's body. Now all we need are some good, strong, tree limbs."

They started to walk into the forest, but Aelundei noticed movement among the dead goblins. He whirled around, and grabbed a goblin by the ankle, pulling him close. The goblin wailed as it was drug backwards towards the elf. Moraina stepped in at the goblin's head to ensure he did not try to escape.

"So, I couldn't help but notice that you and one of your friends were talking about a 'stubborn ranger.' He is being held in the castle, is he not?" Aelundei leaned in, putting on his most intimidating face.

The goblin nodded, but then, realizing what it was doing, it started to shake its head no.

"Well, I see you have knowledge of my friend's captivity." Aelundei leaned in closer, and sneered like he knew something the goblin didn't. "However, just the knowledge of my friend's captivity is not enough." He pulled back his long black hair so that it revealed his pointed ears. "I am an elf!" He roared, his voice slowly increasing in volume, "If you do not tell me where my friend is exactly, then I will use my command of the ancient magics to call a curse down on you. A curse so horrible, that you cannot begin to fathom the pain that you will be in for the hundred or more years that the curse will last!" He started to chant in the elvish language, slowly picking up speed as the wind with perfect timing also began to increase.

The goblin wailed, and immediately started talking to save his skin. "Please, please!" he begged "I will tell you everything I know about the location of the prisoner just as long as you stay your wrath!"

"Now we can do business!" said Aelundei, stopping his chanting just as the wind died down. "Where is his cell? What type of interrogation are they using on him? And where is the interrogation room at?"

"At the top level of the castle is a mighty tower," said the goblin, looking very sincere, "in the top of the tower, one floor below the very top, is a row of cells, he is in the middle one. But they usually leave him in the torturing room on the stretching table. The torturing room is one flight down from the ranger's cell. It's marked by a door with a flame painted on it; the door also has a small barred window on it that should be letting out a red light into the hallway of the tower."

"How do I know you can be trusted?" asked Aelundei, the wind picking up again.

"I swear it, I swear it on my own mother, now please don't curse me!"

"You were cursed to a dreadful life after death when you first sided with the Dark One, twisted elf, I trust your word, but I can't trust you." Aelundei drew his knife and pushed the point against the goblin's neck until black blood began to trickle down its throat. "You will leave here, and go anywhere but the castle of Torrer, or the curse that I began to put on you will come and fill you with pain ten times the amount that you would have felt in the other curse. Now go! Before I change my mind and choose to curse you now!"

The goblin ran as fast as he could away from Torrer, and the two friends set back to work moving the troll's carcass.

*   *   *

Braim watched silently as Grashnir slowly stirred the fire with the poker, obviously not seeing what he was doing. Braim relaxed slightly as Grashnir took the time to let his evil mind scheme. He had almost panicked when Grashnir had used his sword to investigate the spot of the necklace that Eien Moran had given him, but when Grashnir had flicked open the shirt, the leather strap and rose-bud emerald were not there. Braim glanced down again to reassure himself of its re-appearance. It was there again, offering its comforting weight and coolness to counteract the pain of the table. Suddenly, Grashnir stood and walked over to Braim.

"I feel sorry for you, sitting on this hard, painful table, and so tonight I will give you a break." Grashnir's strange mood was starting to worry Braim, this was not at all like the twisted creature. "We will continue the torture for a few more hours, and then resume it at mid-day. Does that sound good to you?"

Braim did not answer, he just kept staring past Grashnir at the ceiling and mulling in his thoughts.

"However," said Grashnir, "I never said anything about diminishing, or not escalating, the torture." He smiled as he opened a cupboard and started pulling out many different torturing devices, all of them appearing well used.

Braim swallowed the growing fear of not being able to keep his mouth shut and braced for the impact of pain.

*   *   *

The sun was just beginning the climb down from her high perch, Moraina and Aelundei reined in the horses as they neared the edge of the forest that had been cleared back by the goblins after they took the castle. They peered out from the forest and across the half-mile of open ground to the foothill on which the mighty fortress was perched. Aelundei suddenly licked his thumb, and slowly raised it so the wet side was pointing north.

"We have certainly timed this right, Orandaur," said Aelundei, wiping his thumb on his green-brown cloak, then setting it on its customary position on the saddle in front of him. "The wind is blowing out of the north, down from the trolls' mountains; judging by the cloud bank that can just barely be seen over the tree-tops," he pointed to the cloud bank that only he could see, "then we will be able to use the cloud cover to get in. If we leave the horses on the opposite side of the castle from where we enter, we should be able to use the same moving cloud cover to conceal our escape. What do you think, Orandaur?"

Moraina leaned forward in the saddle and put her pointer finger and thumb up to her chin, thinking.

"Well," said Moraina, "if it was a castle of humans, I'd say we kill a couple guards and use their armor or clothes to get in, but seeing as we don't have that, then we should be safe using your plan." She leaned out of her thinking pose and looked over at Aelundei, who was looking her up and down.

"Well, you're about the height of a tall goblin, want to give your plan a fighting chance?" asked Aelundei, looking over at a couple of the goblins that were randomly walking around the clear land separating the castle from the forest.

Moraina instantly recoiled, knowing this would mean changing out of the clothes she had worn for the last few months.

"What if I don't know what to do?" she stammered, concern showing on her face before she turned it to the ground. "What if I freeze up or my voice cracks and I'm discovered? That could mean the end of Braim and any hopes of rescue, I'm only an apprentice, and I don't sound like a goblin!"

"Relax," said Aelundei putting a hand on the shoulder of the person he still thought was Orandaur. "You would be doing something I have never done either."

"Yes," said Moraina, "but you're over twenty, I'm only fifteen!"

"Well, yes," said Aelundei, "I'm way, way over the age of twenty. In fact, I'm one-hundred and forty, but like I said, you'll be doing something I've never done before. And you will soon be able to draw an accurate picture of the best escape and entry routes for the rescue operation as well." His reassuring smile and his hand on her shoulder convinced Moraina that she would never win this argument with a clear conscience. She lifted her head and nodded.

"Yes, I can do the task at hand," the concerned face became stern and etched with confidence that she did not feel.

"Good man," said Aelundei, smiling and patting Moraina's shoulder. He dismounted and started watching the various goblins wandering around the field. "Let us hunt some goblins!"

*   *   *

Braim lay on the floor of his cell, wishing he had medicine to lessen the pains of his numerous wounds. Grashnir had started to step up the level of torture by taking several knives and slowly pushing them into Braim's skin. That had been the beginning, and Grashnir had promised an even worse interrogation method tomorrow. Braim was not looking forward to that at all. He decided he wanted to watch the sun set one last time, a favorite activity as a child. He crawled to the window, several broken bones in his bare feet making it impossible to stand. He grabbed the windowsill and pulled himself up, quickly remembering that his arms were cut as well. He shifted from his hands to his elbows, wishing he had a more comfortable place to lean on, but he wanted to view the sunset one more time before he died. He peered out to the west, the sun's brilliant rays of light turning the clouds to shades of purple and orange. He then glanced down to the forest and surrounding fields. A quick movement caught his eye, and he noticed that a goblin that had been walking very close to the forest was not there anymore. Then, a few minutes later, the goblin re-appeared. This time it seemed to wobble around for a moment before slouching over and walking towards the castle, making several rapid movements with its hand to its head to hide the brown hair that Braim could just barely make out.

Orandaur? he thought. Then he realized that the goblin was walking with more of a human's gait, instead of the strange shuffling that the short creatures usually made. He leaned as far as he could out of the window, waving his right hand back and forth before sliding back, trying to look calmer than he felt. He waited a few seconds, noticing that the strange goblin had slowed down and was peering up in his direction. The goblin drew its sword and raised it in the Telnorian salute, then sheathed it to resume its stride, though slightly quicker this time.

Síela aena toivoa en ~ there is always hope, thought Braim, remembering one of Aelundei's favorite sayings. Hope surged back into his veins as he realized his friends had made it past the patrols and were now coming to rescue him.

*   *   *

Why did I have to let myself get talked into this? thought Moraina woefully, as she walked toward the castle. A flurry of movement in a window of the floor just below the top level caught her eye, it was Braim, leaning out the window and waving! Her heart picked up a few beats and the air temperature seemed to rise a couple degrees at the sight of her friend that she hadn't seen in several weeks. She waited until he stopped moving and leaned back before executing a Telnorian salute, drawing her goblin sword and holding it so the flat side was facing him. She then returned the sword to its sheath and resumed a quickened pace. She walked up to the open gate of the castle and stepped through. She headed towards the second gate, sweating bullets and feeling open and bare in the presence of all the goblins. She was thankful Aelundei had been able to get a goblin with a helmet that covered her face. He had also found one with long sleeve clothes to cover her fair skin. He had then obediently turned his back while she went behind some bushes and changed, accepting her story that she just liked her privacy. Her mind snapped back as she bumped into a goblin.

"There you are, you lazy whelp," said the whip-wielding goblin as he turned and noticed Moraina's armor, "Get back in line with that formation until we finish drills or I'll personally beat you!" He jerked his thumb to indicate the formation he was drilling and growled.

Shoot me! Thought Moraina as she scrambled to get in to the back of the formation, *how will I get out of this one?*

She drilled with the battalion for almost an hour when a quiet voice, that she had been ignoring, finally raised the volume a little.

Start a fight, said the familiar voice in the back of her head, the warmth slowly seeping to her body, giving her extra strength.

"Hey, you hit me," shouted Moraina to the goblin next to her, careful to disguise her voice. She looked around to the rest of the goblins who were in formation, all of whom were staring at her now. "That green lump of slime hit me, get him!"

The goblins, eager to fight and not caring who they were fighting, split into two almost perfectly equal factions, and started beating the tar out of each other.

Moraina slipped out of the roiling mass before they could grab her and ran as fast as she could to the point nearest the forest on the north side that Aelundei had selected earlier. She walked up to the wall's stairway, and peered down to the ground forty-five feet below.

That, thought Moraina, shuddering at the drop, *could pose a serious problem.*

She started to walk back to the stairs when she heard a metallic clink, she turned around and noticed a grappling hook firmly wedged in the ramparts. She walked up to the hook and looked over the ramparts. A lone goblin was making his way quickly up the rope attached to the hook. Moraina looked around, confirmed that no one was watching, and seized the hook, twisting it out of position. The goblin let out a small cry as he fell, his top half of the body slowly pivoting around, and landed solidly on the ground with a dull *thwump*. Moraina shivered as she heard the sound of breaking bone. Then she turned and went down the stairs, making her way around the castle until she found a gate to the second level.

*   *   *

Aelundei watched Orandaur walk towards the castle in the armor of the goblin he had killed. His sharp elven eyes also picked up Braim's movement, and Orandaur's salute. He hoped there weren't any goblins that were watching that knew the Telnorian salute, but he highly doubted it. The elf turned and crept through the forest to the spot where it was closest to the wall. His green-brown cloak and hood combined with almost a hundred years in the practice of woodcraft made him practically invisible, and perfectly noiseless. His eyes scanned back and forth, searching for danger, his pointed ears picking up the sound of a goblin walking nearby. Aelundei pulled the cowl of his hood further over his head and froze in the shadows of a pine, using every change in the shadow pattern to his advantage. All of a sudden, a goblin appeared a few yards in front of him. It was moving stealthily and carrying a large coil of rope attached to a grappling hook. Aelundei waited for it to leave the area before following it to the edge of the forest, right to the point where it was closest to the castle. He watched the goblin look across the clearing, waiting until the sentries' backs were turned before slinking across the meadow. It was using the moving clouds to his advantage and staying in the shadows, which were slowly lengthening as the sun set. Aelundei watched from the edge of the forest as the goblin, probably an assassin, made its way to the castle wall. It froze as Orandaur in the goblin armor looked over at the forest before turning away. The goblin threw the grappling hook, which sailed up and landed in the ramparts. The creature tugged a couple times and then started climbing up the rope towards the top of the castle. Aelundei then saw Orandaur walk up to the hook, grab it, and twist. The assassin was about three-quarters of the way up the wall, when the rope it was holding suddenly went loose and it fell, landing on its head.

Well, thought Aelundei wryly, *that takes care of our rope problem, good job, Orandaur!*

Aelundei waited for the guards to look the other way and then started moving across the valley, scooting along with the clouds. He arrived at the rope and the dead assassin, tucked the rope into his cloak and started across the valley again, thankful his father and brothers had taught him wood craft as a child. He made it to the forest and turned around; none of the sentries had seen him; a great testament of his skill in woodcraft. He hoped no one else heard of this, he'd be stuck giving lessons in stealth to clumsy humans for eternity.

Braim fell back to the floor and crawled back to the spot he had been before, feeling satisfied and hopeful. The sunset, and the sight of his friends coming for him, had boosted his morale. He lay there, trying to sleep and regain some of the strength that torture had taken out of him. He could not wait to grasp his sword and his knife. Though he took no joy in killing, they were familiar objects he had longed for. He could not help but wonder if they had his weapons. And he also wondered if they had food. Braim had only been fed a couple loaves of stale bread and a glass of bitter water. He hoped Orandaur and Aelundei made it.

Suddenly he heard voices outside of his door, he listened closely, a goblin was trying to get in and ask him some questions. The sentries drilled him on several questions about their king, which the goblin answered, then the door opened. A lone goblin entered and the door shut behind it. It took off its helmet to reveal Orandaur's face ringed in brown hair.

"Orandaur?" whispered Braim, unable to believe his eyes, "You shouldn't have come; you might get caught. You should leave, now."

Orandaur's eyes clouded over as he slowly approached Braim to sit by his side, then a single tear started down his right cheek. Braim reached up with a scabbed hand and whipped it away. Orandaur's eyes dried up, anger entering them when he felt how destroyed Braim's hands were.

"Orandaur," Began Braim.

"Where is Grashnir's planning room?" interjected Orandaur, a brilliant idea forming behind the dark brown eyes, "do you know?"

"No, I don't know," said Braim, shaking his head sadly. "I wish I did, though. If we could discover the enemy's plans, we would be able to alert our king before it is too late." He paused for a moment as he seemed to study the floor, then looked back up at his young apprentice with doubt in his eyes. "Orandaur, your skin sure is soft and smooth for a man's, even a young man."

"I have to go," said Orandaur, rising to his feet as he struggled to don his helmet with shaking hands, "I will ask the sentries where the planning room is, I have an idea on how to save our kingdom. We will be arriving at your room sometime around five hours after sunset to get you, be ready."

Orandaur pushed the hair back into his goblin helmet and exited the room in a hurry.

*   *   *

Moraina heard the door click behind her and then turned to one of the guards, noticing that he had keys.

"Do you know where the war-room is by chance?" she asked in her goblin voice, "I am new in this part of the castle and Grashnir tol' me to repo't to him there."

"Go down one level," said the guard, indicating that Moraina should go the way she had come, "And then turn left at the bottom of the stairs."

Moraina turned and left without thanking him, and followed his directions. She opened the door and peered in; it was unoccupied. She walked in and started sorting through the various papers and maps until she found what she wanted. She pulled a blank piece of paper from the pile and started copying the other piece that she had found as quickly as possible. She then put all the pieces of paper back into the pile where she had found them, her picture-perfect memory of items and events allowing her to do it flawlessly. Stuffing the piece of paper between her armor and her chest she left the room on the opposite side from which she had entered. She almost jumped out of her skin when a voice behind her shouted, "Halt!"

*   *   *

Aelundei was worried; Orandaur had left several hours ago. The sun had long since disappeared, and the Queen of the Night, with her entourage of stars, made the cloud's shadows extremely dark and blotchy. It was the perfect night for a rescue, but that didn't ensure success. Nothing did. Aelundei scanned the battlements again, surprised to see that all the sentries were asleep save one. Then it hit him, that one must be Orandaur! Aelundei glanced down at his attire and the bundle of clothes that he held. He had changed into clothes more suitable for crawling around in a dark fortress as soon as the night fell. The trousers were of a dark gray color, the same color as the granite that Telnorians used for making their thick walls. The tunic was the same color, only this was of a different material. It was still of the elven weave, only it seemed to grow darker in color to

104

match the shadows and then lighter to match the moon spots. He was glad he had thought to pack it before setting off from the elven lands twenty five years ago. His dark attire was completed by a dark gray bandana that covered his fair skinned neck, his black hair helping immensely.

Aelundei checked to make sure he had everything, then started forward. The only items hindering his movement were Orandaur's clothes, weapons, and the grappling hook. He crawled out into the field, moving with the clouds, staying in the darkest parts of the shadows. He reached the wall and looked upward, *are the sentries asleep? Is it safe for me to proceed?* He barely made out Orandaur's arm as he reached over the ramparts and dropped something. Aelundei caught the falling object, it was a pinecone, the signal that all was safe. Grabbing the hook, the elf threw it upwards; Orandaur caught it, and secured it to the ramparts, careful not to make any loud noises. Aelundei tied the bundles of weapons and clothes to the end of the rope, then tugged twice. At first, Orandaur didn't do anything, but then he caught the meaning and pulled the bundle up. Nothing fell out, a compliment to Aelundei's knot-tying skills. Orandaur untied the rope and sent it back down for Aelundei, who was up it in mere seconds. Orandaur stood silently behind the ramparts, holding the bundle of clothes and a few of the weapons.

"As soon as we find an unoccupied house I need you to change into these," whispered Aelundei, as quietly as possible. Orandaur nodded, and they proceeded to walk quietly down the stairs.

At the bottom of the stairs, Orandaur took the lead, walking over to one of the houses that was missing its roof. Orandaur opened the door and peeked inside; there was not a single goblin at all in the house. They breathed a sigh of relief entered, thanking Vitaren silently for helping them thus far on the mission. Orandaur and Aelundei stepped into the building. Orandaur walked into what had been a different room of the house and changed; emerging as Orandaur the ranger, wearing a gray-colored cloak to better conceal him in the shadows.

"You look much better," said Aelundei.

"Thank you," replied Orandaur with a blush, grateful for the darkness, "I feel much better too. What took you so long to get here?"

"I was waiting for you to return to the forest," replied Aelundei, "Why did you stay here?"

"I was detained," replied Orandaur, looking down, "A goblin caught me in the king's planning room, but I managed to talk my way out of it, barely." Suddenly he switched the subject, "Do you have pockets Aelundei?"

"Not on my clothes," The elf replied, "but I have a pouch on my belt here. Would that work for whatever you have in mind?"

"Yes," said Orandaur, a grateful look sweeping across his face. He held out a piece of paper, "I found the location of the king's planning room, and though I was almost caught, I managed to get out with the enemy's plans."

"Well done," said Aelundei, surprised at how smart and capable Orandaur was for his level of training. "That was well done. Come, we must go, the night and the guards' sleep will not last forever."

Orandaur buckled on his sword, bow, and arrows, then they set out from the house, looking right and left before throwing the grappling hook up to the wall of the second level.

*   *   *

Braim was still thinking of how strangely Orandaur had acted when confronted by the fact that his skin was smooth. For the first time in the three months that they had been training Orandaur, he wondered if there was more to the lad than met the eye. He sat and tried to sleep, knowing that he would soon be required to help in the escape effort; he lay on the floor, the cold seeming to draw the pain out of him, slowly numbing the fire in his burnt and wounded body parts. A vision of Orandaur's face floated through his mind as he drifted off to sleep.

*   *   *

Moraina grabbed Aelundei's arm and helped him over the wall of the third level. Aelundei straightened, there was only one wall left to pass before they reached the tower. But on the wall to the fourth level there were sentries still awake. Moraina and Aelundei looked up at the sentries silently patrolling the wall. If they threw the hook, then they might make a noise loud enough for the sentries to be alerted. But the only other way would be to go through the gate. For that they would need a battering ram, and a large army. Moraina felt Aelundei nudge her shoulder.

"You go around the fortress this way," He indicated that she go left around the circular fourth level, "And I will take this direction," He indicated he would go right, "If you see a spot where there is no sentry, hoot like an owl and wait for me."

They walked in separate directions, until Moraina found a very large gap on the opposite side from which they had come. She hooted a few times and then Aelundei appeared. Moraina silently indicated the two hundred foot gap on the wall by lifting her arm to point it out.

"Very good," whispered Aelundei, but strangely, instead of throwing the hook, he flipped the rope around and tied a knot in the other end of the rope so that it was in the form of a noose about the size of the battlements on the wall.

"What is that?" asked Moraina, not quite getting the purpose behind the noose.

"They call this a Hirlosea, in Elleavemar," said Aelundei, indicating the noose. "I'm going to try to get it around the teeth of the battlements so we can get in without making the noise of iron on stone. It may not work because there's less weight on it, but I think I may be able to solve that." Reaching into his bag Aelundei felt around until he came out with three weights. These he attached to the rope by pushing the jaws of the soft metal together until they clamped on the rope.

"Stand back," said Aelundei to Moraina, she stepped back and he twirled the rope a few times before letting go.

Moraina watched in awe as the rope sailed up and then settled around the base of a merlon with only a dull, quiet click; much quieter than the metallic clang produced by the hook. Moraina walked up to the rope, seized it, and started climbing up the thick, black cord.

Upon reaching the top, she drew and nocked an arrow to her bow, pulling back the string until the arrow tip touched the wood, watching for the first sign of an enemy guard. But none of them had moved, even more of them had fallen asleep. The moon started to set as the time neared for the darkest hour before dawn.

*   *   *

Aelundei followed Orandaur to the door of the central tower, bow drawn. Orandaur drew his sword before opening the door and entering quickly, catching three goblins off guard. Aelundei released the arrow on his bow as Orandaur cut down the goblin nearest him. The third goblin turned to run but was pierced in the back by Aelundei's second arrow.

"We must hurry now," Aelundei said, grabbing his arrows and returning them to his quiver. They stuffed the goblins in a dark corner of an unused armory before racing off in the direction of the stairs to the second floor. The stairs were very dangerous for any attackers trying to make it up. They spiraled sharply to the right, making it possible for a right-handed defender to only expose his sword-arm. A right-handed attacker had to either twist his body or expose all of it to the defender on the stairs, making him an easy target. Aelundei followed Orandaur with an arrow drawn, ready for anything. They ran into only four more goblins, which were too surprised that there were enemies in the central tower to put up much of a fight. Finally they reached the door that opened into the second level.

"Ready?" asked Orandaur, a strange grin on his face.

"I'm ready," said Aelundei, "Are you?"

"I'm a little winded, but I was able to make it up here to see Braim earlier. Thinking of how bruised and destroyed he is has been driving me on."

"Then let us finish this quickly," said Aelundei, pulling the bow back to full draw.

This time when the two rangers burst through the door, there were no goblins to be seen in the hallway. Instead, the pair could hear loud laughter and drunken singing behind a door. It was the door to the banquet hall.

"Anden!" swore Orandaur mildly in the elven tongue, "the stairs to the third level is in on the other side of the banquet hall."

"There has to be another door somewhere!" said Aelundei, a worried look on his face from the thought of having to wait longer for the goblins to go to sleep or leave. "Let's run around the hall here and search for a ladder or stairs somewhere."

They raced down the hall, knowing that if they took too long, then the bodies of the goblins would be discovered, and the first place most of the smarter goblins would go would be to the prison cell in the top of the tower; they would be trapped!

Aelundei's thoughts raced, there were too many odds stacked against them this time, they would be very hard-pressed to get through to Braim with any hopes of getting back out again. On top of that, Aelundei was wondering how much Braim would be able to help with the escape. Finally, they found a door with an ascending staircase, and they paused to catch their breath before hurtling up the steps as fast as they could without making too much noise.

*   *   *

Braim tried to stand again, but could not. The broken bones in his feet accounting for the vast majority of the pain he felt. His arms had been stabbed multiple times by dull knives, hurting slightly worse than the burns that he had received on his chest and stomach. He hoped Aelundei and Orandaur were able to carry him. On the bright side, he had been fed nothing for the past few days, so perhaps he had shed a few pounds. Braim crawled to a position near the door and leaned against the wall. Aelundei and Orandaur had better hurry, each moment increased the chance of an alarm being sounded, and Braim did not want to see his friends hurt or killed on his behalf.

*   *   *

Moraina stabbed the last goblin in the stomach and then continued running. They had reached the fourth level now, they were splitting up. Aelundei would head to the torture room to make sure Braim had not been moved, and then grab any of his clothes that might be there to meet Moraina at the prison cell. She turned right and entered another flight of stairs, while Aelundei went straight and continued on to the torture chamber. Moraina took the steps two at a time, her sword still held out in front of her, and ran straight into a group of four goblins. At first, the goblins were extremely surprised at the fact that there really was a human this deep inside the fortress, and Moraina was able to kill two of them before the other two attacked. Moraina blocked a sword cut to her head and jumped over the other goblin's sword, managing to kick that goblin hard in the jaw and knock it out. She killed the first one and brought her sword down into the second one's heart. She then sped even faster up the stairs to the fifth level, Braim's level.

*   *   *

Aelundei was also having a few difficulties, only he was faced by six goblins that were able to recover faster than the others did. They charged him, swords drawn. The elf shot two of them before engaging the other four with Braim's large broadsword. He made mince meat of the first three with only a few swings of the weapon, and then shot the last goblin as it ran away. The pitiful creature hit the floor with a thud, and Aelundei rushed to recover his arrows. He sprinted to the torture chamber and burst in. There was not a single creature in the small room, but it was still scattered with various instruments of torture, and blood spots. They were red blood patches. He walked over to a cupboard on the other side of the room and opened it, finding Braim's cloak and boots, two very important items. He grabbed them and raced out of the room, where he bumped into eight drunk goblins standing around the dead bodies of their fallen comrades.

*   *   *

Moraina fired an arrow. It flew through the hallway, went into the front of one of the two guards' necks, out the other side, and slammed into the other's. She sprinted through the hallway, removed the keys to Braim's cell from the goblin's belt, and opened the door. Braim jerked awake, an alarmed look on his face before he realized it was Orandaur

"Braim, can you walk?" asked Orandaur, slightly out of breath.

"No, I have broken bones in both my feet," said Braim, shaking his head sadly.

Moraina realized that she would have to carry him until Aelundei arrived.

"Aelundei will be here in a few moments, I'm going to drag the guards in the cell and then we wait for him." said Moraina, trying to look more confident than she felt.

"Orandaur," said Braim, grabbing Moraina's pant leg. "We don't have much time; we should meet Aelundei half-way."

"What if he is forced to go a different route than the one I took?" asked Moraina, hoping Braim accepted the idea, he did.

"You're right, good point," Braim slumped back against the wall again and watched as Moraina dragged the two guards inside the small room.

Just as Moraina finished her self-assigned task, Aelundei arrived. The elf clapped his friend hard on the back, "Why did you have to get yourself captured, Braim? If you wanted to know whether or not we would break into a castle full of goblins to save your neck, you could have just asked!"

"It's good to see you too, Aelundei," replied Braim with a grin.

Aelundei's smile changed to a frown as he examined his friend's disfigured feet. "I will not be able to fix these feet until I can get to my whole medical kit and some firm sticks. Braim, I told you not to kick armored goblins without the proper footgear." said Aelundei, trying to lighten the atmosphere in the room once more, but his face grew hard as he examined the rest of Braim's wounds. "Orandaur, I need to conserve my strength for getting Braim down the ropes, you'll have to carry him."

Moraina was instantly concerned for her cover, if she carried him in her arms he would be pressed against her chest, and he might feel that something wasn't right. Maybe she could carry him over her shoulders? Kneeling down, she wrapped one arm around his knees and lifted him up on her shoulders. She almost dropped him as he screamed in pain.

"I have too many burns and stabs on my stomach for you to carry me that way," Braim was panting, "I should only weigh a little more than a hundred pounds, you can carry me in your arms."

Internally Moraina panicked, *You can do this, Moraina*, she told herself, but she wasn't being very convincing.

"Orandaur," exclaimed Aelundei, "We have very little time, move!"

Goaded to action by the elf's sudden outburst, Moraina squatted down and lifted Braim, one arm under his knees, the other arm around his back.

"I think you weigh a lot more than a hundred pounds," said Moraina with a grunt, she turned to Aelundei. "Let's go, Aelundei, take my sword for me."

Aelundei drew Moraina's sword from its sheath to dual-wield his sword and hers.

"That is a nice blade, Orandaur," said Braim, looking over the weapon with a skilled eye.

"This is not the time to be admiring swords, Braim," said Moraina, almost pushing Aelundei out the door in her newfound haste to get out of the castle.

The three friends sped out of the cell and ran as fast as they could to the stairs. They slowed their pace as they descended the stairs;

Aelundei keeping a steadying hand on Braim to make sure Moraina didn't fall. They reached the door to the fourth level and burst through it, meeting a large group of goblins standing over the bodies of their fallen comrades. Moraina set Braim down and drew her bow, firing arrows into the crowd as Aelundei charged them, engaging them with both swords. The goblins, seeing that there were only two able-bodied people, charged. Half of them were cut down in moments by the singing bow and flashing swords, and the other half soon turned to run. Aelundei drew his bow as well and fired as fast as he could into the backs of the retreating goblins. Eight more fell, but three escaped the arrow storm and ran off to alert the rest of castle.

"We must run," said Aelundei as Moraina picked up Braim. "Do not worry about arrows; we can get more in Telnor."

They sprinted down the stairs to the third level, able to kill two more of the goblins that had run away, leaving only one to sound the alarm. They ran to the stairs to the second level, opened the door, and had to fight their way down, Aelundei carving a path through the enemy with two swords again. They burst through the door to the second level and ran down the hall-way, having to fight hard through most of the long, curved path. Then, with the door to the stairs of the bottom level of the tower in sight, a hoard of almost thirty goblins filed out of the banquet hall. Aelundei fought valiantly, and there were only about twenty goblins left when his strength started to fail.

"Orandaur, I need to take Braim," he shouted as he ducked a cross-bow bolt.

Moraina lowered Braim to the ground and took the swords from Aelundei, who picked up Braim. Moraina fought the goblins until there were only a few left, and then those few ran off. Aelundei gave Braim back to Moraina; they opened the door for the stairs and ran down them. This time, there were no goblins in front of them, but there were sounds of pursuit from behind. Aelundei dropped to the back and prepared to buy Moraina time, but when they made it to the door to the first level, Aelundei had still not seen the enemy; they seemed reluctant to fight the two rangers. Aelundei moved to the front again and then opened the door to the first level's hall-way. They charged out with the Telnorian battle-cry, but there were no enemies there. Aelundei started grabbing chairs and barrels that were lying around in the hallway and blocked the door before running out into the courtyard and the outside world.

The sentries were still asleep at their posts when the rangers opened the door and ran out, shutting it silently behind them. They sprinted across the open ground, took the stairs two at a time, and prepared to go down the rope.

"Orandaur, you go down first, when you get to the bottom tug twice." Aelundei took Braim from her as Moraina put on a pair of gloves and grabbed the rope, sliding down.

Aelundei set Braim down silently, drew his long bow, and prepared to give the first few goblins a nasty surprise. He looked over his shoulder and counted the arrows he had left. Only seven remained in his quiver. He desperately needed replacements, but his only hope for getting more was to get the humans back to Telnor where he could make them.

Moraina hit the bottom of the rope and tugged twice before turning around and drawing her bow and an arrow. She waited as she heard the sound of the grappling hook scraping against the wall as someone at the top pulled it up. A few moments later Aelundei with Braim clinging to his back slowly rappelled down the wall, Moraina returned the bow and arrow to her quiver and took Braim from Aelundei, who grabbed the rope and shook it. The grappling hook came loose and Aelundei caught it from the air before it could hit the ground. They turned and ran to the next wall, the sounds of goblins running out of the central tower urging them on. Going up the stairs to the top of the wall was not a big problem, but the fact that there was a horn blowing and waking sentries surely was one. Aelundei set the hook down as Moraina fired her bow, sending the goblins with crossbows falling to the ground with harsh cries. She hated the fact that the goblins could not be at peace with the humans, and she hated the fact that she had to kill to live. But there was absolutely nothing she could do about it; the goblins sole purpose on earth seemed to be to destroy and subdue. With every arrow that she fired, a life was extinguished, and yet, she felt that there had to be a higher purpose for her in life other than to grow, to fight, to be wounded, to kill, and then to die. There had to be something more!

There is so much more to life than that, said a soft, feminine voice that restored peace to Moraina's mind. *Vitaren put you on the earth for a much higher purpose, my sister, but sadly, most humans and even some of the elves have strayed from his purposes. Return the name of Vitaren to Telnor. Keep faith, my sister.*

Aelundei jerked the hook loose and caught it again before following Moraina's lead to the wall. He dropped the rope over the

113

edge and settled it into a good position. He grabbed Braim, not waiting for Orandaur, he went down quickly. Moraina seized the rope before Aelundei had gone ten feet and raced down after him. Aelundei landed and moved out of the way as Moraina almost collided with the ground too hard. Aelundei handed Braim to Moraina and tugged the rope as Moraina started to walk quickly towards the last wall. He drew his sword as goblin warriors swarmed out of the barracks nearby, they would have to fight their way to the wall. Moraina backed up against him and handed him Braim's sword, wielding her own with one hand, Braim was now clinging to her neck as her free hand supported his legs. They fought for several minutes, Moraina covering Aelundei's back. The sun was rising in the east as they finally broke through to the wall top. Aelundei, with eyes glowing gold, blocked darts with Braim's sword while Moraina and Braim fixed the hook in position and started down. As soon as Moraina was down and well away from the castle, Aelundei did a back-flip off the wall, narrowly dodging three crossbow bolts that sailed not even a hand breadth from his chest. With a thickly gloved hand, Aelundei reached out and grabbed the rope, slowing his fall and making a safe landing. Aelundei raced up to Moraina, who was about halfway across the field and going slowly. He took Braim and yelled as he passed.

"We must put as much distance between us and this castle as we can, pick up the pace, child!" He laughed and raced ahead as projectiles zipped around them, luckily missing their targets, though they got extremely close.

Moraina needed no second bidding. She ran after Aelundei, barely keeping up with the strange second wind the elf had suddenly summoned from some deep reserve of strength. They raced to the horses, Aelundei changed his clothes and Moraina changed her cloak, then they mounted and galloped off. They had rescued Braim, but now they had to make it back to the safety of Telnor.

The Legend of Braim
Chapter XVIII
Executions and Pursuit

Grashnir watched happily as the axes descended on his hapless sentries and a couple of the archery instructors. He then watched as they were thrown onto a huge bonfire before he turned and walked off. He noticed a couple of his couriers standing by, doing nothing.

"Runners," shouted Grashnir; the couriers jumped to attention, "I have an important mission for you. I need you and the rest of your fellow runners to deliver a message to each of the different goblin kings, telling them that we must move the invasion forward a few weeks due to an emergency."

The couriers ran off to find their fellow runners, hoping to get the job done before they followed the other goblins that had been burned that day.

Grashnir then saw Jorguel, his servant, walking towards him.

"Jorguel," barked Grashnir, "run and find the rest of my generals and tell them to prepare to mobilize their troops. Tell them: 'Our victory begins! Exterminate all of the Telnorian pestilence.'"

Jorguel bowed and jogged off to fulfill his master's command. Grashnir was glad that Xim and fifty more trolls would be arriving that day to be given armor and better weapons. He would be glad to have five-hundred battle trolls at the disposal of the kings, but there was one thing that worried him. The rangers that had been in the castle the other night could have had enough time to copy his battle plans. He figured they would have to change. He marched down to the gate at the first level of the castle. The couriers were just about to leave.

"Halt!" commanded Grashnir, the couriers stopped dead in their tracks and looked over to see what their king wanted to do to them. "I have a slight change in the message you must send to the goblin kings. I want you to tell them that instead of gathering in three places as originally planned, we will now be gathering above the middle pass and attacking all from there, able to destroy the divided Telnorian army one section at a time. And tell them also that they may be waiting for us."

The runners looked relieved to not be the subject of the order to halt, and then continued on their different ways.

Grashnir watched them run off into the forest and then turned back to the tower, but not before noticing a shadowy shape roll over the ramparts. He turned to investigate, and the shape rolled off the wall and landed on the roof of a house.

"Who goes there?" challenged Grashnir, a throwing knife in one hand and his drawn sword in the other.

The shape stood up and Grashnir noticed it was one of his assassins.

"It is I, oh King," said the assassin, bowing on the roof, "I am Theraguld, one of your eighteen remaining assassins," Theraguld did a roll off the roof, and grabbed a door sign on his way down, which slowed his fall despite snapping off , unable to bear his weight.

After landing on the ground, Theraguld bowed again, still holding the broken-off sign in his right hand.

"How may I be of service to my king?" he asked, his eyes looking up at Grashnir.

"How fast can you run, assassin?" asked Grashnir, a plan for the escaping humans forming in his black, evil mind.

"I once outran a horse in a long-range chase, oh King," said the assassin, grinning wickedly, "And one of the other assassins ran with me."

"Was the horse lame, or did you tie its legs together?" asked Grashnir with disgust.

"A clever goblin is resourceful," rejoined Theraguld with a grin, "He knows how to sneak into a camp, hamstring a horse, and elude his pursuers well enough to escape. Of course, when one's assistant knows how to set fire to the horsemen's tent, escaping is not too difficult."

"Very well," spat Grashnir, satisfied with the answer, "find your assistant, and pursue those humans, even if you must go deep into enemy territory. I want their heads brought back to me, or at least that young one that was in the torture chamber. You know that one, yes?"

"Yes, oh King," said the assassin, "the one with the red-blonde hair, who will probably be hunched over in his saddle from pain. I will take the other swift assassin and we will hunt them down."

"Good," said Grashnir, "Do not return until they are dead, or you will die as slowly as possible."

Grashnir watched as the assassin jogged off to look for the other swift-footed runner, and then, he too returned to the center of the city

116

to his room in the tower. He marched through several gates and up numerous ramps and staircases, before he finally made it to the central tower. He opened the door and walked in, whistling the melody to an ancient drinking song.

The Legend of Braim
Chapter XIX
Hunted

Aelundei, Braim, and Orandaur reigned in their horses beside the great river. The bridge was destroyed. The storm had caused a flood to come up and wash the bridge away. There was splintered wood everywhere, washed against the shore, snagged against rocks, and clinging to the small island in the middle of the river.

"Well," sighed Aelundei, "we used to be able to cross here. It appears we will have to make for the pass over the Premeleis Mountains; follow me."

Braim leaned back from his seat behind Orandaur's saddle so he could see the huge river.

They rode slower, giving their horses time to rest after the hard ride from the castle to the river. As they rode along Aelundei and Orandaur spoke riddles to each other, each trying to speak a riddle the other could not solve. Braim, never one for riddles, sat and listened as Orandaur spun a Telnorian riddle, every step of the horse increased his pain.

"I am cold as the winter's snow. I am silent as the breath of wind. I am quick as an arrow, or slow as a crawling worm. I drag kings off their thrones, I make messengers silent as stone, I find all. None can escape the knowledge of my coming, I seek out the old and the young, the sick, the wounded, the weak. What am I?"

Aelundei sat upon his horse, thinking as he searched the surrounding woods. "Is it death?" he asked quietly, wary of listening ears.

"Yes," replied Orandaur, hanging his head in defeat, "it is death."

"Try to pick a harder one next time," said Aelundei with a warm smile, "Here is one from my home: I am laughter, I am joy. I bring green and herald warmth, fresh buds and grass lift their faces to welcome me. Who am I?"

"It is spring," cried Orandaur, happy to finally solve an elven riddle after numerous failures over the past months.

"Yes," said Aelundei, quietly, "it is spring, try to be as silent as possible, I fear we are being pursued. I think we have given the horses enough time to rest, we should resume a faster pace."

The riders nudged their horses, and the world faded to a blur of colors, the only clear objects were the mountains in the distance, slowly growing larger as the trio neared the tall range.

"How much farther must we ride?" asked Orandaur, shouting so Aelundei could hear him over the wind.

"Twelve leagues, as the crow flies," cried Aelundei in reply, "but we cannot fly over thickets of thorns or dense trees; these will slow us down and lengthen the trip. About three more hours, plus any times we stop to rest the horses."

The world slowly grew dim as Braim drifted off into pain fill dreams. He tightened his arms around Orandaur's waist and leaned closer.

*   *   *

A tall woman was leaning over Braim, tending his wounds and singing to him in a quiet voice. She had long blonde hair, green eyes, and was wearing a beautiful brown and gray dress.

"Mother?" asked Braim, surprised that he had recognized her.

"Lay still, Braim," said Risallia, "I will care for you as long as you are hurt. Stay still and go to sleep."

Braim closed his eyes as his mother tied more strips of linen around his wounds, but his memory returned to the looming battle and the fact that his country was not safe. He lifted his head, sat up, and then tried to get out of the covers. As he was getting up, his legs were tangled in the blankets, he struggled to get out, and fell to the floor. As he fell he could dimly hear his mother shouting his name. He hit the floor with a thud.

*   *   *

Braim awoke to a face full of dirt and numerous places of pain on his body that had not been there before. He rolled over to survey his surroundings; he was lying on the ground, next to a tight clump of tall pines. He had fallen off his horse. With his arms he dragged himself to a position from which he could see the direction that Aelundei and Orandaur had traveled. Luckily, they had seen him fall and were turning the horses to pick him up. He hoped there were no other humans around; that would be extremely embarrassing, an expert rider having to ride behind his apprentice, and still managing to fall off. He would never have heard the end of it, even if he had been asleep.

The other two rangers dismounted, and helped Braim up into Orandaur's saddle once more. This time Orandaur climbed into the saddle behind him, "What was that for?" He asked, trying to keep a smile from his face. "You almost made me jump clean out of the saddle!"

"Well," answered Braim, "I was having the most wonderful dream ever. How close are we to the mountains?"

"Eight more leagues as the horse runs," replied Orandaur, "we are going to try reaching them before nightfall."

"No," interjected Aelundei, firmly, "Braim is in no condition to ride that far. We must stop and rest for a few days so I can treat his wounds. At the next ravine or deep hollow, we will stop and make camp until Braim is fit to ride."

"Aelundei," objected Braim, "The enemy means to invade Telnor, I can endure pain if it means saving my people."

Aelundei shook his head, "Vitaren sent me to Telnor, He led me to your orphanage, He told me to take you into my protection. If I do not treat you now, your wounds will get infected, and you will die. I must not let that happen."

"Why me," asked Braim, confused, "I am no one."

"Braim," replied Aelundei, "one day your descendants will be seated on the throne of Telnor as kings. Be silent for now, I have something I must explain to you, but it will wait until we are at camp."

Aelundei looked up at the rapidly dimming sky as he urged Valostala forward, they had to make camp soon, or darkness would render that impossible.

*   *   *

A steady drizzle of rain was falling as the trio finally found a ravine to camp in. They led the horses down into the bottom, set up tents, and started a low fire. Under Aelundei's watchful eyes, Moraina made three walls of wood around the little blaze, hiding the light from prying eyes while simultaneously drying the next batch of fuel. Then she watched as the elf set to work with bandages and herbal poultices.

"The healing herbs of the elves have been carefully selected and bred over many centuries," said Aelundei as he applied the mixtures to Braim's burned chest, "They not only heal the wounds with very little scarring, but they also accelerate the speed of healing. Without these, we would have to wait here for at least a week; with the herbs, we should be back in the saddle in three or four days." He finished the burns and cuts on Braim's chest, bandaged him loosely, then moved to the broken feet. "These, however," stated Aelundei with a frown, "will need much more time to heal. I can splint them well enough that you can ride, Braim, but I would stay off your feet for a week." The elf retrieved several large sticks, some thick bandages, and then began tying the feet. "Orandaur," said Aelundei on a whim, "I need to reset a few of the bones in both feet. This is going to hurt quite a bit; you should come restrain our friend."

Moraina, with eyes wide, approached Braim's shoulders with hesitation, placing a hand on each.

"Braim," articulated Aelundei, his mind searching for the right words. "I need to tell you something I should have told you a long time ago." He paused.

"Nothing like taking your time," sighed Braim, impatient, "at least my feet aren't broken and in need of immediate medical attention, or this wait would be really painful."

"The castle you were just imprisoned in is rightfully yours," said Aelundei, speaking fast.

"What?" asked Braim in disbelief, his mouth falling open.

"Your father and mother were the lord and lady of Torrer province," explained Aelundei, "Until the city was attacked by goblins and overrun. Your mother refused to leave your father, and they fell defending the central keep."

While Braim was still trying to comprehend what he had just been told, Moraina saw Aelundei nod, and the elf swiftly reset a bone.

*   *   *

The pain in his feet was excruciating, but could not compare to the wound that had been inflicted deep within his soul. Braim barely contained his howl of pain as Aelundei reset first one bone, then another. *Why did he withhold the knowledge of my parents from me?* Braim's mind reeled, thoughts flying everywhere, *All these years I have been guessing who my parents are, while Aelundei has known all along!* Braim reached up and grasped one of Orandaur's hands as

Aelundei reset a third bone.

"There," said Aelundei, panting, "that is the last bone in need of resetting, but now I need to splint both your feet."

"Aelundei," groaned Braim, "Why did you not tell me?"

Aelundei looked into the fire as he rose to his feet, "I did it to protect you."

"Protect me?" asked Braim, his face growing red with rage, "Protect me from who?"

"From yourself," replied Aelundei grimly, then he started splinting the broken feet. Braim knew from the expression on his face that he would not answer any more questions.

*   *   *

Moraina was sitting next to the fire, staring into the embers as she tried to wrap her mind around the events of the last week. Braim's capture, the rescue, discovering the enemy's plans, riding like the wind, and now Aelundei's confrontation with Braim; she wanted to rewind to when life had been simple, just the three of them without a care in the world. She knew, however, that life would never be the same; there would be no going back.

She jumped in surprise as her train of thought was interrupted by Aelundei sitting down beside her.

"Braim's sleeping now," sighed Aelundei, "I had to spike his soup with an herb that induces drowsiness to do it, but at least he is getting some much deserved rest."

"He needs it," replied Moraina wearily, "Especially after your revelation."

Aelundei dropped his head into hands, then ran his fingers through his hair in frustration, "I should have told him sooner."

"Why didn't you?" inquired Moraina, searching Aelundei's face, yet not sure what she was looking for.

"Not even a year ago it would have consumed him," countered Aelundei, spreading his arms, "He would have ridden down to Teckor, marched right up to the king, and demanded that he do something to help him retake his rightful inheritance."

"What is different now?" asked Moraina, leaning towards the elf.

"The odds are in his favor, now," replied the elf, rising swiftly to pace back and forth, "The enemy is going to strike Telnor, if we can repel the invasion, the king may be interested in eliminating the

122

threat of an enemy presence in Torrer to prevent this from happening again." Seeing that his apprentice was not following, he stopped his pacing and spoke even more animatedly, "Don't you see? Now Braim finally has a fighting chance. The king may be more willing to lend troops to Braim so he can retake his long overdue inheritance."

Suddenly it all made sense. Aelundei had been waiting, watching, honing Braim's skills to prepare him for the right moment, the moment when there was a chance that the enemy force could be driven out of the old Telnorian fortress. Moraina yawned violently, the excitement of the day was taking its toll.

"Go sleep, Orandaur," said Aelundei with a grin, "You have been through much for a young lad your age."

Moraina took her leave, then retreated to the relative shelter of her tent and plopped onto her bedroll. Soon she was sleeping soundly.

*   *   *

The next three days dragged by slowly for the small party. Braim did not talk to anyone, he had retreated into his mind, sallying forth only to eat, drink, and relieve himself. Finally, after what seemed like months to all of them, Aelundei declared Braim fit to ride. The elf and the apprentice packed the gear, saddled, the horses, and hoisted Braim into the saddle behind Orandaur. As the trio rode slowly out of the hollow, Aelundei turned in the saddle to address his friend, "Braim, I know you are angry with me for not revealing the truth about your parents to you sooner, but I had good reasons."

"I know," interrupted Braim with a soft voice, "I overheard your conversation with Orandaur the first night. I was half asleep, but I heard it all. Can you forgive me for being so angry and stubborn?"

"Maybe," retorted Aelundei with a mischievous grin, "but only if you forgive me for not telling you sooner."

Braim smiled back, "You elves drive hard bargains, I fear I may not be able to meet this requirement."

The trio laughed, and continued on their way to Telnor, the mountains looming ever larger on the horizon, waiting like brooding giants to crush anyone who drew too near.

The Legend of Braim
Chapter XX
Failed Assassination

Thorguld and the other assassin watched from behind boulders as the three rangers on weary, mud-splattered horses rode through the entrance of the narrow mountain pass.

"Wait for them to enter, and when they stop to help the middle ranger after I shoot him, hand me one of your two crossbows and we'll shoot them as well," said Thorguld, not wanting to lose his prize but still wanting see them all die.

The rangers cleared the entrance of the pass and continued to ride further down the narrow road. Thorguld raised his special assassin's crossbow, aiming just above the middle ranger's head. He pulled the trigger, and the bolt zipped away towards its target. Unfortunately, Thorguld underestimated the distance to the ranger, and the bolt impaled his quiver, not his head. Thorguld cursed loudly as he watched the rangers nudge their mounts and gallop off. Luckily, Thorguld saw the first ranger's hands flicker just in time. He grabbed his assistant and used him as a shield, just in time to stop the feathered shaft.

Well, thought Thorguld, looking down at his fallen companion, *looks like you're just out of luck*. He turned away from the dead goblin and walked down to the road. Bending over, he traced the hoof prints with his hand. All he had to do was follow these, it would be easy. Thorguld stood and started to jog swiftly down the road, following the fresh tracks of the rangers' galloping horses. He should be able to catch them in a few days. After all, what ranger expects a goblin to pursue his target after losing the first battle?

*   *   *

Grashnir watched as the armies of the first kings who responded to his message marched up to the gate of his castle. He had waited a long, long time for this day. And now it was almost time for him to lead the armies of the goblin kings south to take over Telnor. How he longed to crush the humans who had been a thorn in the goblin's side for years innumerable. He was so excited he could hardly keep the smile off his face. He threw on his battle armor, strapped on his sword, and marched out of his room at the top of the tower. He walked all the way down to the front gates, shouting orders left and right as he went. When he finally made it to the front gates, he saw the first of the goblin kings march in, a flag-bearer at his side holding the black flag of Ankmarn, with a large army at his back. The king walked up to Grashnir and stopped, the whole army stopping as well.

"Grashnir," said the goblin king in a harsh voice, "I, king Maragn-nesh, have come with my army to destroy Telnor. I have over five thousand soldiers at my disposal; they are all eager to fight; when do we leave?"

"Maragn-nesh," replied Grashnir with a slight bow, "we must first wait for the arrival of the other kings. Until that time your soldiers must raise their tents in the field surrounding the castle. I request that your soldiers assemble camp against the west side of the wall. You can sleep with your soldiers or with the rest of the kings inside the tower." He hated bowing to other kings, but it was expected that a host show respect to his guests.

"Very well," said the king, he turned to his general and gave him his orders. The army turned and marched to the west side of the wall, and tents began to appear all over the field.

Grashnir repeated this procedure with the next five kings that arrived, then sent word for the kings to come with him into the castle.

Soon, thought Grashnir with an evil grin, *soon all the pieces will be in place for my great invasion of Telnor.*

The Legend of Braim
Chapter XXI
Lord Esmer

Moraina looked around at the sprawling village surrounding the unimpressive walls of Castle Rochaon. The walls were only about twenty feet high, and the keep tower only twice as high as that. The whole castle gave Moraina the impression of being short and fat, but at least the walls were nice and thick.

The horses' hooves began to clatter as the dirt road turned to one of cobblestone. As they rode through the village, it seemed like every peasant they passed would stop to look at the three rangers. Men stopped their arguing, women stopped their washing, and even some of the children would stop their playing to stare.

Eventually, the silence was broken by a small group of children carrying handfuls of wild flowers. They ran up to each of the rangers, unsuccessfully trying to stand on the tips of their toes so they could give them the flowers.

The three rangers stopped their horses, Aelundei dismounted to get down to the children's level, so Moraina followed suit.

"Do you remember me?" asked a blonde haired girl shyly.

Moraina searched the face of the girl, trying to recall where she had seen it before, suddenly she remembered, "Of course I do! How could I forget such a pretty face as yours?"

The little girl squealed with laughter, then held out a purple wildflower, "Thank you for saving me."

"Oh, you shouldn't thank me," replied Moraina with a chuckle, "Thank the ranger Braim, he stopped the goblins long enough for you to get away."

The little girl looked up at the injured man on the horse, "I can't, I'm not tall enough!" She looked down at the ground with a sniff.

"Hop on my shoulders," said Moraina with a grin.

The little girl hopped on the apprentice's shoulders, one leg on either side of Moraina's neck.

"Hold on," said Moraina with a laugh as she rose slowly to her feet. She walked over to Braim's horse, and the little girl hugged Braim tightly with a giddy laugh.

"Thank you, Brain," said the girl.

"My name's Braim," said Braim as he looked at the little girl on his apprentice's shoulders. His expression softened, as he took one of her wildflowers, "But I guess you can call me Brain if you want to."

Suddenly a bell rang from somewhere in the village, and the children scampered off as quickly as they came.

"I have to go," said the little girl, and Moraina set her down on the ground.

"What is your name?" called Moraina after the retreating form of the bubbly child.

"Snowberry," called the girl over her shoulder. Then she disappeared around the corner of a house.

"What an appropriate name," said Aelundei as he returned to Valostala's saddle.

"Why is that appropriate?" asked Braim.

"A Snowberry is a delicate white wildflower that grows on the slopes of the Premeleis Mountains," explained Aelundei with a grin, "The white flower on the vine develops into an edible berry that is very sweet; much like the personality of that girl."

Aelundei pinned a flower in his broach and the trio rode onward.

They rode up to the gate of the castle, stopping as the two guards dropped into their fighting stances and barred the gateway with pikes.

"Halt," said the captain of the guards, who stepped in front of the three rangers, "state your names and business, rangers."

"I am Aelundei, ambassador of the elven lands, and these are my companions, Braim and Orandaur. We have come with urgent tidings for Lord Esmer."

"State the news and we will inform him of your arrival," said the stern-faced captain.

Aelundei raised his voice so that all in the courtyard could hear, "A large alliance of goblin kingdoms is assembling to invade Telnor even as we speak. Lord Esmer must send news to the king, calling for mobilization of the kingdom's armies, or the country of Telnor will be destroyed."

A look of alarm spread across the Captain's face as he realized the situation that was presenting itself, "Stay here, I will return with my lord's response." He turned, and jogged off.

Aelundei turned to his companions, "Well, my friends, all we can do is pray that Vitaren helps Lord Esmer and our King to act swiftly. Our situation requires his clear judgment and swift action."

After several minutes, the captain of the guards returned and beckoned for the rangers to follow him. They followed him to the central keep, where he stopped. "Dismount, my men will take your horses to the stables and see to it they are well taken care of."

Aelundei and his companions dismounted, and Aelundei turned to Valostala. "Íhl saera," he pointed at the soldiers, and Valostala turned and walked over to the two soldiers who were holding the lead ropes of Rochle and Prince. Aelundei walked up to them, and looked into their eyes. "Tie any ropes on her, and she will kill you." The soldiers looked at each other and gulped.

"Forgive me, captain," said Aelundei, "but my friend here needs to lie down and elevate his feet, both are severely broken. Do you happen to know of a spare room in the keep where we can let him rest while I inform your Lord Esmer?"

Braim started to object, but then realized Aelundei was right. His feet were still badly swollen and needed to be elevated to drain the fluid.

"Follow me," said the captain. He led them into the central keep, up a flight of stairs, and then opened a door to a room with several beds. "This is our sick ward. Luckily for you it is unoccupied, so the three of you can stay here until a better arrangement is made. If you want to settle in, I could return for you in five minutes."

"No," replied Aelundei emphatically, "We have lost valuable time treating my companion's injuries. Now that it is possible, we must move quickly." The elf turned to face Orandaur, "Stay here with Braim, make sure he keeps his feet up. I will return when Lord Esmer has all the information he needs." Then he left the room in pursuit of the Captain of the Guard.

*   *   *

Aelundei surveyed his surroundings. He was in the waiting room outside the Lord's office. To left of the door a bald headed clerk sat behind a small desk that was covered in a mountain of paper. A few torches lit the room, causing shadows to dance and flicker. Aiding the torches in their war against darkness was a small window opposite the desk, casting a beam of light through the millions of dust motes that floated through the air.

The door to the lord's chamber opened, and the guard beckoned Aelundei to enter.

Esmer, lord of castle Rochaon and the surrounding province, sat behind a large, ornate wooden desk. He was wearing a grey tunic and brown pants. He had brown eyes, golden hair, and a full beard. On his right hand he wore a large signet ring which marked his status as lord of the second largest province of Telnor.

"Good morning, my lord," said Aelundei, bowing slightly, "I bring troubling news of the goblins in the north."

"What news is not troubling when it involves the evil goblins?" asked Esmer in his deep voice, a look of deep weariness crossing his face. "Go on, speak this dreadful news."

"My lord, the goblins have united and as we speak their army is preparing to march on Telnor; you must act quickly or our country will be overrun."

The color drained from the lord's face, "How can you be certain this is true?"

"My apprentice and I infiltrated an enemy castle to rescue our friend, the third member of our company," replied Aelundei, "While my apprentice was scouting the fortress before the rescue, he managed to locate the enemy's war room and copy their strategy for an invasion of Telnor." Aelundei handed Esmer the copy of the plans, and the tall man studied them intently. His face grew paler, and he had to steady himself on the corner of his desk with one hand.

"Lord Esmer," said Aelundei, hesitantly, "I do not mean to be rude, but now is the time for action, not timidity."

Esmer suddenly stood upright, the color returning to his face, "You are quite right, master elf." He grabbed a cord hanging from the wall next to desk, a bell rang, and Esmer's secretary entered.

"Jabran," said Lord Esmer, "summon to me all of the messengers in the castle, quickly."

"Yes, my lord," said Jabran, as he turned and hurried out the door.

Lord Esmer grabbed a pen and a piece of paper and began to quickly write out a letter to the king. He placed the letter in an envelope and poured hot wax onto the flap at the front before pressing his ring into it.

As he was finishing the first letter and was starting a second one, the secretary returned, followed by fifty-three men in leather armor and maille. The men crammed into the room and saluted in unison. Lord Esmer returned the salute hastily.

"I need the two fastest messengers from among you." Two men stepped forward, and Lord Esmer addressed them, "Men, this letter must be taken to the king as quickly as possible. Take this envelope that has the letter in it and also this one that does not contain a letter.

If you are stopped by bandits give them the empty one and ride like hell is after you, because it is. Our country is about to be invaded by an army that far outnumbers us. It is up to you to see that the king receives this message as quickly as possible. Am I understood?"

"Yes, my lord," said the two messengers in unison as they turned and ran out the door.

"I have work for the rest of you as well. In my letter, I informed the king that I will be sending letters to the rest of the lords in the upper twelve provinces to ease his burden. I will be sending you out in pairs of two, twenty four of you will go to the provinces, and the remainder of you shall ride through this countryside, mustering our army's full strength.

"Jabran, I have another mission for you as well," said lord Esmer, "bring me my second in command."

"It will be done, my lord," said Jabran as he too exited the room.

Lord Esmer turned to the elf who had been waiting patiently by the desk. "You are dismissed; go prepare for the battle."

"Lord, if I may, I have one final question to ask," said Aelundei.

"Ask away," came the lord's reply.

"How long will it take for the king to muster an army and arrive?"

"In times of need, the army can be raised at a day's notice. And, if he imposes a forced quick march, then his portion of the army will be here in a little over five days. However, we can expect the cavalry to arrive at the same time as my messengers return."

"Thank you, my lord," answered Aelundei. He bowed to Lord Esmer and left the room as the man sat down to write furiously.

*   *   *

Moraina was unpacking some of the essential items from her saddlebag, when Aelundei burst into the room.

"How's Braim?" asked the elf.

"He's fine," answered Moraina, surprised at how soon Aelundei had returned, "What is Lord Esmer doing about the goblin threat?"

"He has mobilized his army," replied Aelundei, talking swift in excitement, "Messengers are being sent to King Mettaren and the lords of the other provinces as we speak. Telnor is mobilizing for war!"

The Legend of Braim
Chapter XXII
The March Begins

Grashnir looked up at the sun through the slits in his war helmet. He looked back down at the army that followed him and the other warlords. In a few spots groups of trolls stood tall above the shuffling goblins. In the course of a week, the rest of the warlords had gathered and they now had about one hundred trolls, led by the great troll Xim. Grashnir could not wait to see the trolls in action; he could just imagine the whole Telnorian Army gaping up at the giant mountains of flesh and iron. The hapless army would be swept aside, and Grashnir would establish his kingdom and rule with an iron fist over the conquered humans.

He could not wait for the cruelty that he had in store for the humans to be unleashed, just hearing women, children and men wailing in despair would lift even his darkest spirits. The rangers would be killed slowly, and the king would be sentenced to a life of servitude. All would hate him, and the goblins would multiply until they were strong enough to destroy the elves, and all other free nations. Then he would be able to murder the man in the imposing dark robe and reject his orders. Grashnir smiled at the thought.

Grashnir turned to his servant, Jorguel, "Send out scouts ahead, I want to know exactly what's in our path, no surprises. Hopefully we will be able to make it to the nearest pass in seven days."

Jorguel turned and jogged off to fulfill his master's wish.

Grashnir returned to his own thoughts of inflicting pain and misery. They would begin in a week, and there would be nothing that the king of Telnor could do to stop him.

Yes, he was finally coming, and soon he would arrive!

A goblin general approached in haste and saluted nervously, "My king, there is fighting among the ranks!"

Grashnir hated setbacks.

$*$ $*$ $*$

Thorguld gazed down at the marching army. His target would soon be in the open. For the past week, the cursed rangers had been housed inside the castle, which was well-lit and well-guarded. But when the army arrived the rangers would be out in the open with the rest of their kind, easy targets for the skilled assassin. Now, all he had to do was wait.

The Legend of Braim
Chapter XXIII
The King Arrives

Braim looked in awe as soldiers in shining scale armor marching in near perfect formation began to appear from around the bend in the road. Great square tower shields and tall pikes were carried by the pikemen. After the pikemen came a much larger group of soldiers, the regular infantrymen. These warriors carried large, kite-shaped shields and light throwing spears. They wore medium length swords at their sides and also a dagger. After them came a third group of soldiers, the bowmen. The archers bore short swords and large quivers of arrows on their backs. Their bows were of various sizes, showing they were self-supplied, most likely built by the archers themselves. After that, yet another group of soldiers passed. These were the famous seventh brigade, also known as the elites. They carried large oval shields, and wore tempered steel scale armor. Long tridents replaced regular spears, and it was rumored that they could use any melee weapon with considerable skill. They were the backbone of the Telnorian army and the royal guard. The brigade always numbered 300 strong and only accepted new recruits after they lost men in battle.

Braim noticed a group of mounted nobles and knights at the center of the 7th brigade formation. At the head of this group rode a man in shining plate armor, with a silver crown resting on his black hair. Braim realized that he was staring at the king himself. Quickly he bowed down on one knee at the sight of his king, Orandaur and Aelundei did the same. After the king passed, the trio rose to their feet and watched the rest of the 7th brigade pass.

All of a sudden, Lord Esmer, mounted on a horse, rode out of the Rochaon army and trotted to the king. He bowed in the saddle, and said something to the king. The king nodded, and Esmer fell into formation behind him.

Behind the 7th Brigade, the nobles, and their accompanying knights, rode an army of one hundred rangers. They mixed and mingled as they rode, for they were not trained to march in one formation. But they all had bows and arrows ready, and they all seemed to be alert, ready for any surprise. Braim also noticed that every once in a while a small group would break off and gallop down the road, checking for anyone who might be stalking the army. That was the rangers' job, to bring up the rear and act as specialized archer-scouts.

Braim looked over at Aelundei and Orandaur. They both seemed to be in awe as well that the king could muster this many troops in a few days time. It had been a week since the messengers went out, and three days since the light cavalry arrived. Braim hoped that the rest of the lords would respond as quickly.

Braim looked up at the sun. It was just past mid-day. Now Braim and his friends could set up their tents with the rangers and wait for the coming battle. But he had no way of knowing how wrong he was. He rose to his feet with the help of his friends, the trio walked and hobbled back to their horses, mounted, and rode to join the rangers.

Suddenly they were stopped by a loud voice calling after them. "Halt!"

Reining their horses to a stop and turning in the saddle, they saw a young courier in light leather armor riding swiftly towards them.

"Are you Aelundei, Braim, and Orandaur of the Rangers?" asked the young man, slowing his horse as he drew near.

"Yes, we are they," replied Aelundei, cheerfully, "To what do we owe the honor of a visit from one of the king's personal couriers?"

"The king has summoned you to his pavilion," replied the courier. If he was surprised at the elf's observation, he hid it well, "Assemble your tents with the other rangers. When the king is ready to see you, he will send some of the Royal Guard to escort you to him." Without waiting for a response, the courier wheeled his horse around and galloped away.

*   *   *

A bruised, battered, and weary ranger walked slowly between his friends, Aelundei and Orandaur lifting him to keep pressure off his broken feet. Around them marched four members of the 7th brigade, though it was clear from the swords at the rangers' sides and the bows and quivers of arrows on their backs that they could defend themselves.

Night was just falling, and only a few more rays of light were left to turn the pine-covered foothills to dull red. While Braim watched the last of the sun set, seeming to promise the army in the valley that she would be back on the morrow, he noticed swift movement in his peripheral vision. Braim turned, and his fears were confirmed, a goblin was rushing towards the trio, and he had just thrown a knife. One of the two guards behind them sank to his knees before falling flat on his face, a throwing knife buried just below his helmet in the back of his neck.

"Clear the path!" shouted Braim as he dove behind a tent, an arrow ready on the string of his longbow, he grimaced as his wounds reminded him that he could not move very well. He found himself side by side with Orandaur, who also had an arrow ready. He looked at Orandaur, grinned, and rose swiftly from behind the tent. He saw the assassin retreating behind another tent, and released the string of his mighty bow.

The arrow, a slender, smooth oaken shaft complete with grey goose feathers, sailed past ten of the three foot wide tents and put a wire thin scratch on the back of the assassin's neck. It slammed into the wood rod that supported another tent and practically lifted it off the two soldiers who were gambling inside. The assassin howled as he clamped a hand on his neck to stop the flow of black blood. The soldiers who had been gambling leaped up and drew their swords. The assassin leaped across the lane between tents, he was now on Braim's side.

Orandaur stood up to check the other side of the tent he and Braim were hiding behind, when the assassin leaped forward and tackled him, a knife raised above his head. The arrow that Orandaur had nocked on his bow flew into the dark sky as the apprentice ranger fell on his back. Time seemed to slow down as the knife descended towards the young lad's neck.

"Orandaur!" shouted Braim, as he rushed toward his apprentice, drawing his sword at the same time.

Orandaur caught the knife in both hands, then twisted his body, knocking the would-be assassin to the ground. The goblin released his hold on the knife, rose to a crouch, and leapt at Braim. Braim, still recovering from his wounds, couldn't dodge the green missile, and he too was thrown to his back.

"I have you where I want you, human," said the goblin with a malicious grin, "Now I'm going to kill you." It drew a knife, raising it for the killing blow.

Suddenly the creature was lifted up into the air and flew with a pitiful wail into the walkway between the tents. He landed in a heap at the feet of the three remaining 7th Brigadesmen, who seized him, roughly tying his hands and feet together. Orandaur stood above

Braim, "Goblins are a lot lighter than I thought they would be, so I hope the landing hurt him." He pulled Braim to his feet, than helped him out into the walkway where Aelundei and the Brigadesmen were waiting.

"We need to keep moving," said the lead guard, "I must report this attack to the leader of our unit. Brone, remain here and escort Taren's body to our camp."

One of the guards bowed to his leader before running back to his fallen comrade.

Braim, Orandaur, and Aelundei followed the remaining two guards to a large pavilion on the crest of a short hill. Orandaur looked up in awe at the Telnorian flag. A red, howling wolf head set on a yellow field, waved in the breeze.

Their escort stopped in front of three more members of the seventh brigade who were guarding the entrance, they raised their swords in the Telnorian salute and the door guards saluted back.

"Taem," said one of the door guards, "What went wrong? Four of you went out to retrieve the rangers, and now only two return. Where are Brone and Taren?"

The escorts bowed their heads, spun their swords so the tips faced the ground, and slammed their hands against the left side of their chests.

"Taren was felled by a cowardly assassin, who threw a knife into his back," answered the one called Taem, "Brone stayed to see that Taren was treated with honor as he is brought here."

The door guards also spun their swords and pressed their hands against their chests, and silence fell as the soldiers mourned their fallen comrade.

The guards raised their heads, and the rangers could see tears in their eyes. The one who had first spoken opened his mouth again, this time addressing the rangers. "I hope we have not troubled you with the death of our comrade, but we soldiers of the 7th brigade are a close-knit group. Now," he continued, struggling to compose himself, "We must not keep the king waiting any longer." He parted the cloth drape that was the door to the pavilion and motioned for the rangers to enter.

As soon as Orandaur's eyes adjusted to the low light he looked around, taking stock of his surroundings, according to the way of the rangers. Lining the inside of the pavilion was an honor guard of twenty elites, standing proud in their heavy armor and scarlet capes.

Directly in front of Orandaur was a large oval table with many people sitting around it. At the middle of the table sat king Mettaren, his tall stature and straight posture making him stand out from the lords, knights, and rangers sitting at the table. Mettaren was a handsome man, with black hair and a neatly trimmed black beard. He wore a bright tan tunic and black pants complete with a large two-hand sword. A simple silver crown adorned the king's head.

Aelundei threw the assassin on the ground as the three rangers dropped to one knee and bowed their heads.

"Rise, faithful rangers," said the king with a smile on his face.

The three rangers rose and Aelundei put a foot on the goblin assassin to keep him on the ground.

"I see you have brought a guest along, how nice." The goblin looked up at the king's words and growled, but the king ignored him and continued, "What use do we have for a treacherous goblin?"

"Your Majesty," began Aelundei, but the king raised a hand.

"Elf, you have been through far more than I, do not look surprised, I have a good guess of how old you truly are, and I know a little about what you did just to rescue your friend. If you must, you may call me sir, sire, or king. Now come, tell me your names."

Aelundei bowed, "I am Aelundei, son of Arenas, keeper of the flame of hope."

"I am Orandaur, son of Saldon."

"And I am Braim, son of Braeln, heir to the province of Torrer."

The king looked surprised, and the other lords seated at the table murmured amongst themselves before the king raised his hand to silence them. He looked closely at Braim and muttered, "Yes, you do resemble your father. If you yet live at the end of the battle, then perhaps I can help you reclaim you inheritance.

"Until then, let us examine our guest," the king rose and strode over to the goblin on the floor, "Tell me your name, filthy creature."

"My name is Thorguld," said the goblin, cringing, "Please, don't torture me."

"Telnorians do not torture," said the king, "However, killing any citizen of Telnor is punishable by execution. If you kill a member of a military unit, then they are the ones who start things rolling, in a sense." The king motioned to the captain of the 7th brigade. He and three others stepped forward, grabbed the goblin, and dragged him screaming out of the tent.

The king turned back to the rangers, "I was told one of you has information vital to the survival of our people. Please, bring it forward for the consideration of my war council."

Orandaur stepped forward, producing the animal skin scroll that had the map and the battle plans on it from a pouch on his belt. He handed it to the king, who laid it out on the table for all to see. The lords at the table leaned in and looked down at the crude map of Telnor, each one calculating in his head how large of an enemy army they would be facing.

The king scratched his beard thoughtfully, "The enemy sent an assassin after you; it appears to me that he at least suspects you discovered his plans. Now that the enemy suspects we have the plans, will he change them? Or will he continue through with them, thinking that we will prepare for a change?"

One of the lords leaned back in his chair, running his fingers through his bright red hair with a sigh, "I believe that it is bloody well impossible for a man to enter the mind of a goblin, and then even more impossible to navigate once in. I say we fortify a castle and hope they don't have catapults."

The king shook his head, "No, Gelbryen, if we do that, then the enemy will bypass us and ravage the country, and that is the last thing I want."

"Sire," said Aelundei, "I know it is not my place, but I have spent the last one hundred and sixteen years of my life studying battles and tactics, may I make a suggestion?"

"Yes, noble elf, you needn't ask."

"Very well, sir," replied Aelundei with a bow, "Grashnir's original plan was to divide his forces into three parts, each entering through one of the three mountain passes. I believe that when Grashnir realizes that his original plan has been stolen, he will react by changing his plans. He will consolidate his army into one massive force, and snap the divided army like a dead twig."

"And if he does not?" asked the king, "If he does not change his plans we could lose half the kingdom in a matter of days."

"Sire, if I could lead fifty rangers over the mountains, then we would be able to observe the enemy's movements and send back a report about what he is doing. Then, we can use guerilla tactics, appearing and disappearing, causing considerable amounts of damage, all the while buying you valuable time."

The king nodded, and looked at the other men at the table, "If anyone has any objections, then they should speak now." The room was silent, and the king nodded, "Very well, it is approved. Orandaur, Braim, you are dismissed; Aelundei, stay so we may discuss your plan in further detail."

Braim and Orandaur bowed to the king and left for their tents.

The Legend of Braim
Chapter XXIV
Aelundei's Ambush

Grashnir was startled from his reverie by the sudden cries of goblins. Arrows whistled around him and gray shafts mowed down several of the warlords around him. Grashnir dropped to the ground and waited for the arrows to stop flying. After the arrows stopped, he waited a few moments before crawling to the body of a troll and standing up behind it.

"Jorguel, are you still among the living?" asked Grashnir, scanning the bodies lying on the ground. One of the bodies moved.

"Master," said Jorguel, holding his arrow-pierced left hand with the right, "What is your wish?"

"Get a count of the dead; I want to know every casualty out there."

"Your will shall be done, master," said Jorguel as he turned to leave.

"And Jorguel," said Grashnir, "Get that arrow removed immediately."

"Yes master," said Jorguel, he pulled a knife from his sheath and began cutting the arrow as he walked off.

Grashnir turned and cursed at the woods, now he would have even worse problems to cope with. First, insurrections and then rangers, they would have to increase the speed of the march.

Grashnir thought for a few moments, and then Jorguel returned.

"Master, there are nine and thirty goblins killed, including seven of the kings that were with us. There are eight wounded, and three trolls died also," reported Jorguel grimly, a filthy rag tied around his left wrist.

"Thank you Jorguel," replied Grashnir, "how many enemies do you estimate attacked?"

"There were fifty casualties, so there are no more than fifty rangers, Lord."

"Yes, that is the same as I thought. They will appear, fire one arrow each, and disappear before we can catch them." The king raised his voice and cursed at the silent forest, "Cowards, why do you not come and fight with swords like real warriors do?" Grashnir threw his glove on the ground and cursed again. "Pile up the corpses and tell everyone to march faster."

"Yes, my king," said Jorguel. He turned and ran off to spread the word through the line.

Rangers or no rangers, the goblins would conquer Telnor!

The Legend of Braim
Chapter XXV
Guerilla Warfare

Moraina leaned as hard as she could against her lever, and heard the grunts of soldiers around her doing the same. The air reeked of sweaty bodies as the group tried to push a huge boulder out of its resting place. They had been instructed by the engineers that they were to make the biggest avalanche possible. Find a giant boulder as high up on the mountain as possible, lever it out of its hole, and send it crashing down the mountain. So far, they'd caused five little avalanches, but not one large enough yet. The boulder started to move, but it did not want to leave the warmth of the sun-baked earth. Everyone leaned harder, and finally they evicted the round stone from its home. The big boulder hit other boulders, which in turn hit other boulders, and soon it seemed the whole side of the mountain was crashing down. Moraina and the others around her collapsed to the ground, panting from exertion as they watched the pile at the bottom grow larger and larger. She turned to the other men with a smile, "Well, now we get to do it on the other side." A general groan went up, but everyone started to climb slowly down the mountain, slipping and sliding as they went. She hoped that the king's plan worked.

*   *   *

Aelundei sighted down the arrow, and said in a whisper: "Fire!" Instantly, fifty arrows zoomed out of the woods and struck the goblins and trolls. This was their fifth strike in the past week, and they had killed almost two hundred goblins, and about thirty trolls. It had not taken long for Aelundei to instruct the rangers where to hit a troll. So far, very few of the rangers had missed, resulting in a few arrows shattering on impact with armor. Aelundei was not worried about a loss of arrows, each ranger had only used five so far, with a further fifteen left. As the rangers turned and headed stealthily towards the horses, Aelundei inwardly debated the idea of retreating to the safety of the mountains. At the goblins' pace it would take four days to get to the Premeleis; the trolls walked slowly and there were plenty of setbacks, such as the hidden pits with sharpened stakes in them that Aelundei and the rangers had prepared. But he had to take into account that they would be needed to help prepare for the coming battle. Aelundei knew that the king would distribute some of the rangers among his archers, in order to combat the trolls and minimize the brutes' damage. The rangers had made it to their horses now, and they rode quickly back to their base camp, well away from where the goblins were going to stop their march.

Once there, Aelundei called everyone around, "Listen to my words, friends. Tomorrow morning we will be riding back to the rest of the army, but before we do we must say goodbye to the goblins, who have so kindly let us practice our shooting." There was some soft laughter, but it soon quieted so the men could hear his plan, "Tonight, as you have guessed, we will sneak into camp and do as much silent damage as possible, however, we must be far more careful than if it were a raiding party. One false move and we could all be killed.

"Once Grashnir has set up camp, we will split into groups of four, which I will assign soon, and then we will enter from four different directions, converging on the center of the camp. Make sure that every goblin is totally and undeniably dead, we must not have wounded goblins raising the alarm. Go in, slit their gray throats, and turn back. If you happen to come across a troll, beware! They have a sense of smell so great they might know you are there before you have a chance to kill them. Slitting the throat will not work for a troll; their skin on the throat is extremely tough and thick. Instead, draw your sword and stab it up under their chin. Do it quickly, and do it quietly.

"Now, I will assign each of you to a group, and if you have any questions to ask of me, then wait until I get to you." The elf walked around and put rangers into groups of four. He did not have to tell them to work as a team; they were trained to do so from the very beginning.

Grashnir beware, Aelundei is on the loose.

*   *   *

Braim looked around at the group of archers that he and three other rangers had been assigned to, most of them were barely even proficient with a bow, but there were a few reasonably good archers among them. Working together as a unit they would pose a serious problem for Grashnir and his armies. In the past several hours, he and the rangers had been instructing, watching and testing the men; Braim could already see vast improvements among some in this unit. When men of Telnor were asked to defend their country, they would learn any task given them; much to their advantage, for it turned every man in the group into an avid learner. Braim and the other rangers dismissed their unit and told them to meet again in the same spot at the same time the next day for more training. He stretched his arms, then his legs, and then rotated his feet. The herbal medicines Aelundei prescribed were doing wonders, and the Telnorian doctors were amazed when they saw Braim was recovering three times faster than a normal human. He subconsciously reached down and touched the necklace. *Aelundei had been surprised to see it, and told him it might have some kind of magical power, perhaps it has some healing properties?*

Braim shook off the thought and turned to the other rangers; he recognized the faces, but for some odd reason he could not remember their names, "Hello," he said, "I get the impression that I've met you all before, but for some odd reason my mind does not recall your names. I am Braim," he stuck out a hand, and shook each of the three rangers' hands.

"I am called Peter," said the one with bright red hair.

"I am Larem," said a man with dark brown hair and a long beard.

"And I," said the last one, who also had brown hair, though not a beard, "am Saeln, it is a pleasure to work with you. Who did you train under?"

"I trained under Aelundei, the elf," replied Braim, "When he returns I will be pleased to introduce him and our apprentice to you."

The other three rangers' eyebrows were raised almost in unison, and before Braim knew it, he had been challenged to a friendly shooting competition.

Four reeds were hung from the branch of a pine tree, and the rangers lined up at fifty yards. The first in line, Peter, nocked an arrow to his bow, drew back, aimed and fired; he missed his willow wand by a hairs-breadth.

Next Larem fired at his reed, and he missed also, this time by a hands-breadth.

Then Saeln fired at a reed, and his arrow actually hit it. But it did not cut the reed perfectly. Instead, it left half the reed hanging by some of its skin, dangling precariously.

Braim was ready. He drew an arrow, sighted, and fired, splitting

144

the reed perfectly in half. He turned around and smiled at the astonished rangers, "You all did well."

"Yes, but we didn't split it," replied Peter, "do it again and we can see if it was not luck that let you split the reed."

Braim fired at one of the other reeds, and again it was split neatly in two.

"Let's see some more," said Saeln.

The remaining two reeds were soon split, and then the rangers replaced them with four more. Braim split them all perfectly, except for one that hung for a second before falling to the ground.

Braim finished and the four rangers walked forward to retrieve their arrows. As they walked, they discussed what they would teach the archers the next day, and Braim told them where to hit the trolls. The other three nodded as they heard that to kill a troll you had to hit it in the eye, but they still wondered if that could be done while the excitement of a battle coursed through their veins.

They retrieved their arrows and were about to head back to their tents when Orandaur ran up.

"My new friends," said Braim, "This is my diligent pupil, Orandaur," He bowed and waved a hand towards Orandaur.

Orandaur smiled shyly and learned their names. He then turned to his master, "Braim, I was talking to the men of the seventh brigade and they told me that they are to be the 'escorts' for the rangers. I guess the rangers who weren't assigned to units will be on one side of the pass and the regular archers will be on the other. I also learned that the rest of the lords and their armies have arrived, which is a bit of good news, but there is bad news along with it," he paused, trying to gather courage for his next statement, "Our whole army amounts only to about one hundred and fifty thousand, and Aelundei's account estimated that there were about one million goblins and two hundred trolls."

"Orandaur," said Braim, patting his friend and student on the shoulder, "It will be alright; our king is wise, has the best military advisors south of the elven kingdom, and he has one elf. I'm sure Aelundei and our comrades are giving the goblins a real good beating above the pass. Besides, the worst that could happen is that we all die and our country is overrun with goblins, so there's nothing to worry about."

"Thank you, Braim," said Orandaur, trying hard not to smile, "I feel much better now."

The five rangers laughed and went back to their tents. Even though there was no more training till tomorrow, there were still things to do, such as sharpening swords and seeing the shield maker for a new shield. Braim was glad Orandaur was a fast learner, most rangers were unaccustomed to shields, and it would take a little practice.

*   *   *

Moraina winced as the straps were tightened on the kite shield. It was cumbersome, and heavy, but she should get used to it. It would probably save her life in the fierce melee battle that would come with the goblins. She drew her sword and gave a few test swings, nothing had changed there, she tried some more complex moves that Aelundei had taught her and realized that they were only slightly hindered by the shield. She sheathed her iron sword and picked up a wooden practice sword. Braim was soon fitted with a round buckler, and she saw that he already had a practice sword in his hand. Braim stepped over to an open area just outside the shield-master's tent and dropped into a ready stance, his shield held forward. Moraina hastily got into position and realized that the hood of her cloak was still on. She removed that swiftly and raised her shield just in time to block a downward cut from Braim's sword. Her left arm buckled slightly under the weight of the hit, but it held. She retaliated from under her shield with a swift stabbing motion, but it glanced harmlessly off the leather covered wood. They dueled back and forth, with Braim constantly giving her tips on how to fight better. The duel ended a few minutes later in a draw, both sides surrendering at the same time.

Braim walked over to the shield master, "I will not take this shield or any shield you have, my sword here will be enough," he reached down and patted his beloved weapon, "Thank you very much for the test, though."

The shield master looked at her inquisitively, "I will definitely take this shield," she said in a hurry, "And I also thank you for the test," she bowed slightly before the man and walked briskly off, following the long strides of Braim.

"Braim," said Moraina, "Do you have need of me?"

"Why do you ask?" replied Braim.

"I've been wanting to visit my cousins ever since the King's Army arrived, but I've been too busy," Moraina stated. "I know

146

which unit they are in, and it has been almost a year since I have seen them last. I just wanted to catch up with them and see how they are doing."

"Very well," replied Braim, with a hint of a smile. "Return to our tents in half an hour, we need to sharpen swords."

Moraina thanked Braim and rushed off to find her cousins' unit. She was nervous about what they would think of her being a ranger, but she felt a strange feeling in her gut that told her to go and meet them anyways.

*   *   *

Aelundei and the other rangers prepared to set out in the falling dusk. They each knew their own part of the mission and they also knew how to carry it out. Most of the groups were going in to kill goblins, a few of the groups would go for trolls, and the rest would go in and cut every bowstring they came across. When all was ready they set out, and Aelundei could only pray that the attack run like clockwork.

They made it into the camp undetected, going soundlessly from shadow to shadow, avoiding the well-lit areas and killing all the sentries who were not standing by fires. Aelundei's group together killed ten trolls and almost thirty goblins in the course of half an hour, then they retreated. They made it out of the camp and then waited for the others. Soon all the groups save three had joined them, but then the alarm was sounded. From deep within the goblin camp came a scream, followed by many yells, and soon eleven dark shapes were seen running from the camp, pursued by dozens of smaller shapes.

"Draw your bows," cried Aelundei, "We must buy them time to escape."

Soon the sound of bowstrings filled the air, and the pursuers were cut down, but more came. The sound of scattered crossbow shots assaulted the ranger's ears, and some of the fleeing shapes were felled. Aelundei and his friends fired back, shooting as fast as they could, soon the crossbows stopped firing. Six rangers staggered into the forest, some with crossbow bolts protruding from their backs, but still Aelundei and his men fired at any shape that came out of the camp. The wounded rangers mounted their horses and started to ride back to camp before Aelundei ordered his men to cease fire and also retreat. The elf did not want to leave the dead behind, but there was no other choice, the bodies would probably be burned, or worse. Aelundei shuddered when he thought about it.

*   *   *

Moraina approached the tent to which her cousins' sergeant had directed her. She heard her relatives' laughter coming from inside the tent, and she stooped down and looked inside the open tent flap.

"Excuse me, gentlemen," said Moraina, still disguising her voice as Orandaur.

The two men looked up from their game of dice, and Moraina was surprised by how much they had changed in the past year.

"What do you want?" asked Silas, the older of the two. His brown hair was matted down in the shape of a helmet liner, his matching beard messy and unkempt.

"Only some company, and advice," said Moraina as she stepped into the tent and lowered her hood, closing the tent entrance behind herself.

Her cousins' jaws dropped in awe at the sight of their cousin in a ranger's garb and armaments.

Matthew was the first to speak. He had recently shaved, and his blonde hair was neatly combed, as usual. "What are you doing here?" He demanded, red-faced.

"Shush, not so loud." She pleaded.

"I demand an explanation," said Silas, quietly.

"My father's ignorance and my sisters' cruelty finally broke me. I had to run away, but if I went anywhere as myself I would be sent back, you know the laws." Moraina explained slowly, choosing her next words carefully. "If I went into the regular archer units in Teckor I would not be far enough away. I needed a branch of the military that did not subject me to heavy combat, yet utilized my skills in archery and stealth. The ranger corps did just that, and allowed me to get as far from home as possible."

Silas and Matthew sat in silence for several moments, digesting her words. Matthew finally broke the silence.

"You could have become a nun, you know."

"Nuns are so boring!" replied Moraina, only half joking, "You know I would never survive that life, I would die of education."

The two cousins laughed. "You have not changed a bit,

148

Moraina," said Silas.

"But you two have, very much."

"What do you expect from two young men hungering for glory, joining the army, and realizing their dreams have been wrong all along?" asked Silas. "All the same, you must not fight in this battle. We will have to turn you in and send you home."

"No!" protested Moraina, alarmed. "You know the law, I would be married to a widower, with spoiled children. It would be better to be a slave in a mine. My instructors will take care of me."

"And so will we," said the two cousins in unison. They looked at each other, surprised by the perfect timing, and then back at Moraina.

"Our sergeant will understand if we explain it to him," said Silas, "our baby cousin joined the rangers and doesn't know what he got himself into, and her – I mean his – father would die of grief if anything happened to him. We would like to go and protect him in the battle."

"He won't let us go," said Matthew.

"What are two less soldiers in the unit to him?"

"He will be suspicious."

"Let him think all he wants, he cannot prove anything."

"We shall see."

Silas stood and left the tent, Moraina pulled the hood of the cloak over her head and followed. Matthew trailed behind.

Moraina put a hand on Silas's shoulder, "Remember, my name is Orandaur."

"Why did you pick such a common name?" asked Silas.

"I liked it," replied the ranger.

Silas stopped before the tent of his sergeant, straightened his uniform, and entered. Matthew and Moraina stood outside and listened.

Muted voices came from inside the tent, and suddenly the two outside the tent heard the sergeant's voice, "You wish to do what?"

There was some more conversing, and then the tent flap opened.

"Orandaur, Matthew, the sergeant wants you two in here," said Silas.

The two cousins entered, and the sergeant looked them up and down.

"Remove your hood and cloak," said the sergeant.

Moraina, heart racing, did as she was told.

The sergeant walked up and grabbed Moraina's face lightly. He

149

looked carefully between Moraina's face and Silas and Matthew's.

"What side of the family are you related on?" asked the sergeant, releasing Moraina's face.

"We are cousins on my mother's side, sergeant," replied Moraina, "I am the only son of my father."

"I see," said the sergeant, "Your face is soft, boy."

"See how young he is, Sergeant," said Silas.

The sergeant turned to him and bellowed, "Did I ask you? I'll give you a clue: no. Now silence!"

He turned back to Moraina, "How old are you, boy?"

"Fifteen, Sergeant. I have been in the forest for only a month."

"I see," said the sergeant. He turned to Silas and Matthew, who were waiting in rigid attention, "I was a young man like you two, once. I thought I could right every wrong by joining the army. But I couldn't, and neither can you. It is not up to you whether this lad lives or dies, what the gods have decided will happen whether you help your cousin or not."

"We must honor our family ties, nonetheless," responded Silas, coolly.

The sergeant's countenance softened, and he looked at his feet for a moment, "And I respect you for that." Looking back up at them he bellowed, "Very well, I can stand losing two men. Move your stuff over with the rangers, and report back to me as soon as the battle is over, or I will hunt you down and kill you myself. With a dull, rusty, sword."

"Yes, Sergeant!" said the two brothers in unison.

"Now get out of my sight!" bellowed the sergeant in their faces.

The trio bolted from the tent, Moraina grabbing her cloak as she ran and buttoned it back on.

The Legend of Braim
Chapter XXVI
Crossing the Premeleis

Grashnir gazed up at the huge, rocky, mountains. The fierce storms that blew down from the north left this face of the mountains almost devoid of trees. Only small, hardy pines were left, their branches wind-swept and twisted. The foothills and the other side of the mountains were sheltered and green though, and Grashnir could not wait to be ruler of that great country. Soon the front of the army would enter the pass; he ordered a halt and walked to the front of the forward legions.

He stepped onto a large rock and opened his mouth, "Goblin warriors, we are about to enter into a great new age. Soon, we will swarm into the human country and defeat their pitiful army.

"We will crush them, for they are far outnumbered by us, and there is no equal to the brute strength of our troll allies. Fight well, and remember, that when we win, there will be limitless gold and food and wine. You will never have to do any work again, for there will be thousands of human slaves. And we will stomp on the conquered humans and laugh. Now, we march into the mountain pass, and so will begin the unending golden age of the goblins and trolls!" He raised his hands for effect, and the goblins and trolls cheered as they moved past him into the mountain pass.

Grashnir shouted encouragement and cheered the soldiers on as they rushed by; soon he saw the familiar face of Jorguel and the few remaining goblin kings. He jumped off the rock to join them. It was almost night, and they would be forced to stop and make camp, fighting would have to wait until morning.

Beware Telnorians; Grashnir is now upon your own threshold!

The Legend of Braim
Chapter XXVII
Far Outnumbered

Braim was roused before dawn by the sound of horns, and a man's voice crying: "Awake! Prepare for battle, the enemy has come. Awake!"

Braim leaped out of bed and pulled on his quiver and bow. He buckled on his sword and drew the cowl of his cloak over his head. In the tents next to him, he could hear Aelundei and Orandaur also preparing for the battle. He stepped out of the tent almost at the same time that his friends did. They looked around and gasped in surprise, the whole valley of the pass was cloaked in a fog so thick they could not see ten feet in front of them. This would greatly hinder their ability to work as a team and to respond to each other, but it would also add to the element of surprise.

From out of the fog came the disembodied calls of sergeants, telling their troops to fall into formation and begin the march to their pre-planned battle positions.

"Well," said Braim, "we better get to the unit that we were positioned with, and we better hurry, it won't be long before the soldiers are ready to march."

Matthew and Silas walked up behind Orandaur, still tightening their shields.

"These are your cousins, Orandaur?" asked Braim, as he shook the two new arrivals' hands.

"Yes," replied Orandaur, as Aelundei stepped forward to greet his cousins as well, "The sergeant gave them leave to honor their family ties and fight alongside us."

"Pleased to meet you, rangers," said Silas with a grin, "If half of what Orandaur told us about you two last night is true, I will feel much safer fighting near you."

A horn blast interrupted the greetings, reminding the group that there was a war happening.

The small group hurried along their way. Braim was glad that he had taken the time to memorize which turns to take, and soon the three rangers and two swordsmen had safely arrived at their destination. They reported to the sergeant that was standing at the head of the battalion, and as they walked to their positions they noticed that the other rangers were already there. They stood for almost ten minutes, watching the light grow slowly brighter as the sun rose. Then a bugle, loud and clear, sounded the march, and each sergeant in turn shouted out the order. The soldiers stepped off, and they walked away from the camp, heading north.

After a further twenty minutes of marching, the army arrived at the site chosen by the king for battle.

Braim listened as the bugle called a halt and the king's voice rose above the noise, giving a speech to encourage his soldiers. The speech was short, for they did not know the location of the enemy army, "Soldiers of Telnor," said the king "soon you will enter into the largest and most important battle since the days of King Fornesaem, when the goblins from these very mountains attacked our kingdom while it was still young and drove us back to the city of Teckor. Therefore, I tell you to fight your very best. Many of you will die, but if we succeed, then the kingdom will be preserved, and you will be remembered as the heroes that you are. Today you will be fighting an army that will give no quarter, extend no mercy. You are fighting for the freedom of all Telnor, and no worthier cause exists. Prepare yourselves; remember your wives and children as you fight. Now go, for glory! For honor! For freedom!"

With a cheer, each battalion marched off to their preplanned positions, and then they waited in nervous anticipation.

*   *   *

Aelundei sighted down the dark shaft of his arrow; the enemy was so close that the sound of their boots drowned out all others. He hoped that the rangers on the sides of the mountains would hear the sound of the army stopping and begin their fire as well. The fog had lessened slightly, now he could see twenty feet instead of ten; large dim shapes began to loom in the mist.

*   *   *

"Remember, aim for the eyes of the trolls," said Moraina to the archers around her. She said it more to remind herself and calm her nerves than to remind the soldiers. Her hands shook violently as she waited for orders. The sergeant whispered for the archers to load, then to aim, and then they waited for the cry that they were to fire.

"Fire!" called the voice of a general far down the line, and the air was filled with the sound of bowstrings twanging and arrows whizzing through the air. They heard several loud cries as arrows slammed into trolls' eyes and then even more cries as their falling bodies crushed the goblins around them.

"Pikemen, forward," called the voices of the sergeants in charge of the pikemen. Soft boots marched forward, the soldiers pressed the butts of their pikes into the rocks of the embankment that had been made by the avalanches. The dark shapes of more trolls rushed toward them, but the creatures impaled themselves on the sharp blades of the Telnorian pikes. Arrows came whistling down from the mountains above and slammed into the goblin army, Moraina heard dozens of goblins scream, then the world erupted in a storm of noise and activity. The sergeants of the archer units kept a withering fire on the trolls that had impaled themselves on the pikes, the rangers bombarded the army that was trapped in the pass, and the swordsmen began to move forward to defend the pikemen. In some places the trolls broke through, bringing a swarm of goblins with them. A horn high in the mountains sounded three times, and the Telnorian cavalry that had lain in wait outside the pass charged in, hammering the rear of the goblin army.

The archers continued firing until their first quivers ran out, then retrieved their extra quivers and launched the arrows in those as well. The rangers also fired until they ran out of arrows, then they drew their swords and charged down the mountain sides with the swordsmen and members of the 7th brigade that were with them. Every swordsman threw his javelin and drew their swords as they ran to meet their foes.

Moraina saw Braim, Aelundei, and her cousins draw their swords, so she drew hers as well and grabbed her shield. They formed a triangle and charged into battle, blocking each other from receiving blows, striking out as well, a spinning triangle of death. They cut a trail through the enemy, Telnorian soldiers following in their footsteps. Soon there was a large wedge cut into the goblin army, and still they pressed slowly on, until they met the trolls that had been held back in reserve.

*   *   *

Aelundei looked up to the sun as he jumped over a troll's club. It was about noon, and the fog was almost gone. He landed and did a combat roll between the legs of the troll, then jumped and grabbed the troll's shoulders. He pulled himself up and threw his left arm around the troll's neck, stabbing and slashing at the arms that reached up to pull him off. Swinging around, he stabbed the troll through the eye. As it toppled over he jumped from that troll to another and sliced open its neck with a mighty swing. He fell back to earth, rolled, and found himself standing next to Orandaur and his cousins.

"So," he shouted over the din of the battle as he blocked swords and slashed out at his attackers, "What do you think of your first battle, Orandaur?"

"It is a lot different than anything I thought battles to be," replied Orandaur between swings, "I always imagined men lining up and firing arrows at the enemy and winning with nobody dying, but I've already seen many men die today, I know that many more will. I never want to see anything like this again."

"I agree," replied Aelundei, slicing a crossbow bolt out of the air with a flick of his sword. Bending down he picked a goblin sword up off the ground, "Having two swords was very nice when rescuing Braim, I should fight this way more often."

The battle continued on for hours, neither side gaining an advantage, until finally the sheer weight of numbers began to push the men back slowly, foot by foot. It looked like the battle would be lost for the Telnorians after all.

*　　　　　*　　　　　*

Braim was in a battle rage; imaginary pictures of his parents lying dead in a burning castle overrun by goblins had driven him past the point of mere anger. He barely felt the numerous cuts that he received on the parts of his body not covered by the maille. He did not feel exhaustion; he did not feel hunger or thirst, all he felt was rage and a need for vengeance. He barely heard the sound of the Telnorian battle horns calling for a retreat; and when he caught sight of Grashnir it was almost impossible for Aelundei and Orandaur to pull him away from the fighting. The rage left him when Aelundei slapped him lightly across his face and yelled at him to snap out of it. His vision refocused, he was behind the front lines and in a spot where there was no fighting. Braim was suddenly aware of pain, hunger, thirst, and exhaustion. He reeked of blood.

"Braim," said Aelundei as he moved his head to the side to avoid an arrow, "The army is in full retreat, and all rangers have been summoned to assist the 7th brigade in an effort to buy the main army time to escape. We will need every man."

Braim's knees buckled, so Aelundei and Orandaur helped him up.

"Braim," said Orandaur, "I know you're tired, we're all tired, but we will need every single man to help cover the army's retreat. Besides, you used to say that we'll have all the rest we want when we're dead, let us be strong."

Braim mustered the strength to walk on his own, and followed Aelundei to the banner of the 7th brigade.

What the trio found there was just short of chaos. A few other battalions, and most of the knights, had been assigned to assist the rangers and the 7th brigade in holding off the enemy until nightfall, which was still a few hours away.

"Listen to me," shouted the commander of the 7th brigade, "We are about to engage in a time-buying procedure, there will be no retreat, we will all probably die, but we will buy the rest of the army enough time to escape. Form up, let us move to the frontline, to glorious death!"

The last of the rangers arrived to refill their quivers, then the small force moved into position. The frontline withdrew until it passed them, thus began the longest period of fighting any of them had ever endured.

Braim, Aelundei, Orandaur, and the rest of the rangers and archers present, fired arrows until their quivers were empty. The knights, in their full plate-body armor, were indestructible terrors to the goblins.

But the most fearsome warriors among the defenders were the soldiers of the 7th brigade. They were like gods of war. They stabbed with their tridents until the weapons were ripped out of their hands, then they drew their swords and cut down their enemies until they went dull to the point of uselessness. After that, they either grabbed a fallen goblin's weapon to use, or they drew their own second weapon and continued to fight.

This remnant of the army sustained heavy casualties, but they fought on, knowing that every minute the main body of the army was getting further away.

Braim looked over to Aelundei and shouted over the din of the battlefield, "How much longer will we be able to fight? How much longer will we be able to hold off these creatures? How much longer, until these valiant men are able to retreat?"

Aelundei faced Braim, "Not much longer; but look! The sun will soon set, it is getting low over the western sea, and we may be able to retreat in the cover of darkness, if we are not overrun by then."

Braim looked; the sun was halfway down into the ocean. Then the horns sounded for the army to retreat.

*   *   *

Grashnir watched as the tiny army grew smaller in the distance. He turned to his bugler and ordered the call to halt. The goblin raised the large black ox-horn to his lips, sounded the simple melody, and the giant army ceased its pursuit of their enemies. Grashnir stepped up on a boulder and raised his voice for all the army to hear.

"Loot the dead and pitch camp here, the enemy is no longer a threat to us. Tomorrow we shall carry on, to crush any further resistance in Telnor, but tonight we feast!"

*   *   *

The Telnorian army fought backwards, and to their amazement, the enemy army did not pursue for long. The small group of defenders retreated several miles and set up a temporary camp. Of the six hundred elites, knights, rangers, archers, and swordsmen who had remained to hold off the enemy, only two hundred and forty nine remained. They had lost fifty one rangers, ninety five members of the 7th brigade, seventeen knights, seventy archers, and sixty seven swordsmen.

They set up camp and posted scouts for the night to ensure the enemy would not pursue, then the leader of the 7th Brigade, a captain named Feariden, summoned all of his men and the rangers to a quiet meeting.

The Legend of Braim
Chapter XXVIII
Death

L isten up, we only have one chance, and that is to take the offensive." Feariden was only a young man, no more than thirty, but he had risen to the rank of captain swiftly for one his age, "We will be falling back even further before the sun rises tomorrow morning, and then tomorrow night, we will pay a little visit to our guests, the great goblin army. I want all of you rangers to go and harass the enemy army, slow them down and buy us some time. The king was wise enough to leave us a large cache of arrows here in the valley, and that is what I want you to use." The captain looked at those gathered around him, "If we diminish their forces enough, and then eliminate their leader, we may have a chance of causing them to withdraw back to their own lands. However, it will take much precision and a lot of help from above. We will have to work as a tight-knit team, and nothing must go wrong, listen only to me, and those who I put over you. You are dismissed, get some rest, but be ready to move out in a hurry tomorrow morning. Aelundei, Braim, and Orandaur please remain behind."

The three rangers, followed by Silas and Matthew, walked up to the captain of the 7th Brigade and saluted. He returned their salute and then began to pace.

"Who are these two?" asked the elite captain.

"Do not worry about them," answered Orandaur, "They are my cousins. They were temporarily dismissed from their unit because they wanted to guard me."

The captain looked at Orandaur suspiciously and then at the two swordsmen, "What unit are you from?"

"We are from the third Teckor regiment," replied Silas, "Do you have news of them? We were ordered to report to our sergeant after the battle."

The captain's face went grey, "They were directly in front of my brigade during the beginning of the battle. They were totally annihilated by trolls."

"No," said Matthew, alarmed, "Our brothers in arms!"

"I am afraid they perished, I am sorry," the captain bowed his head, and then turned to address the rangers. "I asked you to remain because I have a problem," stated the new commander, "I am in charge of this operation only because the three officers above me all died in combat, and because the knights who volunteered to remain behind placed themselves under the command of the 7th Brigade. Every single soldier in the Brigade is trained in battle tactics, but I am as of yet untested in the planning of war. I know that you three have far more knowledge than I. I am placing you in charge of the planning. You will still submit and explain your strategies to me, but I will only look through them for major errors before passing them along to my men. If we receive victory, I will ensure you get a large piece of the credit."

"Very well, we will think in our sleep tonight and have at least one plan by tomorrow morning," replied Aelundei, "Vitaren be over us all."

The elite nodded, and the three rangers returned to camp. They set up their tents and fell asleep, each dreaming of ways that could halt the enemy advance.

*   *   *

Braim strapped on his sword and grabbed his un-strung long bow and quiver of arrows before stepping out of his tent. He looked up at the low flying clouds; it would probably rain later that day, a blessing and a curse. The sound of the rain would allow the rangers to move about unheard by the goblin army, and it would mask their scent from the trolls. However, it would also ruin the strings of their long-bows, preventing the rangers from killing any of the trolls from a safe distance.

Braim turned as he heard the opening of a tent flap beside him. Orandaur crawled out of his tent and stared up at the sky, the flame of defiance burning in his eyes as he beheld the dark clouds.

At that very instant, Aelundei also crawled out of his tent, a large sack in one hand and several scrolls in the other. He tossed the sack to Braim with a grin.

"Rub this oil on your bowstrings, and pass it on to the other rangers. It will prevent the missiles of those mischievous clouds from making your bow-string go slack," said Aelundei, "It is the extract from the leaf of the Zalen-Draeo that grows by the lakes around our beautiful city of Vilien." A far-away look came into the eyes of Aelundei, and a solitary tear rolled down his check before he brushed it away.

"Do the elves have an herb for everything?" teased Orandaur, just as his cousins emerged from a nearby tent, blinking at the sun.

Aelundei snapped back to the present and looked at Orandaur with a smile, "Indeed. But this oil is not from an herb, it is from the glowing leaves of the weeping willow that grows beside the shimmering lakes. It only lives near our city, this jar of oil was hand-picked by my love and I. Use it sparingly, it is all I have; very precious." The sad look returned to Aelundei's face, and he hurried off to present his scrolls to the captain of the 7th Brigade. Orandaur, Braim, Silas, and Matthew rushed after him.

They found the captain of the Elites standing over a map, dressed already in his full battle armor, surrounded by his advisors. The three rangers approached the captain and saluted. He returned the salute, then pointed at the scrolls.

"What are those, good elf?" asked the captain.

"The only elvish writings of mine that human eyes are allowed to see," replied Aelundei, "Some of the battle tactics from my homeland of Elleavemar; I selected only the ones concerning how to attack a significantly larger force and emerge victorious. Not all of the methods will apply, but I feel that most will help us immensely." Aelundei unrolled the scrolls and began to read sections of it to the commander. He nodded at the descriptions of the movements and positioning of different units, clapped Aelundei on the shoulder.

"Very well, these plans will work. Tell us what we must do next."

*   *   *

Braim looked over at Aelundei and spoke nervously, "You know that if this doesn't work we're all dead men, right?"

"It will work, trust me," said Aelundei from his position atop the sharpened log, "Now get up here, ready to cut the rope?"

Braim, Orandaur, Silas, and Matthew scrambled up on the log and Braim nodded to the elite, who moved over to the rope that held the log in place and drew his sword.

"Is your friend mad?" asked Matthew.

"Silence," said Aelundei with a slight grin, "On my signal." The elf peered through the trees as the troll drew nearer to the spot that the log would swing through. "Now!"

The elite slashed through the rope with his sword, and the log hurtled down towards the troll's neck. The four humans and the elf clung tightly to the ropes that the log swung from. The sharpened end of the log slammed into the troll's neck at the same instant that fifty arrows from fifty rangers cut down many cross-bow goblins. The five friends were flung off of the log as it jerked to a stop and fell in a heap on the ravine floor, except for Aelundei, who drew his two swords as he landed on his feet and charged back into the enemy ranks. The humans shakily returned to their feet and did the same, cutting down many of their foes.

"Time to run, here come their reinforcements!" yelled Aelundei over the din of the battle. The rangers in the trees around them sent down a withering cover fire, and the five warriors in the ravine withdrew safely into the forest, leaped onto the waiting horses and galloped away. The fifty rangers on the other side of the ravine fired a few parting arrows, then leaped onto their horses to retreat as well.

The two groups of rangers and the few elites who had accompanied them regrouped a safe distance from the enemy, embraced and shook hands, happy to still be alive.

"How many casualties in your group?" asked Aelundei.

"The three rangers on the second log were almost taken, but they managed to escape with severe wounds. Also, three of our men took poisoned crossbow-bolts in the back as they were retreating, it will not be long now for them, they cannot ride further," replied Peter.

Aelundei looked where Peter directed, there were three men lying on the ground, bandaged but very bloody. Ranger healers attended them, clearly doing all they could do, yet unable to do enough. Nearby three other wounded men sat on their horses, one with a sling and two with numerous bloody bandages on their chest and head. Bowing his head, the elf slowly articulated, "Try to move them out of the path of the coming army, we will wait for them to perish, and if necessary we will defend them."

Three ranger medics moved over to the mortally wounded rangers and knelt over them. "Our brothers, may you go to the halls of Vitaren and sleep peacefully. You have fought bravely, know that your families will remember you with honor."

It didn't take long, but one by one the wounded warriors slipped away from life to immortal dreams.

All present lamented as the three dead men were covered with blankets and draped over their horses. The entire company set out again, and returned to the main camp.

The entire camp was in uproar, tents were being taken down,

quivers loaded, swords sharpened, and knights in shining armor gripped their lances as they sat atop their fearsome war horses.

Aelundei approached the young captain and saluted. "Greetings, Feariden. I see the men are already in preparation for tonight's battle."

"Aye, tonight we will defeat the enemy or die in the attempt," replied the towering man in armor, "But I made several changes to the plan."

Aelundei began to protest, but Feariden held up his hand to silence him.

"I believe you will be pleased with the change. It will throw the enemy into confusion and kill many of their soldiers at the same time.

"Instead of merely firing arrows into the enemy camp during the middle of the night, then charging with all of the remaining elites and knights mounted on horses, I have decided that all of the rangers will be armed with fire-arrows. Some of the rangers will go into the camp as silently as possible to mark the position of all the flammable barrels in the camp on a map, and the rangers will target those."

Aelundei's face lit up with delight at the plan, "Feariden, that's truly brilliant! I volunteer to be one of the rangers that go into the camp. I am the best at stealth in the entire army, and I would be able to accomplish this task easily. This will truly add to the confusion and chaos of the enemy before the cavalry strikes."

Feariden smiled at the joy on the elf's face, and replied, "Aye, you have my permission to enter the camp and take with you two other rangers of your choice; the enemy camp is large, too large for one ranger, be he even an elf."

"Very well, I will take two rangers with me. We will enter the camp at midnight, and remain for an hour. At that time, we will have all the rangers look at the map, and two hours past midnight we will begin our fire upon the enemy camp."

Aelundei thought for a moment, then continued, "I would also like to make a change to the strategy. Give every single man a war-horn and a torch. When the sound of chaos rises from the enemy camp, have all of your men blow their horns as they charge, and when they enter the camp have them throw their torches onto the tents of the goblins, blow their horns one more time, and continue their charge through the enemy ranks. This will greatly increase how large the enemy thinks our forces are, and add to the terror."

"Very well," replied Feariden, as he ran a hand through his golden hair, "I will pass the word along to my men. Now go, the sun is setting, and your rangers will need all the time they can get to maneuver into position unseen and unheard."

Aelundei grinned as he clapped Feariden on the shoulder, "Farewell, my friend. Three days ago, you knew little of battle tactics. Now you are about to lead an army outnumbered ten-to-one into the greatest victory in Telnorian history."

*   *   *

Moraina watched silently as Aelundei, Braim, and Peter silently inched towards the enemy camp. She offered another prayer to Vitaren as a tear rippled down her cheek. Being only a first-year novice, she was not allowed to participate in something requiring this great a feat of skill, and all she could do was pray that Braim and the others would emerge alive. She fingered one of her arrow tips, but quickly returned it to her quiver when she was reminded by the sticky black substance on her finger that her arrow was coated in tar. Moraina was nervous and scared, and all she could do was wait.

*   *   *

Braim looked slowly to his left and then to his right to check the progress of his companions. Seeing that they were still slightly behind him he decided to wait until they moved forward again. Goblins might be bad sentries, but they weren't blind. The young man began to inch forward again, but froze as one of the sentries shifted and whimpered softly. The goblin was asleep, they were blind after all. Braim stayed perfectly still while he glanced at the other sentries. Not all of them were asleep, but most of them. The rangers had never attacked during the night, only the day, and the goblins had grown confident that that pattern would continue. Braim began to crawl forward again; he was only a few yards from the first sentry now, and the rest of the camp was totally silent, all its occupants sleeping. Braim slowly eased his knife from the sheath, and Vodasie eased the sentry into the deepest slumber in life, death. Braim rolled the sentry under a nearby tarp that hid barrels of tar. Braim marked the location on his map and then continued further into the camp, marking every position on his map. He continued doggedly on

163

towards the center of the camp, and the tent of his mortal foe.

*   *   *

Aelundei's knife Nelya silently stopped the goblin's heart-beat. The elf scanned his environment, his pointed elven ears detecting no sound of alarm. He marked down the location of the explosive ammunition that the goblins had brought along for their catapults, and then continued on into the camp. He was only a few yards now from the opposite side of the camp, the gate to freedom. It had been nearly forty-five minutes since they entered the camp, and if all went well the three rangers would rendezvous in the forest to distribute their three maps to the rangers waiting for the signal to attack. He marked down another location on his map, killed a sentry, and began to inch his way out of the camp towards the safety of the forest.

*   *   *

Braim stood next to Grashnir's tent, sword in hand, a battle raging in his head. Every fiber of his being wanted to burst into the tent and kill his former tormenter. Yet there was something unexplainable holding him back. Orandaur's face kept floating through his mind.

Why am I thinking of Orandaur? Thought Braim, silently, *why am I attracted to a man?* Braim was repulsed by the thought. *Some people in Telnor may be attracted to those of the same gender, but I certainly am not.*

Out of nowhere a new voice entered his mind. *What if Orandaur is not a man?* Scenes of Orandaur weeping at Braim's side accompanied the voice, followed swiftly by memories of changes in the pitch of Orandaur's voice, and the way Orandaur seemed to constantly remain near Braim. Then he remembered the two cousins, who were fiercely protective of Orandaur. Braim shook off the idea with a silent laugh. *My lack of sleep is affecting me in strange ways!* Somehow he sheathed his sword and marked another location on his map, Grashnir's tent. Then the young man silently glided away.

*   *   *

Aelundei, Peter, and Braim passed out the maps to the other

rangers, who quickly memorized them before moving into position. Torches were lit, hidden behind shields so the remaining goblin sentries would not see them. The rangers were ready to send the goblins a message, of fiery importance.

*   *   *

Feariden sat atop his horse and fingered the lip of his war-horn. If all went well, the rangers would soon send a barrage of burning arrows into the enemy camp, signaling the men of Telnor to charge the enemy and send their foes running with fear out of the kingdom, back to the dark holes from whence they had come. The eighty mounted men that waited behind him held unlit torches; he was the only one with the torch lit, and from his flame all of the others would be kindled. Suddenly, the sky lit up over their heads as sixty-one flaming arrows flew out of the forest and slammed into the explosive barrels. Columns of fire rose into the sky as the arrows hit their marks and kindled the flammable materials. Feariden rode past the first row of knights and elites, igniting their torches, preparing their hearts for the battle to commence. The men turned in their saddles to pass the flame to the next row. As the flames moved backwards, Feariden addressed them one last time.

"Listen, my brothers, you are men of Telnor, and today, you will accomplish a feat that no one in the history of Telnor has accomplished before," the men looked at their leader, the flames of the torches reflecting in their eyes and giving them the appearance of fierce armored demi-gods. "Now ride with me, to glory, and death!"

Feariden raised his horn to his lips and sounded out the call for a charge, all of his men doing the same. And they charged.

"For Telnor, and for death!"

*   *   *

The rangers in the forest around the camp fired arrows as fast as they could, and the goblins ran screaming about as their camp was consumed in flames. Then the cavalry, led by Feariden, burst into the clearing. The cavalry blew their war-horns, throwing their torches into the nearby tents before drawing swords and slaying the few goblins that had rallied to face the charge. The rangers fired their last arrows and charged out of the forest, led by Braim, Aelundei,

Orandaur, and Orandaur's cousins. The goblins fled from the wrath of the five friends, and it seemed that the battle would soon be won, until a huge, pitch-black troll slammed his giant hammer into Feariden's mount.

Aelundei watched in horror as the wounded captain flew fifty feet and landed in the forest, pinned beneath his mount. The Great Troll began moving towards him to finish him off and eat his body, which would crush the hope of all the elites. Aelundei did something he had never done before. He sprinted after the troll on the heads and shoulders of the goblin army, and leaped onto the back of the monster. He stabbed Raeva Reavel into the neck of the troll and yelled at the top of his lungs, "Íhl alleas reavel!"

This would be the greatest foe Aelundei had ever fought.

* * *

Braim cut his way through his foes, rangers at his back, and Orandaur and his cousins at his side. He was on a mission, and none could stop him. He cut all the way to the center of the camp in ten minutes, making full use of the chaos, goblins either fleeing or being cut down by his sword. Braim did not slow his disastrous pace until he emerged into the center of the burning camp, and found himself face to face with his arch-enemy, Grashnir. "Grashnir!" he shouted as loud as he could, "I am coming to kill you!"

* * *

Grashnir heard a familiar human voice yell his name and a threat, then noticed goblin weapons flying as Braim fought his way towards him. He drew his sword and prepared to meet his foe. This human would have a lot to reckon with.

* * *

Aelundei's sword bit deep into the neck of the troll. The elven blade was sharper and stronger than any human weapon, and it now proved itself to be superior. Suddenly, Aelundei was batted off of the troll by a mighty swing of its arm. Despite being almost knocked unconscious the elf managed to land on his feet. He rolled to the side just in time to miss being made into red paste by a blow of the troll's giant hammer.

"You are face to face with Xim, ruler of the trolls in the Northern Mountains, and the only Great Troll south of the frozen wastes. Come now, I bring your doom!" The troll stepped forward, raising his giant war hammer and preparing to crush Aelundei.

The elf ducked, and the hammer missed his head by a matter of inches. Then Aelundei jumped, and the hammer flew by just beneath his feet. He rolled underneath the trolls legs and stabbed upwards, but he and his blade were knocked to the ground by a swift kick. This was no ordinary troll, and it would take all Aelundei's skill to defeat.

*   *   *

Braim stopped in front of Grashnir, his sword held ready in both hands.

"Now is the time of your death, boy," said Grashnir as he brandished his sword.

The two began to circle slowly, exchanging probing cuts, each trying to find the other's weaknesses. Braim launched the first serious strike, stepping in and swinging wide, trying to cleave Grashnir at the waist. Grashnir stepped back, and the blow passed harmlessly by. Then he stepped forward with a mighty swing of his arm, aiming for Braim's head. The young man ducked and stepped backwards. Back and forth they dueled, for several minutes, before Braim's strength began to triumph over the strength of his opponent. Grashnir tried every trick he knew, and all were foiled by deft moves. Grashnir had only one trick left. Bending down, he scooped up some of the trampled dirt, and threw it in Braim's eyes.

Braim stumbled backwards, blinded and in pain from the dry dirt. Grashnir stepped forward, raising his sword for the final blow, but yelled in surprise as a knife barely missed his head, knocking his sword out of his hands, sending it flying far into the still-panicking goblin army.

*   *   *

Aelundei could not worry about missing Grashnir for long. He sidestepped a hammer blow and watched as it made a huge dent in the forest floor. The troll bled everywhere, but the more it bled the harder it fought. Aelundei dodged another blow, a fool-proof plan began forming in his head.

*   *   *

Grashnir snarled and threw his knife at Braim, who was starting to recover from the dirt in his eyes. There would be no-one to help him now.

*   *   *

Moraina caught the glint of a knife flying towards Braim and leaped. The knife hit, stars of pain exploded in her eyes before she blacked out.

Braim recovered just in time to see Orandaur fall to the ground, a knife protruding from his left shoulder. Silas and Matthew yelled in alarm. Braim looked back up at Grashnir, snarling as he leaped towards the goblin king.

*   *   *

Aelundei stabbed his sword through the eye of Xim, and was thrown off of the troll. He had been holding on to the shoulder of the beast, but now he was falling through the air. The elf landed on his feet, and ran to retrieve his sword from the corpse of the troll. He picked up the hilt of the sword, but it was melted off at the hilt by the heat and acidity of the troll's blood. Aelundei dropped the hilt as it began to burn his hand. He grabbed two goblin swords and fought his way to the side of Feariden. He knelt beside the once strong and proud figure, now trapped beneath his own horse and barely breathing.

"Aelundei," said Feariden, "I go to Vitaren's halls."

"Not while I am here, Feariden," replied Aelundei, unpacking his medical kit. "Do you have a family? Tell me about them. Hold on to life, Feariden."

"Aye, I have a family," replied Feariden weakly. "A beautiful wife, and a handsome little son, Faleden, who wishes to join the 7th brigade as I have."

"Good, tell me more."

"Aelundei," said Feariden, his voice growing weaker. He reached up and grabbed Aelundei's forearm. "Give me the final prayer. The

168

elves are the greatest healers, but they have no medicine for internal bleeding. Your skill is needed elsewhere. I go, now."

Blinking away tears, Aelundei's trembling hands closed the eyes of the dead captain. He muttered a prayer in elvish before retrieving his swords and sprinting towards the center of the camp.

The few remaining trolls had seen the death of their leader and were now running, some of the goblins with them. The tide was turning once more in favor of the Telnorians.

*   *   *

Grashnir barely had time to draw his final two knives as Braim leaped at him with an inhuman roar. The goblin king blocked furiously, blows seeming to rain down upon him from every side. Braim severed Grashnir's left arm at the elbow, taking a blow from the other knife at the same instant. Then he severed the other arm at the shoulder and sliced across both of Grashnir's thighs. The goblin staggered and then fell to his knees. Braim rested the tip of his sword on the goblin's shoulder and spoke.

"I, Braim, son of Braeln, find you, Grashnir, guilty of murder, plotting assassinations, and of war-crimes against the kingdom of Telnor, my parents, and myself. By the power invested in me as heir to the province of Torrer, I condemn you to death and order you to be executed on the spot." Braim lifted the sword and brought it down on Grashnir's neck, severing the head in one swing.

*   *   *

Aelundei cut down three more goblins and finally found himself in the area of Grashnir's tent. Braim, Silas, and Matthew were kneeling over a human body, he rushed over to them.

"What happened here?" he asked.

"I fought with Grashnir, and he threw a knife at me while I was blinded by dirt. Orandaur took the blade in my place," replied Braim, his voice taut with grief.

"Get on your feet and defend me while I work," ordered Aelundei, "This will take all of my skill."

Braim and the other two men leaped to their feet, brandishing their swords. The entire goblin army was in full panic and running for their lives, with the Telnorian army in pursuit, but the terrified creatures still lashed out at any human they found. Braim and the two cousins of Orandaur had to be in twenty places at once in order to keep the creatures away from Aelundei and the wounded ranger.

Aelundei worked furiously, he started to cut away the shirt around the wound with Braim's knife, but stopped quickly as he realized the lie that Orandaur had lived. He sat stunned for a moment, then quickly turned away and pulled off his cloak, draping it over Orandaur's chest. Next he slowly worked the knife out. He was able to remove it without causing any more damage to the shoulder; a remarkable feat, for the wound was deep. He washed the wound quickly with water from a water-skin that he had brought into battle, and then took some of the elven herbs that he had brought when he left Elleavemar, crushed them into a powder, and sprinkled them into the wound. Producing a needle and fine thread from the bag, he stitched the wound tightly shut. The herbs would clean the wound and also fight infection, but that was still the greatest danger. Many men with lesser wounds died from the infection, and there was only one herb that totally prevented it. It was also the one herb that Aelundei didn't have. All that Aelundei could do now was to pray and have faith that Vitaren would heal her. He stood, drawing his sword and laughing in the face of the innumerable enemies that were charging towards him.

The Legend of Braim
Chapter XXIX
The Champion's Loss

Moraina slowly opened her eyes, but quickly blinked as bright sunlight blinded her. *Why am I in a tent? The battle, Braim, the knife!* It all flooded back to her, and she sat rigidly upright, clutching the blankets like a bulwark to her chest.

"It's too late," The unexpected appearance of Braim by the side of her bed startled her. Moraina retreated to the opposite side of her bed like a hunted animal.

Braim's voiced was charged with emotion as he spoke, "Aelundei told me of his discovery." He faltered for a moment, and then whispered, "How could you?"

"Braim," began Moraina with a sob, but she was cut off.

"I trusted you!" bellowed Braim as he stood to his feet, his face dark with rage, "I lived with you, I trained you, I protected you, all to find out that you are not who you said you were!"

Moraina was weeping now, barely able to see through her tears, yet he continued.

"What were you hoping to do by leaving your family and joining the rangers? You know the law! You know the consequences of deserting your family! Why did you still leave?"

Moraina struggled to control the sobs that racked her body as Braim, trembling, sank into the chair by her bed. "I wanted freedom," she began timidly, "I wanted to know what it was like to live away from the oppressions of my sisters, and the ignorance of my father. Then I decided that I liked your way of life; I wanted to live that way for the rest of my life." Growing bolder, she queried, "Why do you treat me like this? I thought we were friends."

At this Braim rose to his feet and strode to the entrance of the tent. Looking over his shoulder, he replied in a hushed tone, "I thought I had a good friend named Orandaur, but it appears he never existed. Goodbye, Moraina."

She watched in despair as he exited the tent. "Braim, wait!" she wailed in desperation. But Braim did not wait, he did not stop; he only marched forward, his shoulders square and back rigid.

*　　　*　　　*

The rest of the day went by in a blur for Braim. The king arrived around noon to present him with a new set of armor, but it did not bring any joy into his grief. A feeling deep within him urged him to forgive Moraina, but he smothered it, extinguished it like a tiny flame.

You were deceived by a woman! Screamed a voice in his head, *She used you as a tool to run away from her family, and you believed every lie!* Every time that voice spoke, the feeling of wrong tried to rekindle itself, but Braim, in his anger, clung to the voice that affirmed him, let it drown out its counterpart every time.

When evening came, he crawled into his bed, weary from the battle the evening before, and emotionally drained by the war that still raged in his head. As he drifted into dreams, he was haunted by the despondent face of Moraina. The weaker voice seized its opportunity, *She saved your life.*

*   *   *

Braim awoke early in the morning, his tousled hair and horribly wrinkled clothes attested to his night of fitful sleep. As he pulled on his boots he heard the sound of hooves nearing his tent. Grabbing his sword, bow, and arrows, he left his tent, curious to see who was leaving the camp at this hour.

Moraina, slumped in Prince's saddle, rode slowly down the path next to Braim's tent, led by her cousins, who were also mounted. She wore her ranger's clothes, her disheveled hair indicating she had slept as poorly as Braim. Then he looked into her eyes, swollen from the tears they had shed, and for the first time in his life he felt moved deeply by compassion.

When she saw Braim staring at her, she stopped Prince in front of him. He could barely hear her as she whispered, "Braim, I'm so sorry."

Unable to bear seeing her grief any longer, Braim wheeled around and walk away. As he retreated, he heard Silas say, "Come along, cousin, we need to leave."

The Legend of Braim
Chapter XXX
Retreat of the Goblins

Jorguel ground the dirt with one foot, and tightened his grip on the hilt. Squinting across at the last of Grashnir's surviving generals, he grinned wickedly before lunging at his opponent.

The surviving goblins of Torrer had left the rest of the retreating kingdoms the day before, and Jorguel had seized the opportunity to assassinate all of Grashnir's surviving generals. All of them except for this one, he needed an example. So there Jorguel was, beginning his fight to the death with an enraged general. He was ready.

The sound of metal on metal rang throughout the forest as the two combatants attacked, parried, and lunged. Jorguel could see his opponent growing weak, it spurred him on. The general was a skilled warrior, but he was old, and Jorguel's youthful vigor soon dominated the fight. Dodging an overextended lunge, Jorguel stepped forward and pinned the general's arm beneath his. With a wild grin on his face, the young goblin dropped his sword, drew a knife from his belt, and plunged it into the neck of his foe. He stood there for a moment, twisting the knife and relishing the bewildered look that was frozen on the old general's face, then dropped the limp corpse and turned to address the watching goblin army. He raised his hand, black with blood, and shrieked his victory, the surrounding goblins joining in. As soon as they quieted down, he spoke.

"You have seen my prowess in battle; I defeated an opponent much wiser and more skilled than I. Are there any who yet challenge my desire to rise to the throne?" He glared into the eyes of the front row of goblins, the wild grin still plastered on his face, inviting any who dared to challenge he who so relished killing. Seeing no one willing to accept his offer, Jorguel continued, "The humans will pursue us. One has arisen who believes that Torrer is rightfully his. I say then, let him come to take it, if he so chooses!" The goblins laughed, as if he had suggested that only one man would try to take the castle, "If we prepare the way that I have envisioned, any human that tries to take our home from us will wish he had never ventured north."

Jorguel basked in the adulation of his troops. *I know you're coming, Braim,* Thought Jorguel, smugly, *I'll be looking forward to meeting you.*

The Legend of Braim
Chapter XXXI
The Retaking of Castle Torrer

The army that followed the tall young man in bright armor marched proudly, for they knew that they marched behind a great leader; even the horses seemed to sense it as they held their heads high. Though the army had marched for almost a week, spirits were high, and the anticipation of paying the goblins back for years of misery added to that feeling of joy.

Even though the mood of the army was proud and strong, the young man and his elven companion knew that the need to know what lay ahead was great, and there was always a party of seven rangers riding on the road ahead.

Suddenly on the trail ahead, they heard the sound of galloping hooves, and one of the rangers burst around a turn ahead and reigned in before Braim; it was Peter.

"My Lord!" said Peter, but he could not go on before Braim raised his hand.

"Peter," said Braim, "I am not a lord yet, and you know me. Now come, tell me what news you bring."

Peter paused for a moment as he calmed his excited horse, and then he went on, "The forward scouts have sighted Castle Torrer. You and your men are only a few hours march from the castle."

"Thank you for the information, friend. But now I have another errand for you. Ride forward and tell the rangers to come back, except for three. Those three that are left behind are to watch every move the goblins make, and report back here to me if the goblins leave the castle. When you come back, turn to your right off the path and ride until you find where we are camped."

"Yes, sir!" said Peter as he turned and rode back down the road in the direction from which he had come.

Braim turned and faced the army, "First battalion in line, there is a large clearing off the road to the left here. Follow me, every battalion after the first turn exactly where they did. Sergeants, call the march," Braim turned left off the road as the sergeants raised their voices and commanded their units to start forward.

They walked for twenty minutes before Braim broke through the clawing pines and found himself in a clearing. It was a fairly large clearing, just barely large enough for all the soldiers to camp in.

Braim kept walking until he was on the other side of the clearing, and then he turned and started calling out where the units were to stop. The last battalion made it into the clearing and was just starting to set up camp when the rangers arrived, led by Peter, Larem, and Saeln, who had all survived the battle with their bodies relatively unscathed.

"Welcome to the new camp," said Braim, "Go ahead and set up your tents and get ready to eat, the food is almost done."

The rangers set up their tents and gratefully filed into the line that was in front of the cook's tent, bowls and spoons at the ready. That evening's dinner was a fine stew, full of savory venison and cut potatoes, complete with fresh herbs that had been found by the cook's assistant.

As the sun set, Braim and Aelundei began to talk in whispers, and after awhile, Braim left and began to select men from the troops.

"Alright, listen up," said Braim, and instantly heads began to turn, "These men," gesturing to the captains whom he had selected, "Will be in charge whenever Aelundei and I are gone. You will listen to what they tell you to do, and will cooperate. I have given them instructions on what needs to be done. That is all, carry on." Everyone resumed what they were doing and wondered where he was going.

After Braim finished the announcement he joined Peter, Larem, and Saeln. They walked to where Aelundei patiently waited and watched as he began unfolding an old map of Torrer.

"There is a legend," began Aelundei, "That in the days of Lord Braeln's father, Lord Bernhard Goblinsbane, a tunnel was constructed from the keep courtyard out into the forest. Recently I came across this map which proves the myth to be truth," Aelundei paused to point to the end of a line that had been drawn from the castle into the woods, "First we need to find the old exit, it was made to look exactly like the forest floor. It has been about two decades since the tunnel has been used, so the disguise has either become even better or started to fade. I personally hope for the second, but we must assume that it has blended in even better by now. When we arrive on the scene I will be able to further instruct you about what we should search for, but for now we march," the humans followed the elf into the forest, well armed with shovels and eager to begin their work.

We are about to find a path into my father's castle! Brimming with excitement, Braim was caught completely off guard by the sudden rebellious voice, *If only Moraina could share in your victory.* He crushed the thought with the bitterness in his soul, and stomped onward, until Aelundei held up his hand.

"The tunnel should end in this area," said the elf softly, "Spread out and stomp the ground with your feet until you hear a hollow sound."

Eager to get his mind off Moraina, Braim began stomping around the area with vigor, hoping like a child waiting to open a gift to be the first to find the tunnel, but it was Aelundei's sharp ears that finally found it. He pointed to the ground, "Start digging here," the five friends began to dig furiously. The wooden door was only two feet below the surface, and it was not long before it was entirely uncovered.

Braim stepped forward and grasped the iron handles. He lifted hard, but it would not budge.

"If human arms cannot forge a path," said Aelundei as he stepped forward, "Then perhaps an elf could be of assistance," he grasped the handles and with one great heave he lifted them open. He gestured for Braim to enter first, and then stepped in behind him, the three other rangers following him. They lit a torch and Braim lifted it high, using its flaming end to brush through the spider webs that barred the tunnel. The map told them it was three hundred yards from the entrance of the tunnel to the castle. They walked along for several minutes, with no conversation and no light other than that of the torch. Finally, the five companions began to feel the tunnel rise gradually, and the previously dirt floor turned to one of cobblestones.

Then, out of nowhere loomed a stair, rising up into blackness. "Here is where we begin to climb," said Braim, excitedly, "Soon we will find the door that allows us to come in to the midst of the enemy, all we must do is test it, we will not open it today. In a few days' time we will attack, and enter into the land of our fathers. Now, we climb!" Without a second glance he stepped on to the first stair and began the walk to the top.

They walked for about five minutes before they reached the top of the moss covered steps, a giant wooden door barred the way above them.

Braim grabbed one of the shovels from Peter, and used it to knock softly on the aging wood. It produced a hard solid noise, but the shovel did stick in about half an inch. He pulled the shovel out and turned to his friends, "The door appears to still be mostly solid, in fact, it feels that there is hardly any rot at all. Tomorrow, we will come back with chisels and hammers to weaken the door for the attack. When the battering ram is finished, we will be able to take this castle back from the goblins that slew our brothers in arms. Let us return to the camp and rest tonight," They turned around and began the long walk back.

*   *   *

The camp rose before the sun, instantly everyone began preparations for the coming battle. The soldiers put finishing touches to a battering ram and prepared for the battle that would come that evening. Peter, Saeln, Larem, and six engineers carrying packs on their backs followed Braim and Aelundei into the forest.

They marched to the entrance of the tunnel and stepped through it, Braim leading all the way to the end. The engineers stopped and looked up at the old door, the only thing between them and the castle that had once belonged to their fathers. One of the engineers stepped forward and tapped on the wood.

"Aye," said the engineer with a nod, "It is thick oak, just as I thought. The top of this door will probably be slightly rotted, whereas our side still appears to be good," The other engineers came forward and produced chisels and hammers from their bags. They wrapped the hammers in cloth and began to chisel away at the oak door. Braim watched with satisfaction as large hunks of semi-rotted wood fell away before the engineers' skilled hands; they were that much closer to the invasion of Torrer.

*   *   *

The band of two hundred soldiers and twenty rangers marched quietly through the woods to the entrance of the tunnel. These soldiers were only one battalion in the army that had been sent with Braim, and the rangers were only one third of the force that had volunteered to assist him in the retaking of castle Torrer.

The soldiers and their leader halted before the entrance of the tunnel; Braim turned to them and raised his voice, "Soldiers! Friends! Comrades! We now stand before the very tunnel through which our fathers, mothers, aunts, uncles, sisters and brothers once fled; forced to leave their homes and their sons, brothers, fathers behind to defend an overwhelmed castle. Today, we will take back that which was once ours, we will finally repay the goblins for the blood of our families, the blood that ran and quenched the thirst of a dry ground. Soon our friends and fellow soldiers will begin the battle at the gate. We will march down this tunnel, tear the ancient door off its hinges, and crush the goblins that now occupy the realm of our ancestors!" He finished his speech just as a ranger on a sweating horse galloped up.

"The fighting has begun!" he cried, before wheeling his horse and racing back towards the gate.

Braim turned to his soldiers, "Now my friends, we march to victory, or death!" With a quiver of excitement, he turned and entered the tunnel.

*   *   *

Aelundei dropped his hand, and a volley of arrows flew from the bows of forty rangers as the soldiers that carried the battering ram charged towards the gates. The elf watched the sentries on the wall above the gate fall before he whistled shrilly and urged his horse into a trot. The rangers also urged their horses forward, picking off any other goblins that dared to show their heads above the ramparts.

The battering ram slammed into the gate with so much force that the ground shook from the sound of it. The gates buckled and the soldiers heard the locks on the back cracking, but the gate still held. The battering ram struck five more times before the gates finally broke off their hinges and came crashing down, narrowly missing the soldiers that held the battering ram.

Aelundei fired another arrow and watched with satisfaction as another goblin dropped his crossbow and fell, then he turned in the saddle and whistled three short blasts. With a mighty roar, the soldiers that had been waiting in the woods burst into the open, and charged through the ruins of the gate. Aelundei and the rangers led the charge, before splitting up and heading down opposite sides of the castle. Riding at the head of a mass of soldiers, they picked off goblins as they rode. The two parties met at the middle, then went back to get the battering ram. The army rode up to the second gate and prepared to knock that one down as well, but they were unaware of the danger that lay in wait.

"For Telnor!" yelled Braim and the army in unison as they charged out of the tunnel and prepared to meet the unsuspecting enemy. The goblins that had been facing out towards the army that attacked the gate now swung round to meet the army that had suddenly appeared behind their backs, but they were cut down by dark brown shafts from the bows of the rangers. Braim and most of the soldiers sprinted to the door of the central keep and bashed it down. They found a small battalion of goblins, caught unaware by an army that was supposed to be attacking the main gate. The large group of soldiers split up, half of them prepared to go through the door in front of them, and the other half with Braim raced up the stairs, splitting into even smaller groups to go through each room.

Meanwhile, Peter and the rangers spread out and battled their way to the top of the walls. They killed the goblins at the top of the wall and began firing arrows down on the backs of those below. For the army at the top of the castle, the battle was going extremely well.

*   *   *

Aelundei winced as the crossbow bolt sliced across the side of his neck. That one had caught him while he was trying to dodge a ballista missile. He drew an arrow from his quiver, aimed at the string of one of the giant crossbows, and fired. The tight string snapped and wounded its crew. Aelundei thanked Vitaren for helping him before reaching up for another arrow, but the quiver was empty. Only two of the five ballistae were left, but Aelundei was the only archer capable of hitting a target that narrow, and the only other way to disable a ballista would be to take a sword and hack through the string. Aelundei drew the two swords that he had borrowed from a Telnorian blacksmith, and charged towards the ring of spears that the goblins had fastened to the ground. He was grateful that he had left Valostala behind, his horse would not have been able to leap over these spears. Swinging with all his might he hacked through eight of the spears and then leaped over the rest. Soldiers poured in behind him, following in the path of wreckage that he had left to form a wedge, widening it until the whole group could fit. Aelundei ran up to one of the ballistae, fought his way through the crew, and aimed the ballista at the one that was on the other side of the spear fence. He pulled the cord that held the string and watched as the large projectile slammed into the other ballista. It smashed through the machine and killed most of the crew. Aelundei picked up his sword, ready to enter back into the battle, but the soldiers had just finished killing the goblins. Only a few goblins outside the ring of spears were left. The elf turned to the soldiers that were standing around him, "Pick this ballista up and carry it to the next gate, if there are more of these there then they will find that we know how to use one, too." They did as he bid; the army from the gate was coming.

*   *   *

Braim burst through another door without knocking, then dropped to the ground as a crossbow bolt flew over his head; these goblins were terrible hosts. But then again, the men weren't the best guests either. He rolled out of the forced fall and up onto his feet, this room was empty as well, except for the crossbow that had been rigged to go off when the door was opened. Braim had lost several good men to these hidden enemies, but they were nearing the top of the castle, and they would repay the goblin leader for all his wicked deeds.

*   *   *

Peter fired the last arrow from his quiver and looked down from the ramparts with satisfaction. The goblins in the castle had not counted on an enemy appearing behind their backs, the army from the tunnel had caught them completely off guard. The force of crossbow-wielding goblins had been entirely destroyed in the next level below them, and so had most of the sword-goblins. Peter and the rest of the rangers leaped down the wall as the ranger called out in a loud voice, "Charge, soldiers of Telnor! Open the gates and meet the enemy face to face, today they will pay for the blood of our fathers!" With that the gate was thrown open, the soldiers and rangers charged out like the rising tide, roaring the battle cry of Telnor. The few goblins left were no match for the soldiers in bright scale mail, and fell like wheat before a scythe. The rangers retrieved their arrows as they ran, and were soon on top of the walls firing down at the goblins on the level below. The goblins below found themselves

180

caught between two foes. Aelundei and his men had just broken through their gate, and were fighting the foes that had surrounded it with a fence of spears. Peter heard a loud twang, and saw that Aelundei's men had salvaged a ballista, and had brought it up from the second level of the city. He paused his shooting and turned around, "Soldiers of Telnor, find the ballistae that we passed on our way down to this gate and bring it here, it may help our comrades who are fighting on the level below!" The small group of soldiers raced off, gathering others as they went, and soon returned carrying four intact ballistae. They carried them up onto the wall and began to crank the levers that pulled back the strings of the massive cross-bows. They set the great bolts into their slots and fitted them to the strings. Then, they lifted up the ballistae and set them on the walls. They aimed at the ballistae that the enemy were using to fire at their friends, and pulled the trigger. The noise of four giant bowstrings firing four giant bolts made Peter jump, and the soldiers holding the ballistae almost dropped them onto the heads of the enemy. But when Peter looked over the wall, he was very pleased with the wreckage. They needed to do that again, the results were amazing.

*   *   *

Braim and his dwindling band of soldiers charged the small group of goblins with swords raised and battle cries in their throats. The two parties slammed into each other and there was a brief engagement. The goblins put up a weak resistance and were crushed almost immediately. Braim was about to congratulate his soldiers when one of them dropped his weapon and fell to his knees, a growing pool of red liquid appearing at his feet. Medics rushed forward and stripped the boy of his armor to bandage him, but there was only so much that they could do. Braim counted heads inwardly, and was shocked to find that only twenty of his soldiers were left standing, it was time to pull out and wait for reinforcements. He ordered the medics to make a stretcher out of spears and leather strips, then the men formed up and Braim led them out of the room. They stepped out of the door and found themselves surrounded by almost a hundred goblins.

"Get back into the room and grab spears, we need to hold out until Aelundei and his men show up," Braim yelled, and the small band raced back into the room to set up a row of spear men in the door. Braim hoped they could last long enough for Aelundei and his men to show up; they could be there in a few minutes, or longer, and by then it might be too late.

*   *   *

Aelundei shook hands with Peter and looked around at the carnage of the battle. "Medics!" he yelled, "Comb the battlefield for wounded men," medics began to run from patient to patient, and Aelundei turned back to Peter, "Peter, where's Braim? I do not see him among you."

Peter turned and looked up to the central keep, "Last I saw, he led a band of fifty soldiers into the central tower, I think we should gather every available man and get in there to assist."

Aelundei looked up at the tower in alarm, and then began yelling orders to various sergeants, who in turn ordered their troops to fall in and begin the march to the central keep. If Braim was in trouble, Aelundei wanted to get there to help him as quickly as possible.

The army reached the base of the tower and halted, they could hear the sounds of fighting, but they were distant and muffled.

Peter turned to Aelundei and asked, "How will you find him?"

And Aelundei turned and replied, "I figured I'll just follow the trail of destruction, that should lead me to him," He ran through the door, and the band of soldiers followed him. The elf halted and bent down to the ground, "They split up, half went through the door on the right, the other half went through the door on the left, and Braim was with the group that went left."

Peter raised his eyes in amazement, "How did you figure that Braim went left?"

"This," said the elf, as he bent down and picked up a spear that had been cut in half, "Was not done by a regular infantry sword; it would have taken a sword much larger to do that. I fear to do the same thing that Braim did, but I fear that there is no other choice if we wish to save both groups." He paused briefly, weighing his options before speaking swiftly, "Take your soldiers and go through the door on the right. I will take my soldiers and head through the door on the left," Before waiting another moment, Aelundei and his troops ran through the door on the left, working their way quickly towards the top. The sounds of battle grew slowly closer.

182

Braim looked around at his shrinking band. They had inflicted many wounds, killing about forty goblins by his reckoning, but still the enemy pressed in, and it seemed that more were coming out of the surrounding rooms. The soldiers had formed a shield wall in front of the door, and were using goblin spears to stab at the enemy, but for every goblin that they killed, another five seemed to take its place. They were fighting a losing battle, and the goblins were driven into a frenzy by the knowledge of it.

Braim watched in horror as three more of his men fell, he and two others took their places. Two more fell, then the goblins began to stream into the room. Suddenly, from out of nowhere came Aelundei leading fifty soldiers. Braim heard Aelundei yelling above the others, "For Braim, charge!"

The weakened force defending the room had hope driven forcefully into their hearts and they surged forward, the goblins that had driven them back were cut down, trampled underfoot. The goblins in the hallway turned to meet the new threat, and discovered themselves facing a much larger force. The ugly creatures realized that the tables were turned and ran. The two Telnorian forces watched the goblins run away; there was no point in pursuing them, there were only a dozen of them left. The medics from Aelundei's group rushed in to help the medics of Braim's group, and the two friends walked up to each other, Braim wiping the black blood off of his sword.

"What were you thinking," demanded Aelundei, fuming, "Why didn't you wait for me and my reinforcements? Was it the need for revenge? I tell you now, anger and a want for revenge will only get you or others hurt."

Braim looked down at the ground, and thought of the cost of his action. Aelundei reached forward and put his hand on Braim's shoulder.

"Friend, many men were hurt or killed for your actions, but thanks to you, we did not have to clear out every room when I came to find you. You have made a mistake, even elves do, but the key is to learn from what you did wrong," he removed his hand, "We still have a lot of work to do to make it to the top of this tower. Go, tell your men to prepare to press on."

Braim turned and walked away, thankful to have such a good

friend as Aelundei. He gave the orders to the men, and watched as they formed up and prepared to move on through the castle.

*   *   *

Peter and the rangers ran through the castle, firing arrows and slashing with swords. They were almost to the top of the tower when they found the remnant of soldiers gathered in a circle in the middle of a hallway. They were surrounded by almost a hundred goblins and they were slowly losing men. The rangers charged into the fray, the men in the front had drawn their swords and were carving a path through the enemy to their surrounded comrades. The men in the back of the formation started firing arrows into the goblins that were on the other side of the circle of men. The goblins that were getting shot realized that the tables had turned and ran down the hall, getting hit by arrows as they ran. But the goblins that were closer saw that they had no way to run, and they were cut down by shining swords.

The leader of the group of soldiers walked up to Peter and shook his hand, "Well ranger, I gotta thank you, 'cause you just saved our lives."

Peter looked the captain in the eyes and grinned, "It seems you army types could always use a hand, I'm happy to be of service. Captain, see to your men, then prepare to march onward, we will meet up with our friends at the top of this wretched tower."

The captain saluted and marched off among his men, snapping orders confidently as he went.

*   *   *

Aelundei and Braim stood before the door to the highest room in the tower, at their backs stood one hundred soldiers.

Aelundei turned to Braim, "Well, Braim, this is it. We've cleared every other room in this tower, and behind this door is the room that used to be your father and mother's. Waiting behind this door is a foe of unknown size, but I would guess that there are no more than thirty or forty. Goblins are tricky creatures, they honor no agreement or treaty, and you cannot expect them to go out peacefully. If they surrender, then do not turn your back, and expect nothing but treachery; for their father was the father of treachery, and that is the only way they know. Now go, and retake that which is rightfully

184

yours."

Braim drew his hand and a half sword and kicked through the door. But Aelundei sensed danger just Braim's foot hit the wood. Entering Illnorean, he grabbed the human by the back of his cloak and pulled him to the side. Instinctively ducking, he saw a large orange and black mass hurtling towards him. *Is that a tiger?* He had read about them while preparing to be sent to Telnor, but he never thought he would actually see one. As the creature began to fly past him, the elf cut upwards with his sword and cut the beast from its chest to its groin with almost surgical precision.

Exiting Illnorean, Aelundei turned swiftly around, ready to fight the wounded creature. One of the soldiers, however, had instinctively thrust his spear forward to protect himself. The great beast had been pierced through the heart.

Aelundei helped Braim to his feet, and the young man once again kicked open the door. He found that he was facing a group of twenty goblins. He looked at them and asked, "Who is your leader?" the goblins split down the center, almost as if they had been told, and Braim found himself looking at a short goblin with a cruel-looking face.

"What do you want of us, human?" asked the goblin leader.

"You or your fore-fathers took this castle from my parents," replied Braim, "and killed them in the process. I am here to take back what is rightfully mine by inheritance. I give you the choice of surrender, now; you will be escorted to the northern border of this province. But if you choose not to accept these generous terms, then my elf friend and I will cut you down and rid the earth of your evil and twisted existence."

"We would never surrender to scum like you, human!" said the goblin leader. He raised his sword above his head and slashed down at Braim, but the young man blocked it easily and ran his sword through the goblin's ribcage. The other goblins charged towards Braim, but were stopped short by a volley of arrows. Braim turned around to see who had fired, and in the back of the room was a rank of rangers, with Peter at their front. Braim turned back to the ten remaining goblins and cut three of them down with one blow of his sword. Aelundei finished the other goblins off, and the battle for Torrer was finally over.

The Legend of Braim
Chapter XXXII
Conflict at the Golden Lamb

Braim brushed his soaked hair out of his face and peered through the pouring rain at the warm-looking village. Smoke rose from small chimneys and light shone through the windows. He patted Rochle on the neck.

"Well, my faithful friend, only a little further to warm stables and sweet hay." The tired horse nickered softly in reply to his master's voice, and it stepped forward with only a slight increase of pressure from Braim's legs.

Braim rode silently down the main road that went through the village. It had grown quite a bit since his last visit; but the road was still dirt, and now Rochle's hooves made sucking sounds as the mud tried to bind them in its cold embrace. Braim halted again before the inn; the sign dangling from the eaves had a lamb with golden fur painted on it. The ranger grinned up at the familiar symbol; the paint had faded, but it was still the same sign that had dangled there three years ago when he had tracked a band of goblins to this very village. He grinned again as he remembered the friendship that had developed between him and the inn keeper's son as a result of rescuing the village and especially that inn, whose lamb-potato-cheese pie was known throughout the province.

Braim dismounted and led Rochle to the stables in the back. He ensured his faithful steed had good bedding, a blanket, food, and drink. The tired brown horse munched on the oats with gratitude before settling down to rest. Braim left the stables and walked back through the rain to the front of the inn.

As soon as the stranger stepped through the front door of the inn, all heads turned. Travelers were rare at this time of the night, and especially in this weather. Twenty sets of eyes took in the tall form of the ranger in the soaked green cloak. Everyone noticed that he was a handsome young man, and most even noticed the keen grey eyes through the smoke that wreathed the ceiling. Some of the men noticed that he wore a sword at his side and a bow at his back, and from his ready stance and graceful movements they knew he was skilled with their usage.

Braim closed the door behind him, walked over to a corner booth, and sat down. A waitress walked over and asked him if she could get him anything to eat and drink. Her accent was lilting and had the graceful sound of the central provinces of Telnor.

"Mmm, I'd like to have a glass of milk, please. Is there any of that fine Lamb Pie that you're famous for?"

The waitress smiled at him and nodded, "Yep, momma just pulled one out of the oven. I'll get you a plate of it."

Braim looked gratefully up to her, "Thank you; it's been a long cold ride through the storm out there. Could you tell your father that an old friend is here and would like to visit for a spell?"

"Sure, but would you mind givin' me a name to recognize you by?" said the girl with a hint of doubt in her eyes. "He's been a little busy lately."

"Tell him that Braim is here and wishes to catch up on the events of the village."

The young woman looked at him surprised, "Braim? Father has told me so much about you; I'll fetch 'im right away!" She walked off quickly and went through the double doors of the kitchen. Braim settled back and waited, but not for long. The young woman came back through the doors carrying Braim's order, as well as a few others. She set Braim's food and drink before him and smiled again.

"Papa will be right with you. He's bottling a new batch of Filbert Nut Ale and testing some wine."

She hurried off to check on the other men in the tavern common room as Braim dug into the steaming pie with gratefulness.

Braim was about half done when a large man in plain clothes covered by a stained white apron walked through the kitchen's double doors. He looked around the smoke-filled room and soon caught sight of Braim.

"Hey there, Braim!" said the man as he walked over to Braim's booth.

Braim stood up and was wrapped by the larger man's arms in a warm embrace. He hugged back, and the two friends sat down on opposite sides of the booth.

"So, how have you been these last four years?" asked Braim, "I heard the village was attacked by some human bandits last year, but I couldn't make it down to help. I was busy tracking a goblin raiding party when the news arrived." With a grin he added, "Them goblins probably wouldn't have gotten much here, though."

The friendly man, who went by the name of Laeln the Brewer, smiled back at Braim and nodded, "Aye, that they wouldn't have," his voice was deep and it rumbled like an avalanche, but the words still had the same graceful lilt as his pretty, red-headed daughter. Braim knew that she didn't get that red hair from Laeln, his locks were coal black, but evidently she had inherited his stocky build and hazel eyes.

Braim grinned at the man, "They would probably get more here than they would from my new province, though."

Laeln threw back his head and roared with laughter, "Aye, that too. We heard tales that you and an elf had gone back north with an army to retake Torrer. By the way, where is that pointy-eared friend of yours right now, and what business tears you away from the talons of your new position? Anything that can do that must be something mighty important."

"Well, it's a long story, 'tis," said Braim, settling into the accent of the area as he usually did around his old friend, "It all started when I forgot to tie some provisions up in a tree. Since 'tis so long, you'll have to settle for a summary."

Laeln leaned in and listened to the tale with nods and a grunt of surprise when he heard of Braim's torture at the hands of Grashnir, but being a good listener, he waited until Braim finished the story to ask questions.

"So, that is why I ended up here in your little village, I need to find Moraina and apologize for being so quick to anger. I also need to tell her something that has been weighing on my mind a lot recently; and hopefully, she will forgive me and say the same thing back to me, else ways I will feel stabbed through the heart, I will," Braim smiled grimly, "Now that I know who Orandaur really is, I feel as if I must have her as my wife, and my heart hurts that I told her to leave and was so stubborn." Braim grinned, "But I have a feeling that the father wouldn't have been too happy with me if I had kept her without asking."

Laeln laughed again at that, "You can be sure of that my friend, a father can be a bit of a problem when it comes to who gets his darlin' girl. Take me advice as a father: when my daughter walks through town, them boys look stricken at the sight of her beauty, and I want to run them over with my horse! Someday, a man may come who is worthy of her hand, and I'll still want to run him over with my horse; 'cause in me mind, no man is worthy of her hand, 'cause she's me darlin' little girl. Do ya catch what I'm saying?"

Braim frowned for a moment to work through the words, then

nodded, "So, in the eyes of a father, no one is worthy of his daughter's hand, because she is so precious to you. Therefore, they should all be run off with threats of being run under a horse's hooves."

"Exactly."

"So, how will you know when the right man comes?"

"Well," he said with a slight grin, "I guess I will have to evaluate the ones that stay any way and make sure they are brave, dedicated and *smart,* as opposed to brave, dedicated and *stupid.*"

This time Braim laughed as Laeln shook his head and continued, "Love can make a man do stupid things, and some of these boys here don't need the extra help."

"Is there any advice you can give to a novice in this art?" asked Braim with a smile.

"Well, there are quite a few things that a man should do. The first, is to be honest, if a women suspects you of cheating, things become like hell pretty quickly. On the other hand, though, whenever your wife asks a question, make sure that you always smile, nod, and be sure to say 'Yes, honey m'dear!' that way she's always happy."

"You just smile and nod and say 'yes m'dear?' Isn't that breaking the rule of always being honest?"

"Well, the way I figure it, it's better if she's happy than if she knows she can't buy that new dress at the market or get that cat she's want for the mice, and so she's happier. I'll show you how to do it right, ask me some questions a wife would ask."

"Well, I guess," replied Braim, feeling awkward but not knowing how to say no, "Um, Honey, there's this new dress at the market, can I buy it?"

Laeln smiled and nodded, "Yes m'dear, of course. See, 'tis an easy matter! Go ahead, ask another question if you are not convinced!"

Braim thought for a moment before he smiled a little, "Honey, does this dress make me look fat?"

Laeln smiled and nodded, "Yes, m'dear, of course! See, 'tis easy!"

"Laeln, did you even hear what I asked you?"

"Something about another dress, right?"

"I just asked you if the dress made me look fat, you big tub o'lard!" said Braim as he roared with laughter, "What type of husband are you?"

Laeln shared the laugh with his old friend for a while, before he grew serious once again. "On a more serious note, Braim, you must be able to realize the needs of your wife and work to meet those needs. You must respect her as an equal, yet treat her as weaker, out of respect and honor for her as a woman. Treat her as the most beautiful and special person in all creation, because she is."

Braim nodded, and was about to reply when the door opened and two men in dripping clothes walked into the tavern, bringing with them a gust of wind and drowning rain before the door was closed. The two men looked around the tavern, and walked directly to Braim.

"We here heard you's were the new lord of Torrer, so we came to you for help," said one of the men, "You see, I's a farmer of this good province, and I's aint never done no-one any harm," the man who was speaking looked over at the other man angrily, "But this 'ere man is from 'ere in the village, a lowly leather tanner. He's been stealing my sheep for the past year now, ever since he lost a big bet on a horse race. I want him dealt with; the law says they can't find sheep bones near his house - and there are no bones near my farm - but this one's too clever for that."

The other man looked as if he had had enough of this man's accusations and insults. Braim took a sip of milk and looked up.

"How often do you lose a sheep, man?" asked Braim to the farmer.

"Why, every two to three days."

"That's a lot of sheep for one man to steal and use," said Braim skeptically.

"You should see the size of 'is woman! She eats as much as you and me put together I reckon, judging from her shape!"

The man standing next to the farmer turned and spoke for the first time, "Fred, I keep tellin' ye and tellin' ye, my wife is not fat! In fact, she is smaller than your woman, and your wife has no children to feed like mine does!"

Braim raised his hands to quiet them, "Children, stop your bickering! Now, Fred the Farmer, how long has it been since the last sheep was carried off?"

The farmer looked up at the ceiling and thought for a moment, and then he looked back down, "Well, two days; I'd reckon that I'd lose another sheep tonight, but they're in the barn out of the storm now."

Braim sighed, and pulled the cowl of his cloak up over his head,

"Go sit down somewhere, and let me think. I'll call you when I come up with a plan."

The two men looked over at each other, scowled, and walked to opposite sides of the tavern and sat down. It was only a few moments, though, before Braim called them back again.

"Here is my plan for tomorrow," he said with a scowl, "It is really simple, so it won't be too hard. Tomorrow evening I'll stay as a guest of the leather worker here. I'll sleep downstairs on the floor by the door, and if you still lose a sheep, it's not his fault. If you don't lose a sheep from the pasture, then the leatherworker is guilty. But, just to ensure fair play on your part, Mr. Fred the Farmer, I think that Laeln's son should go visit your farm and watch you run through your routines."

The two men nodded, scowled at each other, and walked out the door of the tavern, heading to their different destinations.

Braim turned to Laeln and grinned, "Well, that was a simple plan in the end, but it took me a little bit to think of it. Now I'm delayed another day, which is another day I can't spend riding to the capitol. At least Rochle will be able to rest."

"Well, simple it was, but hopefully the wolves are hungry and haven't gone somewhere else to eat," said the tavern keeper grimly, "Else wise you'll have the blood of poor John Tanners on your hands."

"I highly doubt it will come to that," said Braim as he took another drink.

The Legend of Braim
Chapter XXXIII
The Quest

Moraina looked out from the corner of the dance room. She sat in the chair, wishing she had her old ranger cloak and could sink away into the depths of its hood. She watched the couples dancing merrily, hoping that the man who her father wanted her to marry wouldn't come. She despised the man, some middle-aged fool with six snotty, mean-tempered, bickering kids. His name was Ferthrin, most women thought that he was extremely handsome, but underneath his slick looks was a personality that she found unbearable. Over and over she found herself praying to Vitaren above to send Braim riding Rochle to rescue her, but the more she did, the less and less likely it seemed that he would. Right now, he was probably fighting to retake his parents' castle above the Premeleis Range. She looked out from her thoughts and found that Ferthrin was walking towards her. She forced herself to not scowl at the man, but it was too difficult. By custom she was required to stand and greet him, but she remained in her seat.

"Why, hello there, Moraina," said Ferthrin, "It is a lovely evening, is it not?"

I know a person that would make it even lovelier, thought Moraina, but she forced herself to look up, "Yes, it is a lovely evening."

Ferthrin looked around awkwardly for a moment, and then he turned back to Moraina, "Shall we dance?"

I'd rather fight a hundred trolls then dance with you, the girl thought, but again she forced herself to speak something slightly nicer, "No thank you, I would prefer to sit here and watch, perhaps you could find another girl who would like to go with you."

"Moraina, come walk with me."

Moraina was grabbed by the hand and pulled out of the seat. She followed Ferthrin out the back door of the hall and onto a trail through a small garden. It was extremely quiet, and there was not a soul around. Ferthrin threw an arm around her and they walked side by side. Moraina hated the fact that she had to put up with this man, and she wished they would go back inside. It may even have been better if she had agreed to dance with him, but she marched steadily onward. They walked to the point farthest from the low building and then Ferthrin turned towards her. He put his hands up on her shoulders and touched the top of the scar that ran down her shoulder and into the top of her dress. He looked into her eyes and smiled down at her. She glared back at his and then glanced down at the ground; he lifted her head back up and leaned in to kiss her on the lips. She drew slightly away from him, "Ferthrin, I'm cold; I think we should go back inside."

"I can warm you up," said Ferthrin, and he reached to pull her close, but she twisted away. She began to walk briskly back to the dance hall, with Ferthrin following at her heels. He realized that he had not played his cards right, but he knew he would have another chance.

Moraina sat down in a chair that was in the darkest corner of the room. She wished again that she had her ranger cloak with her, but her father had burned it. She sat thinking about her adventure as Orandaur, and began dissecting her actions one by one. She was so wrapped up in her thoughts that she barely noticed Ferthrin sit down beside her. She turned to look at him; he had drawn quite near, so she responded in turn by sliding away. He had pursued her to the edge of the seats when they were both startled by a loud commotion at the front of the room. A tall man walked into the room. Though she could not see his face, Moraina instantly recognized him. She leaped from her seat and began moving towards her friend. Moraina could not make her way through the mass of dresses and pretty faces, all trying to meet the young warrior. She pushed against the women, and was pushed back. She was slowly being pushed away from the one she loved, and she was desperate for him.

*　　　　*　　　　*

Braim realized that he was fenced in by the mass of large dresses and faces that he did not know. The noise was almost unbearable, and he found that questions flew at him like enemy crossbow bolts. From far off, he heard a familiar voice, and he turned towards it. He shouldered his way through the crowd, pushing and shouting pardons at everyone that he accidentally knocked down. All of a sudden, he realized he was getting nowhere, and he stopped. Raising his hands to his mouth, he yelled at the top of his lungs, and the room went quiet; even the band stopped in the middle of the waltz they were playing and turned to see who it was that had interrupted them.

193

"The only reason I am here," said Braim to everyone in the room, "is to find Moraina. Does anyone here know her?"

A tall girl with brown-blond hair walked up to him and looked him up and down, "I'm her sister," she said snobbishly, "Moraina is promised to a different man; you'd have to talk my father into changing his plans."

"I have already talked with your father, and he said that if she agreed then he would tell the man that she has been ordered to marry that the bride-groom has changed. Now, tell me where she is."

She looked at him again with a weird half sneer, "Who are you that would dare make demands?"

Braim could feel anger rising within him as he replied swiftly, "I am Braim, son of Braeln, son of Bernhard; Lord of the Province of Telnor, and defender of the northern borders of this kingdom." Leaning toward the shocked woman he continued slowly, "Where is she?"

Moraina's sister merely pointed toward the back of the room, and Braim brushed past her without thanking her. Knowing Moraina, he headed for the darkest corner. But when he arrived, he found a man holding Moraina in her seat, her back against the wall.

"Come now, soon we will be married, you will spend the rest of your life with me and my children; you will have to learn to love me one way or another," said the man before leaning in to kiss her lips. Braim stepped in and pulled the man off his friend, throwing him to the ground.

"Braim!" shouted Moraina, "You came!"

"Moraina," said Braim as he helped her out of her seat, "I'm sorry that I sent you back here to be with your sisters and this man; will you forgive me?"

She nodded, "Braim, you know that I would forgive you!"

"Thank you, Moraina," Braim turned back to check on the man, who was still lying stunned on the floor, and then he looked back to his love, standing before him. He took her hands and looked into her eyes, "Moraina, I stopped to talk with your father on the way here, and I asked him a few serious questions. He told me that you had been promised to the man standing behind me. Your father said he would reconsider, as long as you accept my next question," He dropped down to one knee, and reached into his pocket, "In my home province of Torrer, it is the custom for the man to give the woman that he wants to marry a ring. If she agrees, they become like the ring,

194

which is made into one item from two pieces of metal. He pulled the golden ring out of his pocket, and put it into her hand. "Moraina, will you accept this simple and small token of my love?"

Moraina looked down at the ring. It was such a tiny thing, but dazzlingly brilliant, and at its top there was a beautiful blue sapphire. She quickly rammed the ring onto her finger and wrapped her arms around Braim's neck, "Yes, Braim, you didn't even have to ask. Let's go find Father!"

She practically dragged him onto his feet and spun him around. She was about to take off running with Braim in tow, when she saw that Ferthrin was barring their way with a sword in hand.

Braim's hand dropped to the hilt of his sword as he stepped in front of Moraina. With barely restrained anger coloring his voice, he intoned, "Ferthrin, think about what you are doing, it makes absolutely no sense. I give you one chance, stand down and move out of our way."

Ferthrin stepped closer to Braim, "No, that is the girl that was promised to be married to me, and I will see that happen, I need the dowry her father will provide."

"Ferthrin, she and her father have agreed that she will no longer be promised to you. Can you not see that she does not love you?"

"She loves me, she just hasn't realized it yet. Now, prepare to fight!"

Braim raised his hand, and Ferthrin stopped moving forward, "If there is to be bloodshed, let it at least be done outside."

"Very well," spat Ferthrin.

The two men exited the building, followed by Moraina, a throng of dancers, and musicians. They walked until they were a good distance apart from each other, and then faced each other with harsh looks frozen on their faces. Ferthrin was red and angry; he looked ready to tear Braim's arms from their sockets. But the young man stood across from him, calm, ready to defend.

Ferthrin charged at Braim with his sword above his head, and swung it as hard as he could down at Braim's head, but Braim was no longer there. He had stepped casually to the side, and brought his sword down hard on the back of his opponent's blade, knocking it out of the man's hands. The weapon fell to the ground, and Ferthrin turned just in time to see a fist in his face, then the world blacked out.

*　　　　*　　　　*

195

Braim sat in front of Moraina's father, listening as the old gray man told him how he should treat his daughter. Saldon talked for about fifteen minutes, and Braim drank up every word of advice that he had to offer, then he called Moraina in. The young couple sat side by side on the narrow bench holding hands and planning the wedding date. It would be two weeks from then, and every friend of Moraina's family was to be invited. Braim wanted the wedding to be a soon as possible, for he still had to attend to his province. He still had not told Moraina that he planned to name it in honor of her; he hoped she approved of the name, *Morenelath*. His thoughts were turned back to the room as Saldon began to finish, "Remember, always forgive each other, and if you do not give your love a reason to need forgiveness, then you will never go wrong," Braim realized that it would take a little more than that to keep a relationship together, it would also take a common love for their creator, Vitaren.

*   *   *

Braim and Moraina stood at the door to the banquet hall in the king's palace, waiting for the roll of the drums. Nervously he straightened his dark red tunic, then checked his grey pants. He looked at his bride, her soft blue dress complemented her brown eyes perfectly, and she smiled at him, just as the drums began to sound. The huge, intricately carved oak doors opened outward, the bride and bridegroom stepped onto the red and gold carpet. They walked past the crowds of guests, who rose in honor of the couple, until the pair – hand in hand – stopped before the throne of the king. The drums ceased rolling as the king entered the room and took his seat on the throne. Braim and Moraina knelt before their king.

In a clear, commanding voice, Mettaren recited the traditional vows, "Moraina, do you hold true to the laws of the land, and pledge to serve Braim as your husband, bound to him by these events today?"

A shiver of joy surged up and down Braim's spine as Moraina replied, "Aye, I know the laws of the land, and I pledge to follow them. All the days of my life I shall serve my husband, bear his children, and follow him faithfully. In plague or in good health, in poverty or in bountiful harvests, in warfare or in peace, I will remain at his side until old age ends me. These things I swear by all that is good.”

Turning to Braim the king continued, “Braim, do you also hold true to the laws of the land, and pledge to lead and protect Moraina as your wife, bound to her by these events today?”

With joy welling up within him, Braim replied, “Aye, I know the laws of the land, and I pledge to follow them. All the days of my life I shall lead and protect my wife, provide for our children, and love her faithfully. In plague or in good health, in poverty or in bountiful harvests, in warfare or in peace, I will remain at her side until old age ends me. These things I swear by all that is good.”

The king smiled, and raised his eyes to view the assembly, “Then let their union be postponed no longer. Rise, husband and wife, the laws of the land deem you wedded!”

The crowd cheered and applauded as Braim rose to their feet, helped Moraina to hers, looked into his wife’s eyes, and kissed her. When they were finished, Braim turned to the people gathered before him and cried out, “Let it be known that henceforth, the province I have inherited will no longer be called Torrer. In honor of my new bride, and with permission from the king, I have renamed it, *Morenelath!* Now, let us celebrate!”

The Legend of Braim
Chapter XXXIV
More Plotting

The man in the imposing dark robe watched as the goblin king of Gartsamn, a neighboring kingdom to Torrer, slammed against the stone wall and fell to the ground. He walked up to the cowering goblin king and roared, "You will gather your whole army and march on the castle of Torrer, now! Or, I will kill you and do it myself."

The goblin king nodded, "It shall be done as you have commanded, great lord."

In the hidden depths of his black robe, the man smiled. The creature leapt to his feet, looking like a hunted deer, and ran to do as "lord" had bidden.

The army mobilized, prepared to march to Torrer and catch it unaware.

*   *   *

The man in the dark robe walked through the confusing streets of the goblin-built city. He finally made it to the stables and retrieved his horse. Then he left the city and rode away.

The goblins will not retake that castle, thought the man, *and I wish I could go to see them get crushed once again, but now it is time to report to my master of our defeat.* He cringed at the thought, but continued riding anyways. The penalty for desertion would be worse than that for report of a failure.

The Legend of Braim
Chapter XXXV
The Siege

Aelundei watched as the engineers worked on the new gate. He was worried that the enemy would try to retake the castle before they could hang the new gate. His men would be almost defenseless against an angry horde of goblins. With this in mind, the engineers worked quickly, also wanting to protect their friends. They felled trees, sawed them into boards, and bound them together with iron bracers. Unfortunately, Aelundei didn't think they had time to use oak trees, the wood was too hard and would take longer to cut and shape, therefore, the engineers were using thick slabs of pine until it was confirmed that there was no threat of a goblin counter-attack. Aelundei searched the surrounding woods again for signs of the enemy. Nothing, that was good. He had posted Peter, Saeln and Larem in the forest at strategic points, and he trusted the three rangers with his life, but he was still nervous. He looked back down at the engineers, busy chopping, sawing and hammering. They worked quickly; Aelundei only hoped it was quickly enough.

*   *   *

Peter ran a hand through his bright red hair, he was starting to get tired from a long night of little sleep, combined with a long period of standing watch. His eyelids drooped, and he slapped himself. *Whew,* he thought, *gotta stay awake.* Suddenly, he heard a noise. It was the sound of many feet jogging swiftly towards him. He pulled the cowl of his cloak over his head. Adrenaline coursed through his veins, and he decided he was no longer tired. That was when he heard the harsh goblin-cries and whoops, as they started running through the woods in his direction. He whistled loudly three times, and then ran fifty yards to where his buckskin horse was tied. Peter untied the lead ropes of the now nervous horse, and leaped into the saddle, galloping swiftly in the direction of Castle Torrer. *I have to warn Aelundei!*

*   *   *

Aelundei's pointed elf ears picked up the noise of three galloping horses slightly before the humans also heard the noise. He grabbed the engineer in charge, and looked him in the eye, "How long until you have one half of the gate finished?"

The engineer looked at Aelundei with fear in his eyes, "Ten minutes."

Aelundei thought for a split second, "Good, get half the gate done and hang it quickly. Fell three more trees, drag them to the front gate, I will send horses to help." The engineers started working even faster than before, some running to cut down the trees, but most continuing to finish the half of the gate.

Aelundei started sprinting as fast as a cantering horse towards the castle, which was only about a hundred yards away. He reached the castle walls quickly, and shifted out of Illnorean, the world slowed down. He jogged up to the rangers that were standing just inside the gate and they jumped to attention.

"I need you men to buy us at the castle ten minutes of time," said Aelundei, "The enemy is on their way, and in a moment we will know their exact location. When we do, you must hurry and attack them as far away from the castle as you can. Do not risk a frontal assault, but do what we rangers are best at!"

The rangers jumped into action, they grabbed swords and longbows, and got ready. They heard the sound of approaching hoof-beats, and suddenly three rangers burst through the hole where the gate should be. They reigned in their horses in front of Aelundei, and Peter reported, "Aelundei, hundreds of goblins are making their way to the castle; they are a mile out to the east of this gate still, but nearing rapidly."

"Can you three fight?" asked Aelundei, looking into their weary faces.

"I believe we still have enough energy to give the enemy a good whipping!" replied Saeln enthusiastically.

"Good, lead these rangers to the enemy, strike hard, strike fast, and be sure you don't need to shoot at the same foe twice," Aelundei moved to the side as the rangers mounted horses and galloped off in the direction of the enemy, before he turned and ran towards the center of the castle. He had more tasks to complete before the attackers arrived.

*   *   *

Braim looked round at the forest that was passing by him, then back at Moraina. He certainly hoped that there would be no fighting ahead of the company; he didn't want to have his first big disagreement with Moraina this soon. But Braim was more worried that they would arrive too late to save Aelundei and his troops if there was a goblin counter attack. Braim turned in the saddle and looked back. Behind him were a hundred archers, fifty cavalry men, fifty more pike men, and over a hundred swordsmen. *The king had definitely wanted to reinforce our new hold on Morenelath*, thought Braim, *Now, if only I had some more rangers, too.* Braim reached over his shoulder and fingered one of the twenty-five arrows in his quiver, and felt comforted that the king hadn't taken them away. He looked down at the new scale armor, and then down at the large two-handed sword that was slung on his saddle. Moraina now had his old hand-and-a-half sword hidden under her saddle bags. He looked ahead again, and even stood a little taller in the saddle, he recognized several landmarks. *Good*, he thought, w*e are about an hour and a half away from Morenelath.*

He felt a hand on his shoulder, and turned to see Moraina looking at him with a slight smile playing on her lips. He reached up and put one of his own hands on it.

"Nervous?" asked Moraina, a look of concern replacing her smile when she saw the worry on his face.

"Yes," answered Braim. "I'm nervous that we may be too late, nervous that we may be caught unawares, and even more I'm nervous that you will get hurt." He looked into her eyes, "If we are attacked, or if we arrive and see the castle under attack, then you must promise me that you will not go into the battle. I need you to take forty archers and fifty swordsmen to guard the civilians that are following us," he saw stubbornness enter her eyes, and her face hardened. *Brace yourself, Braim!*

Moraina took her hand off Braim's shoulder and put it on her hip. "My place is with you. You asked me to be your wife, and I accepted. I will do anything that you tell me to do, except for this!" she looked even fiercer than she had in the middle of the great battle, if that was possible. "Also, why have me do that when you could have a captain or sergeant-in-arms do that, they would probably be more capable at leading the men than me."

"Moraina, this is no time to be fighting each other when there are plenty of enemies waiting for us. But still, you're not a ranger anymore, you're a delicate woman!" *Wrong word choice, brace yourself again!*

"Delicate? How am I delicate?" Moraina punched him in the shoulder, and even with the armor, Braim winced. Moraina shook her fist, tempered steel was not the softest item, and her knuckles throbbed slightly. "Braim, you are not an invincible warrior, and you have something to live for now, me. I want you to return to me after the battle. And your chances of succeeding at that quest would be much better if you had someone to watch your back closer than a regular soldier!"

Braim rubbed his shoulder, "I guess you're not really *delicate*, I chose the wrong word there. But I still don't want you in the coming battle, if there is one."

Moraina realized that Braim would not give in to her arguments, he was worse than Aelundei, so she nodded and looked down at the road, a new plan already forming in her mind. Braim looked forward and took note of the surroundings. They were only an hour away.

*   *   *

A thousand goblins or more charged up the hill towards Torrer castle, with the king of Gartsamn at the head of the noisy horde. They made it to the gate and leapt through the half that was open, having to climb swiftly over the barricade that was waiting for them. The goblins in the front of the army tried to stop as they saw the danger waiting for them at the bottom of the pile of rubble, but they were pushed forward by their comrades behind them. They fell five feet and impaled themselves on the sharpened stakes planted between the cobblestones; the goblin army walked across the dead backs of the former soldiers. The first living goblins to set foot within their old fortress looked up to the walls above. Between the ramparts of the second wall they could see the backs of battered Telnorian helmets. The Goblins raised crossbows and fired, the helmets were pierced by the short bolts before falling off of the poles that were wearing them.

Aelundei rose from behind a rampart and began firing arrows swiftly, "Fire all arrows! *Íhl ahleas reavel!*" the rangers and Telnorian archers also came from behind the tooth-like ramparts, firing arrows as fast as they could, knowing that with every goblin they killed they increased their chances of surviving.

As Aelundei fired his last arrow he leapt off the inside of the wall and landed half way down a wide stairway. He ran to the gate of the second level, made sure that the pike men were standing ready, then jumped over them and made his way to the barricade between the first gate and the second. He drew his sword and waited. The first goblins rounded the bend of the wall, and plunged towards the barricade. Aelundei and the men crouched below the edge, waiting for the enemy to try jumping onto their side of the low wall.

Braim, you better hurry, thought Aelundei as he shifted into Illnorean, and the first goblin flew over the wall. He sliced upwards and the goblin was dead before it started its descent.

*   *   *

Aelundei fought as hard as he could, he had run out of the energy to sustain Illnorean, he was now fighting just as well as any human could. The enemy had pushed them back to the gate of the third level, he and the army were running out of strength to fight. Out of arrows, the rangers joined in the fray. The pike-men threw the remains of their shattered spears and splintered shields at the enemy, and the swordsmen wielded notched swords with bloody red and black hands that were almost too weak to lift in battle. Aelundei withdrew from the fighting and began to tie bandages on gaping wounds, the men were giving as good as they got, but for how much longer? Then he heard Telnorian horns, rising above the sounds of death and destruction.

*   *   *

The goblin captain was growing impatient, his soldiers wanted to kill humans, not sit outside of the castle wall and wait to enter the fight. He looked around and noticed that over half the army was still sitting outside of the castle walls, what a stinkin' waste! All of a sudden, he heard a mighty battle cry, and he turned to see a row of cavalry with a human boy sitting on a horse at the front. The young man turned to the soldiers and started riding back and forth in front of them, giving a speech to rally his men. The goblin captain turned to his soldiers with a far different leadership style. He screamed at his troops with a harsh voice, "Come on, maggots, form ranks or I will kill you before the cavalry can," a slow moving pike-goblin was walking by, so the captain grabbed him by the scruff of the shirt that was sticking from beneath his armor, "Didn't believe me, eh?" The captain drew his sword and ran the soldier through. He grabbed the short pike from the hands of the falling creature and handed it to a sword-goblin. "Move to the front," said the captain, "and you better be quicker than your friend, or you'll be joining him in the funeral pyre later." The captain grinned savagely as his troops began to fall in quicker; his way always seemed to work.

*   *   *

Braim reigned in his horse at the sight of the goblin army, and turned to the sergeant at his side, "Sound the calls for battle formation." The sergeant lifted his ox-horn and blew a combination of long and short blasts. The army fell in behind him, the cavalry in front, the swordsmen behind, and the archers following them. Braim turned to them, and rose in the saddle, lifting his voice so that all could hear his words. He began to ride his horse back and forth in front of his men, letting all of them see his face, "Soldiers of Telnor look into my eyes. I tell you the truth, our enemies are numerous, and they blot out the ground near our ancestor's former lands! They will do this no longer! Today, I give you a chance to help me purge this land of evil! Now let us ride, for freedom and justice!" Braim wheeled his horse around, "Archers, fire your arrows until we reach the enemy's front ranks." He lowered his voice and addressed the sergeant, "Sound the charge," the man raised his horn again to his lips, and the horses surged forward, their riders eager for a fight.

Arrows zipped over his head as Braim raised his two-handed sword over his head and roared at the top of his lungs, hundreds of throats joining him.

"For Telnor!"

*   *   *

Moraina threw the scale-mail armor quickly over her dress and readjusted her sword. Then she grabbed the Telnorian cavalry helm and buckled it on, glad that her hair had not yet grown back to the length that Telnorian women preferred. She stepped out from behind the bushes and mounted her horse. She had given instructions to a captain for the civilians to be escorted back one mile down the road. She galloped down the road after the army, and joined the ranks of cavalry close to her husband just as he turned to face the enemy,

204

perfect timing. She drew her sword and charged with the army, her feminine voice drowned out by over a hundred other shouts. She would keep Braim close in her sight.

*   *   *

The front ranks of the cavalry charge jumped their horses over the wall of spears and slammed into the faces of the goblins. Then they threw their spears at the foes and drew their swords. Braim's remount was cut from under him and he fell to the ground, barely able to kick his legs clear of the falling body. He stood shakily, and looked up just in time to see a glittering arc of beautiful cold steel cutting towards him. Braim leaped to the side and ran his opponent through with a two-handed thrust beneath the armor. He jerked his sword out and blocked the blade of another opponent, then brought his sword down into the side of the soft flesh of a goblin neck. Braim paused for a moment and turned to the bugler, who had miraculously stayed with him, "Sound: cavalry, fall back."

The man raised his horn to his lips and blew the call. The remaining horsemen pivoted their horses and split to allow the infantry to engage the enemy.

Braim shouted again, "Sound: archers, advance one hundred paces, and, fire at will."

The bugler blew again, then dropped his horn and drew his sword.

Five goblins saw Braim and charged as the last note of the horn faded. Braim scowled angrily at them and rushed forward, sweeping one of his foes off its feet and stabbing it through the throat. Then Braim launched himself with a will at the enemy, his sword a black stained vessel of death. But for every foe he killed, eight more seemed to step in and take its place, and Braim knew he could not continue for much longer. A blade slid past his defenses and caught him in the gut. The scale armor turned the blade aside, but Braim still felt the impact and surprise. Then another blade slipped past as he blocked three more weapons at once. This one cut across his left cheek below the eye, and he reeled from the pain. A goblin leaped on him and sank teeth into his neck as it tried to stab a blade up his armpit. Braim went down beneath a pile of writhing bodies, and this time he could not get up from beneath.

Thoughts swarmed through Braim's mind at an alarming rate.

Things he never thought he would think as he prepared to die. The loudest thought was actually regret, regret that he had not told Moraina that he loved her more often, and the look of hurt on her face as he had left her behind. As the hungry blades started to taste his flesh, he realized that he would miss her. He would miss her warm hand on his shoulder. He would miss those deep brown eyes looking into his. And most of all, he would miss her smile, yes, her smile and her laugh. A solitary tear rolled down his bleeding cheek as the world began to black out from pain, and Braim hoped that Moraina would be able to move on after his death.

The world went black, but not until after a Telnorian soldier with curling brown hair slammed into the goblins that held him down, bringing with her the rest of the army. *Moraina?*

*   *   *

Moraina slammed into the goblins that covered Braim, using her shield as a battering ram. She screamed at the top of her lungs, it was a scream born of desperation; knowing that if she didn't get to Braim soon enough, he would die.

She shoved the last of the goblins off of Braim's pale, bloody form and sent the soldiers ahead of her. Screaming for a medic, she began frantically stripping Braim of his armor. The scale armor was held together by leather straps on the back, but her hunting knife sliced through the tough hide like butter. She pulled the mail off and threw it to the ground, then ripped his shirt off and began making bandages from her dress. She reached down to the medical bag at her side, it had rudimentary items such as small bandages, but it lacked the herbs and cutting tools needed for Braim's injuries. She called for a medic again, and started to tie the bandages on the lesser wounds. *Where is Aelundei when I need him?*

*   *   *

Aelundei tilted his head to the left, a crossbow bolt whizzing through the space where his head had been a moment before. He gutted a goblin with a flick of his sword and dodged another bolt. He was panting and tired, he had killed three times as many goblins as any of his soldiers, and this was the price to pay. He silently thanked Vitaren for creating elves with extra strength; it had carried him through the worst of the fighting. Now, the small band of Telnorian soldiers that were left to defend the castle was slowly pushing the enemy back out of the castle, and they were gaining speed.

Aelundei tilted his head to the right, but fatigue slowed his reflexes, and a blow aimed to impale his throat with a three foot sharpened steel stick did manage to put a small cut under his chin. Aelundei lashed out with his own three foot sharpened blade. *Ha-ha!* The elf thought, *number seventy-six!*

One hour and ninety-three goblins later, Aelundei and his remaining men shook hands and exchanged hugs with their rescuers. Aelundei turned and watched the remaining few goblins running as fast as they could, Telnorian cavalry cutting them down with no mercy.

No mercy for those who gave none and feel none, thought the elf grimly, *but it does not make my work any easier to think that way. Killing is killing, and goblins were once elves.* He was startled out of his reverie as a courier rode up next to him on the back of a sweating horse. "My lord elf, Lord Braim is severely wounded, and Lady Moraina requests that you come as quickly as you can."

"Does your horse have enough strength to bear two riders?"

"It would be an honor, my lord, Paervin has well more than that left in him, hop on." The courier extended a hand, pulled Aelundei up behind him, and they were off.

*   *   *

Moraina watched the skilled hands of the medics with anxiety. *If only I could have been there sooner, then maybe Braim would be standing next to me now.*

She turned around at the sound of hoof beats behind her, and saw the courier on his sweating horse galloping towards the tent, Aelundei sitting easily on the saddle behind him. The courier reined in his horse, but Aelundei was already out of the saddle, running for the tent, his own personal kit of herbs held tightly at his side. He brushed past the Telnorian medics and examined Braim's wounds with a frown.

Moraina walked up behind the elf, "Will you be able to save him, Aelundei?"

Aelundei looked up from his work for a second and put a hand on her shoulder, "Moraina, that matter rests in the mighty hands of

207

Vitaren. I will do everything in my power, but there are three things that you can do to help me. First, I need you to trust me and look brave; those soldiers outside need a strong leader. Second, order the men to begin clearing out the castle and finding their wounded before it is too late; tell the medics to clean a room, so Braim can be moved there when he's ready. And third, I need you to pray. You've talked to Vitaren before, and now you must do it again. Ask him for strength, you'll be surprised how much he gives you." He clapped Moraina on the shoulder and set about his task with grim precision.

Moraina took one more look at the still, pale form of Braim, then turned and walked out of the tent, crying out with a silent plea to Vitaren as she did. A great peace enveloped her, and she set about the tasks, yelling orders as she went.

*   *   *

Images and memories flashed before Braim's eyes. He refought the battle of Morenelath Pass, saw every mistake in his life, all of his tears and joys. Suddenly, he was standing at the base of a giant stairway; peering up at its magnificent height. The stair stretched up into the clouds. As he looked, the clouds seemed to roll back. A great light shone from the clouds, and he had to turn his eyes from it, blinking like a man who emerged suddenly from subterranean passageways to behold an unclouded day. A voice boomed from the light, in awestruck worship he dropped to the ground. Suddenly, Braim heard the voice of the messenger who had come to greet him in the torture room of Grashnir.

"Welcome to the stairs of Vitaren. These stairs lead you to the Free Kingdom, in which the walls and streets are made of gold, as pure as glass. Vitaren is prepared to have a great feast in your honor, mighty warrior, but there is one task he would like you to fulfill before he calls you home. This is what he requires-."

*   *   *

Braim awoke in a soft bed, staring up at the ceiling of a room in a castle. He was weak, hungry, and thirsty. He opened his mouth to ask for a drink, but all that came out was a croak.

Moraina nearly jumped through the roof, but she guessed what he needed, and gave him a drink of water. He looked up at her, her eyes full of joy. Her arms wrapped around him, and he breathed in her wildflower perfume as she kissed him. After several minutes she released him, went to the door, and called to several people outside. Aelundei, Peter, Larem, Saeln, Silas, and Matthew walked into the room; Saeln was walking on crutches, his broken leg still not fully healed.

"How long have I been asleep?" Braim asked.

Aelundei smiled at him, "Glad to see you're better, you've been asleep for two weeks and four days; you've given Moraina and I quite a scare. We thought we were going to lose you until just six days ago. Suddenly, your fever broke and you started getting better. There's some resilient blood in your veins, Braim, and lots of help from Vitaren."

Braim's head sank back wearily into the pillow; the effort of looking up at his friends had drained him. He smiled, and they slowly walked out of the room, leaving him and Moraina alone in the room. He took her hand and she bent over to listen as he whispered in her ear, "Vitaren sent me back Moraina. I was dead, and he sent me back. He asked me to bring his name back to Telnor.

"Moraina, I should never have left you behind; I'm stronger with you guarding my back. But I was worried that you would get hurt, and here I am sliced to ribbons, while you are without a scratch. I guess I'm no longer the fearless, untouchable warrior I used to be, whose only thought was to die for his country. I love you!" Exhausted, Braim slipped back into the realm of dreams.

*   *   *

Two weeks later, Braim took some halting steps with Moraina and Aelundei on either side of him. Most of his wounds had healed well, but the deepest ones were still giving him pain. The trio hobbled over to the door of the wide balcony which had been recently installed, but before they went through the curtains, Moraina turned to Braim and smiled. "Your people want to tell you something."

As the two humans and the elf stepped out onto the balcony, Braim was taken aback by the sight of civilians and soldiers alike crowding around the keep tower at the center of the fortress. At his appearance, they all began cheering, the soldiers thrusting their swords and spears above their heads. He heard mixed cries of *Lord*

Braim, Thank you, and *Lord Braim for Telnor!*

Braim slumped against the railing, partly from the effort of walking, and partly from gratitude for his people. Aelundei and Moraina leaned in as Braim whispered silently, almost to himself. "I will try to deserve this, I must lead them well."

The Legend of Braim
Epilogue
Things Yet to Come

Braim looked around at the beautiful garden he was walking through. It was full of every beautiful flower that bloomed in his province, and more. This garden had become home to many herbs of healing, which had been planted as seeds by Aelundei. He left the garden and walked towards the central tower, where his love was waiting. It had been ten years and a week since their marriage, and the bond between them had grown stronger with each passing day. He opened the door to the keep and was greeted by a chorus of cheers from a group of rangers that had stopped in to pay him a visit. Among them were Peter, Larem, and Saeln, his old friends. He shook hands with each of them and reminded them of the feast that would take place that evening; he would see more of them then. He continued energetically up the stairs, greeting every one he passed with a cheerful hello. Finally, he arrived at the door to Moraina and his chamber. He saluted the two guards at the door and walked through. His nine year old son Caeldrean ran up to him with arms thrown wide, "Daddy!" Braim scooped up his son and spun him around. He hugged the boy and then walked over to the crib that contained their sleeping newborn baby girl. Moraina walked up behind Braim and embraced him and Caeldrean.

"How are my men doing?" she asked with a small smile on her face, "I see you are home a little early, there must have been fewer appellate cases for you to judge than yesterday."

"Yes, there were quite a few less cases than yesterday," said Braim with a look of relief on his face, "I was ready to quit yesterday, but I don't think Aelundei or the king would have let me."

At the mention of the elf's name Caeldrean looked up at his father's face, "Where is Aelundei, daddy?"

Braim looked down at the dark hazel eyes of his son; every time he looked at them he was reminded of how much he looked like Moraina, "He's talking to Peter in the hall of the second level, do you want to go see him?"

"Peter's here!" cried Caeldrean excitedly, Braim set him down and the boy ran off, his soft leather boots making hardly a sound.

Braim and Moraina looked at each other and laughed quietly. Except for his parents, Peter and Aelundei were Caeldrean's two favorite people in the world. Whenever Peter visited the castle, he would bring Caeldrean a bow that was slightly more powerful than the one he had brought the last time, and he would also give him five more arrows with it. Under Peter and Aelundei's instructions, Caeldrean had grown to be a proficient archer, and in a few more years he would probably join the rangers and patrol the northeastern borders of Morenelath.

Braim turned back to Moraina as the door closed, and hugged her tightly. She looked up at him with her beautiful eyes, her face framed by her long brown hair.

"What are you going to wear to the celebration feast tonight?" she asked, a smile playing on her lips.

"Well, I was thinking I would just go wearing what I am now." He looked down at his clothes. He was wearing a tan tunic with dark green pants and a green cape of the same color. At his side hung an impressive two handed sword, which had been given to him as a gift from the king to replace his battered ranger one.

"You can't go like that, here, come take a look at what I have picked out for you!" Moraina grabbed Braim by the wrist and dragged him back to the wardrobe that contained their clothes. Lying on the bed were two sets of clothes, one for Braim and one for Moraina.

Moraina had chosen a dark red tunic for Braim, and grey pants to go with it. Next to his outfit there was a beautiful emerald dress and a gold necklace. Braim looked on the clothes with satisfaction, and knew in his heart that they would go well together. Braim led Moraina to the window, and threw the shutters wide. They stood there, each with a hand over the other's shoulder, and watched the courtyard below. Twenty knights in bright armor stood in a circle around a training arena and watched two dueling combatants with wooden training swords. One was Sir Tomneis, wielding his large two-handed training sword easily. The other was a small figure holding two short swords, expertly dodging and parrying each swing of the larger knight's sword. In the center of the ring was Aelundei, yelling tips to the young Caeldrean as the boy slowly worked his way towards the knight, trying to get in close to lessen the advantage of the large sword. The boy was doing extremely well, not only parrying the light thrusts and chops of the larger knight, but also landing a few attacks on the grinning man.

Braim turned to Moraina, "We certainly raised our first child right, he is a strong lad, and he knows the value of good friends, just as I value you."

Moraina drew closer to her husband, and looked up into his eyes, "I hope he and his wife are as close to one another as you and I, but I hope she doesn't have to break into a castle to rescue him like I did."

The couple laughed, hugged each other, and kissed. Moraina had been joking about their son being in danger in the future, but neither of them knew what would befall their son in his life. The sun began to set, and the castle prepared for the feast. Everything was peaceful. For now.

*   *   *

The man in the dark robe walked into the chamber of his lord and king, and knelt before him.

A great voice came from high above the kneeling figure, "Ah, my faithful servant, Gramod; what news do you bring of your mission in the south?"

"Oh, glorious father of truth," replied the man in the dark robe, "I regret to tell you that the invasion of the human land of Telnor has failed. The combined efforts of the goblins and trolls were thwarted by the rangers, who were led by an elf and a human known as Braim."

"Fear not, Gramod," said the thundering voice, "There is more than one way to crush a cat, as I like to say. I have a new task for you, to destroy the Telnorians in a different way. But for that you will need a new steed; come, follow me."

Gramod followed his king further up into the tower, keeping his eyes averted; the Great Prince, as he was known by his subjects, talking to Gramod the whole way, "Long have my servants toiled trying to catch these fearsome beasts, it is a difficult task, but finally we were able to capture five of them, and I subjected them to my will."

They emerged onto a platform high on the tower, and the man in the dark robe looked out across his master's realm. Almost as far as the eye could see there were goblin spawning pits, and the ground itself seemed to crawl with the wretched creatures. Gramod wrinkled his nose, their stench found its way even here at the top of the tower. His attention was returned to his master as the Great Prince began to speak again.

213

"Look at this beast, Gramod; look, and be amazed." All of a sudden, a giant winged beast flew from below the platform, and settled silently on the hard stone. Gramod gasped with amazement. Before him stood a proud beast, with a long neck, bright scales, and leather wings.

"I thought Dragonin only existed in children's tales," whispered the astonished man.

"See, and believe, my faithful servant," said the Great Prince, "They are subject to my will, and so they will be totally obedient to you, but it will take some time to master riding and guiding them. For the next few years, we will train them and you, and then we will strike."

"Do they breathe fire?"

"No," replied the Great Prince, "Only their ancestors, the Great Dragons, breathed fire, but these will prove deadly enough without it. Now, return to your room, you will need rest."

"Yes, my master."

The End, For Now

About the Author

Joseph Anderson is a 20 year old author and college student. When he isn't busy at school or church, he enjoys hiking, playing music, writing, world developing, improving his elvish language, and visiting with friends. After finally finishing his first book, he plans to write a sequel, as soon as his schedule permits him to do so.

Made in the USA
San Bernardino, CA
17 January 2014